W9-CED-956

Clear! Clear! Dear! by Ron Benrey
Faith Wright walked away from NASCAR for good after a horrific accident ended both her rookie year and her promising career as a driver. Now she's back—as a spotter for Tony Griffith, an overconfident driver who keeps losing races but refuses everyone's help. Could the partnership neither of them wants turn out to be the best thing in their lives and bring them love, success, and renewed faith?

The Remaking of Moe McKenna by Gloria Clover
Moe McKenna enjoys fast cars and the men who drive them—so much that she dedicated one summer to the racing circuit. Fourth generation race car driver Boedy Sutherland spots Moe when she starts dogging his team. Only when he's forced into issuing an ultimatum does he realize how involved his heart is. Then the entire Sutherland family takes the job of turning Moe into a lady. . .and a child of the King.

Over the Wall by Becky Melby and Cathy Wienke
ER nurse Camela Eastman arrives at the Darlington Speedway with hopes of more than just working on a medical team, but a trackside wedding proposal isn't on practical boyfriend Joe's to-do list. When comical Tommy Garrett, a pit crew jackman with puppy-dog eyes and a heart for God, literally falls for her, Camela resists. But a life-threatening pit row accident forces her to take a leap of faith.

Winner Takes All by Gail Sattler
Rob loves NASCAR so much that even though he didn't qualify to drive, he has a second best—a computer racing game to play when he's not cheering for his favorite drivers. Lynda also loves racing, and when she's not cheering from the stands, she sells NASCAR licensed merchandise. When Lynda starts selling Rob's game, a race of another kind starts—a race for the heart of a righteous man, where the winner takes all.

Race to the Altar

Four Romances Come Full Circle at Racing Events

Ron Benrey

Gloria Clover

Becky Melby & Cathy Wienke

Gail Sattler

BARBOUR
PUBLISHING

© 2007 *Clear! Clear! Dear!* by Ron Benrey
© 2007 *The Remaking of Moe McKenna* by Gloria Clover
© 2007 *Over the Wall* by Becky Melby and Cathy Wienke
© 2007 *Winner Takes All* by Gail Sattler

ISBN 978-1-59789-847-8

All rights reserved. No part of this publication may be reproduced or transmitted in any form or by any means without written permission of the publisher.

All scripture quotations are taken from the HOLY BIBLE, NEW INTERNATIONAL VERSION®. NIV®. Copyright © 1973, 1978, 1984 by International Bible Society. Used by permission of Zondervan. All rights reserved.

This book is a work of fiction. Names, characters, places, and incidents are either products of the author's imagination or used fictitiously. Any similarity to actual people, organizations, and/or events is purely coincidental.

Cover design by Kirk DouPonce, DogEared Design

Published by Barbour Publishing, Inc., P.O. Box 719, Uhrichsville, Ohio 44683, www.barbourbooks.com

Our mission is to publish and distribute inspirational products offering exceptional value and biblical encouragement to the masses.

ecpa Member of the
Evangelical Christian
Publishers Association

Printed in the United States of America.

Clear! Clear! Dear!

by Ron Benrey

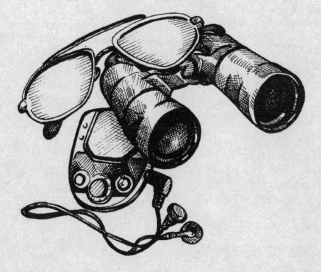

Dedication

For Pat Crandall

Listen to advice and accept instruction,
and in the end you will be wise.

Chapter 1

W hy me?" Faith Wright tried to put just the right touch of astonishment into her question. She leaned back in her chair and hoped that the expression on her face looked unreservedly puzzled.

Maybe Emmett Grant would get the idea, on his own, that offering a job to her on his racing team was crazy. That way, she wouldn't have to tell an old family friend—and one of the richest men in North Carolina—that she would never, ever again work within a hundred miles of a NASCAR racetrack.

I burned enough bridges three years ago.

Emmett peered at Faith for a few moments and then smiled slyly. "Well now, I can think of three possible answers to your question. For starters, I could say that a woman of your experience and temperament will add valuable capabilities to my staff." His smile deepened. "Of course, we both know that would be an exaggeration. I currently have all the engineering talent I need on my team. Moreover, we both know how you feel about NASCAR."

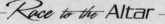

"With good reason!" she said, before she could stop herself.

Whoops! No need to complain to Emmett. He already knows my whole story.

Emmett ignored the interruption and went on. "Or, I might remind you that your father worked with me for thirty years. . . that I feel a strong sense of obligation toward him. . .and that I've known you since you were a baby." He gave a small chuckle that Faith thought sounded more like a grunt. "All of that would be true—but also irrelevant as far as offering you a job is concerned. My racing team is a business, and I never base important business decisions solely on friendship."

He looked squarely into her eyes. She willed herself not to blink or be the first to turn away.

"Or"—he spoke louder—"I can simply tell you the truth. Tony Griffith needs a world-class spotter. You are the perfect person to do a disagreeable job that must be done well."

"So you admit you've offered me a rotten job."

"I said *disagreeable*, not rotten. Many of the jobs on a NASCAR team are unpleasant—like toting seventy-five-pound wheels during a pit stop or driving for three hours inside a race car that gets hot as an oven." He made a face. "Tony's spotter will also take a lot of heat. From Tony."

She sat up straight. "Emmett, you have dozens of experienced people on your staff. Choose one of them to spot for Tony." She added, "I can't imagine why you think I'm right for the job."

Emmett tapped his vast desktop with his index finger. "I know *you* know that a driver won't make it through a full NASCAR race without the help of an effective spotter talking to him over a radio. That second pair of eyes high above the racetrack is essential for. . ." He hesitated. Faith noticed he no longer looked directly at her.

"A good spotter is a must for avoiding accidents," Faith said, softly. "I'm a big girl, Emmett. I don't mind remembering what happened to me." She took a breath. "We both agree—spotters are essential. What's your point?"

Emmett made a slow sigh. "Tony Griffith doesn't feel that way. He mostly doesn't listen to his spotter when he's driving."

"He sounds like an arrogant jerk."

"Well, let's just say that Tony Griffith is a special kind of driver who requires a special kind of spotter. Specifically, someone like you." Emmett began to count on the fingers of his right hand. "Point one, Tony doesn't seem to respect the other spotters on my staff. But he will respect you because you've had recent experience racing in the Nextel Cup Circuit—"

"I don't drive anymore," Faith broke in. "My. . .ah, accident was three years ago. I left NASCAR halfway through my rookie year. I'm a retired has-been—actually, a retired *never*-been."

"True. In fact, your current status is my second point. Because you're not an active NASCAR driver and apparently have no intentions of being one again, Tony won't feel threatened by you—although he'll have to admit that you know your stuff, particularly when he finds out you just earned a master's degree in automotive engineering." He wagged his fingertip to emphasize his second point. "Tony has a bachelor's degree in mechanical engineering. The pair of you should have lots to talk about."

"Well, maybe. . ." She shrugged. "Keep going."

"Point three, a good spotter has to be a good coach. You

have oodles of teaching experience."

"Teaching at an engineering school doesn't count."

"I disagree. College kids are great at detecting phonies. You have a great reputation at Michigan State. I checked. Coaching skills are important when you spot for Tony. He started his racing career as an open-wheel driver. Tony became a NASCAR driver about two and half years ago, but he's still burdened by lots of non-NASCAR ideas and philosophies."

"What's point four?" Faith was surprised to feel curious. There weren't that many NASCAR drivers who'd begun their careers driving open-wheel Formula One cars. Tony Griffith might be more interesting than she'd imagined.

"You're available. I know for a fact that you won't start your PhD program and your new teaching fellowship until next fall. You sorely need a job for the next seven or eight months." He grinned. "Would you like me to tell you your current bank balance?"

She felt herself frown. How much had it cost Emmett, she wondered, to get around the laws that were supposed to protect her privacy?

"I'll survive," she said.

"Sure. By waiting tables or flipping burgers." He smiled again. "Except—and this is point five—you're a sensible gal. Much too smart to fail to take advantage of an exceptional opportunity."

"Emmett, you say that you know how I feel about NASCAR. Well, I suspect that NASCAR feels pretty much the same way about me. I don't think they'd give me a license to be a spotter."

"Not a problem. I checked that, too. Everyone believes you

made a simple mistake two years ago—albeit a mistake that caused a serious accident. Drivers make lots of mistakes every Sunday, and sometimes people get badly injured—or worse." He reached over and touched the top of her hand. "I've already started the paperwork to get your license renewed."

Faith spoke as evenly as she could. "I did *not* make a mistake two years ago."

"I didn't say that you did. I said that's what people believe."

"What do you believe?"

"I *know* that Faith Wright is smart, skilled, and professional." He tapped her hand again. "Come to work for me. You'll earn a great salary, and we'll give you an office one floor down, with a nice view of Concord. When you're on the road, we'll pay all your living expenses. You'll share a deluxe motor coach with two other women who travel the circuit."

"A motor coach?" Faith heard her voice squeak.

"Yep! Parked in the owners' and drivers' lot at each NAS-CAR racetrack."

Faith couldn't help but smile. She'd stayed in hotels during her rookie year. Only the owner, the crew chief, and the senior drivers qualified for palatial motor coaches parked in a private area at the speedways, a short walk from the cars.

Emmett continued, "I travel to the track by helicopter every Sunday, so I turned over my personal motor coach to Jessie McKnight, my car chief."

"You have a female car chief?" Another squeak.

"Correct! She started three weeks ago. And also a female media relations manager." He laughed. "So why not a female spotter?"

Faith found herself thinking, *Why not, indeed.* She steeled herself not to give in to Emmett's charm. *Keep remembering that you don't want a racing job.*

Faith decided to change tacks. "You overlooked one important detail about me, Emmett. A spotter needs to develop a great rapport with a driver. These days, I'm not so swift in the relationship-building department."

"Glad to hear it. Tony doesn't need a new relationship. He has a serious girlfriend back in Oregon, so he won't get amorous with you." He winked at her. "And if you were my daughter, I'd tell you to stay away from the thousand other good-looking guys you'll see at the racetrack every Sunday. A woman with a good career can run into problems married to a man involved with NASCAR. He'll spend half his life on the road, away from home."

"That's not what I meant, and you know it."

Emmett gave a disparaging wave. "Don't kid a kidder. You have to develop a coaching relationship based on trust with every student you teach. Do the same thing with Tony and you'll be fine. It may take awhile, but Tony will come to like and respect you." He added, "And while that's happening, you'll have my full support. You'll report to me, not Tony. And you make all the decisions related to spotting. He can ignore you, but he won't be able to order you around."

"Look, Emmett, I appreciate your thinking of me, but for the next four years, I'm a student."

"I agree. But you don't have to make a long-term commitment to Grant Racing. All I ask is that you join my team for seven fun-filled months. You'll work hard, travel to NASCAR tracks across the country, see some great stock car racing, and go back to school with a significantly fatter wallet. How can you possibly say no?"

"Well. . ." Her mind filled with images of NASCAR stock cars zooming around her favorite speedways. And she'd have the best seat in the house. Faith abruptly realized that Emmett was right. She simply couldn't say no. Working for Grant Racing would be a godsend—a perfect way to rebuild her dangerously depleted savings account.

"Well. . .okay, I say yes."

"Wonderful!" He stood up, marched around his desk, and gave her a big hug. "I want you to begin work next Monday morning. We'll set aside a couple of weeks to get you up to speed with our racing program and to finish your paperwork. You'll spot your first race on the first Sunday in April, at Martinsville Speedway, in Virginia."

She began to smile. "I hate you, Emmett Grant."

"Nah! It's too soon for that. Wait till you've worked with me awhile."

Faith felt a shiver whiz along her spine.

Oh boy, what have I done?

Tony Griffith reached deep into the engine compartment of the Dodge he would drive next Sunday and felt the armored hose that connected the oil cooler to the engine block.

"It seems in good shape," he said.

"It *is* in good shape!" Larry Connors said, two notches louder than Tony. "In fact, it's brand-new. My crew always replaces

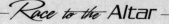

critical hoses before every race. It's Grant Racing policy."

"Still, it doesn't hurt to make sure."

"That's where you're wrong, Tony. You go over our work so often that my crew is becoming convinced that you don't trust us."

"Well, that's their problem, not mine," Tony blurted. He immediately looked around the huge, brightly lit garage to see if any of the mechanics were within earshot. Thankfully, the four other mechanics at work on other Grant team cars were more than a hundred feet away. They didn't give any indication that they'd heard an imprudent exchange between Tony and their boss. The soft hum of machinery, fluorescent lights, and overhead blowers effectively soundproofed the big room.

Tony scolded himself under his breath. It was incredibly dim-witted for a driver to offend his team's chief mechanic. But these days, for some reason, he often felt on edge. He frequently started fights with people he wanted to keep as friends.

You know better. Stop being a jerk!

Tony smiled at Larry. "I promise—I'm not trying to insult your crew. I only want to be certain that I don't have any problems on race day. I've had bad experiences with exploding hoses."

"Sheesh, Tony! Last year, you had *one* lousy water hose pop during a race. It wasn't anybody's fault; the hose had an internal flaw that was invisible when we installed it. You coasted into the pit, and we replaced it in less than two minutes."

"I finished in forty-second place because of that broken hose."

"Yeah? Well, that's the thing about NASCAR racing— sometimes you're lucky, sometimes you're not."

"Luck is for people who don't work hard."

"What? That's the silliest thing I've ever heard come out of the mouth of a NASCAR driver."

"Whoa!" Tony took a step back from the race car. "Seems I keep putting my foot in my mouth this morning. What I meant to say is that the best way to lose a NASCAR race is to rely on luck to overcome sloppy work. A winning driver needs more than luck. He needs a solid commitment to avoid mistakes—from himself and from his entire crew."

Larry let out a noisy sigh and then began to chuckle. "Tell you what, Tony, it won't bother me if you personally squeeze every hose and pipe in every race car we operate. However, I have to get back to productive work."

Tony watched Larry walk away, across the spotlessly clean floor, and head to his office. *I have to be more careful when I speak to Larry. I need him on my side.*

"Just the man we want to see." A commanding voice behind Tony caught his ear. He spun around and saw Emmett Grant walking toward him accompanied by an exceptionally attractive woman. She looked to be in her late twenties, with short, curly, ash blond hair, a compact athletic build, and large brown eyes that stared at Tony with unabashed curiosity. She moved in an unhesitant way that signaled her total self-confidence.

I wonder if she's married. . .or has a boyfriend? Tony pushed the question from his mind. What difference did it make if a pretty girl was available or not? Everyone at Grant Racing knew that he was committed to Kathy Mullins, who lived nearly three thousand miles away in Medford, Oregon.

"Good morning, Emmett," Tony said, cheerfully. "What

brings the boss to the garage?"

"The fact that you spend most of your spare time in and under my race cars. I assumed you'd be here—and I was right." Emmett gestured gallantly toward his companion. "Tony Griffith, meet Faith Wright, your new spotter."

Tony felt a jolt of disbelief that morphed into an ache of astonishment. Emmett had done it! He'd followed through on his threats to hire a new spotter—without asking for Tony's input.

"Faith is an engineer, like you," Emmett said. "Plus, she has NASCAR driving experience. She's the perfect spotter for you."

Tony groaned inwardly. Emmett had acted precipitously, outrageously. So what if Tony had dragged his feet a bit? So what if he hadn't looked for a spotter himself? Big deal! Grant Racing had plenty of people who could serve as spotters. What was the rush to bring in an outsider? He didn't need, or want, an assigned full-time spotter.

I won't put up with it! Tony focused his mind and began to choose the words of protest he would deliver when his boss was finished talking.

Emmett went on, "I searched high and low until I found Faith. Her qualifications for the job are remarkable. I know that you and she will get along splendidly."

Tony opened his mouth to speak. . .then snapped it shut. It wasn't so much what Emmett said, but the way he said it that changed Tony's mind in an instant. The commanding tone of his boss's voice—coupled with the forcefulness of his expression—convinced Tony not to argue. Instead, he made himself smile.

One day, when he'd won a Nextel Cup or two, he'd have enough clout to give the orders, but today he had to be a good soldier. Too many other good drivers would love to have his job. It would be foolish to give Emmett a reason to fire him.

"Welcome aboard, Faith," he said calmly as he extended his right hand. "I look forward to working with you."

Faith shook his hand and returned his smile. "Same here." Tony saw a glint of uncertainty in her eyes that matched the way he felt about her.

She doesn't want to be my spotter.

"Where did you get your engineering degree?" he asked.

"Bachelor's degree in mechanical engineering at Penn State, master's in automotive engineering at Michigan State."

"I'm impressed," Tony said, really meaning it. "And you were also a NASCAR driver?"

She nodded. "But I never got beyond my rookie year."

"In what division?"

"Winston Cup Racing, before the name changed to Nextel Cup."

"Now I'm more impressed—in fact, I guess I don't understand why someone with your training and experience wants to be a spotter."

Emmett jumped back into the conversation. "Save your answer for later," he said to Faith. Then he turned to Tony. "You'll have plenty of time to get acquainted with Faith this afternoon. Right now, she has to meet with the folks in human resources."

Tony acknowledged their departure with an unenthusiastic wave. Faith seemed pleasant enough. . .and her lack of

enthusiasm might be a good thing. But the idea of a full-time spotter continued to rankle. Moreover, something else had begun to bother him. The name "Faith Wright" seemed vaguely familiar. And not in a good way. Where had he heard it before? What was her story?

If anyone knows, Jimbo Davis will.

Tony walked quickly through the garage and took the steps up two flights to the third floor. Seen from above, the three-story Grant Racing building looked like a big H. The left vertical bar housed the garage, workshops, and parts storage warehouse; the right vertical bar held most of the offices; and the short cross bar was given over to an auditorium, a cafeteria, and a well-equipped exercise room.

Tony turned the corner and found Jimbo Davis working in his office. Jimbo's official title was Special Assistant to the Chairman—an intentionally vague description that camouflaged his real role as Grant Racing's expert-at-large. Jimbo, a spry, white-haired septuagenarian, had done everything one could do on a racing team, from designing race cars, to driving them, to being a crew chief. He was a walking encyclopedia of NASCAR information and often helped develop racing strategy for Clint McCabe, Emmett Grant's senior driver. Today, his desk was covered with maps and diagrams.

"Can I bother you for a minute?" Tony asked.

"It's no bother." Jimbo looked up and smiled. "I'm refreshing my memories of Martinsville Speedway so I can help Clint McCabe prepare for the race. I make the same offer to you, if you're interested. Although, it's probably a waste of time to read this stuff. The track is so short—and I've been there so often—I know the place by heart." He added, "Take a load off your feet and tell Uncle Jimbo your problem. I can tell by the unhappy look on your face that you have one."

Tony moved a visitor's chair close to Jimbo. "The boss hired a spotter for me today. He went out and found her by himself."

"Hey! Don't say I didn't warn you. Emmett is serious about dragging you into the real world. You're the only NASCAR driver I know who thinks he can succeed without a smart spotter looking over his shoulder." Jimbo abruptly looked puzzled. "Did you say 'her'?"

"I did. She is a former NASCAR driver named Faith Wright."

"You're kidding!"

"No, I'm not. Emmett marched her into the garage to meet me."

Jimbo leaned forward. "A pretty gal. Curly hair. Big, *big* eyes."

"That's her."

"Uh-oh."

"What's wrong? Do you object to female spotters?"

"Not at all. It's Faith Wright I'm not so sure about. Given her driving history, I don't think I'd want Faith Wright spotting for me."

"Do you think I can change Emmett's mind?"

"Do you think pigs can fly in North Carolina?"

Tony slumped in his chair. *Great! This is going to be a miserable racing season.* "Tell me what I should know about her."

"Well, once upon a time there was a young woman from

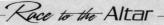

Montgomery, Alabama, who could drive NASCAR race cars with the best of them...."

The human resources manager, a vivacious redhead named Gloria Barker, smiled at Faith. "You realize, of course, that every unmarried woman at Grant Racing will be jealous of you."

"Because I'll spot for Tony Griffith?"

"No, silly! Because you'll spend endless hours of quality time with the most eligible bachelor in the company. Tony is gorgeous, smart, rich, and single. And, compared to most NAS-CAR drivers, he has a manageable ego. What more could a girl want?"

"But I thought he has a girlfriend."

"He does. A woman who lives clear across the country and whom he never sees." She shook her head, making her red tresses swing. "Some relationship!"

"It does sound a bit strange."

"I'll say! She's crazy to let a man like Tony live so far away from her."

"Has anyone tried to, ah, separate him from her?"

"Only all of the unattached women in this building—including me." She sighed. "I'm sorry to say that Tony doesn't break records for being amiable. Oh, he's friendly enough when he wants to be, but he always seems slightly on edge. He doesn't warm up to people easily."

"More good news!" Faith murmured, under her breath. "Not only does he dislike spotters, he's also touchy."

"Did you say something?" Gloria asked.

"Oh, don't mind me. I'm just thinking that I should probably track down the man in question and tell him what Emmett Grant has in mind. I have the feeling my unexpected appearance in the garage came as quite a surprise to Tony."

"Look in the garage. That's where he spends most of his time. If he's not there, try the exercise room."

Faith checked both locations, without success. She finally found Tony seated on a bench in the patio area behind the Grant Racing building. He seemed lost in thought.

"Hi!" she said. "Is now a good time to chat about my new assignment?"

Tony looked up at her, an ugly glower on his face. "It's probably as good as any," he said. Faith noted that he didn't ask her to sit down.

He's going to be difficult even before I officially start my job.

She sat down near the end of the bench. "I thought we could begin by figuring out the best way to work together. Emmett wants me to begin spotting for you at Martinsville Speedway."

"Ever drive there?" The words spit from his mouth.

"No. Although I know it's the shortest NASCAR track and one of the most difficult."

"I'll bet you read that on the back of a NASCAR sponsor's cereal box."

Faith felt her temper rising; she took several deep breaths. *Let him act like a childish nitwit. You be the grown-up.*

"Look, it's important that we talk about our working relationship, but I'll be happy to do it tomorrow if you have something more important on your mind right now. When is a good time to meet?"

"Never!" His piercing glare became more powerful. "I don't intend to develop any kind of working relationship with you. As far as I'm concerned, you'll be a voice on my radio. A one-way voice. Don't expect me to respond to what you say. I'll listen to your advice, think about it carefully, and make my own decisions."

Faith hoped that Tony didn't hear her soft gasp. She paused a moment to compose her thoughts. . .and let her heartbeat return to normal.

"Fair enough, Tony," she said. "The driver is always in control of his car. You don't take orders from your spotter. But let me ask you a question. Why the sudden hostility toward me?"

"Hostility?" Tony gave a scornful laugh. "Look at the situation from my perspective. Emmett Grant found me a new spotter who's known throughout NASCAR for demonstrating awful judgment, causing a near-fatal crash, and ending a promising driver's career. To make matters worse, you kept insisting that it wasn't your fault, even though the evidence against you was crystal clear." He laughed again. "Why would any sensible driver listen to you? Or build a working relationship with you?"

Faith felt light-headed. She hadn't expected this kind of attack, not at her first private meeting with Tony Griffith. She had intended to tell him about the accident, tell him her side of the story. But now he'd never believe her.

Who cares what he believes? I report to Emmett Grant. "Now that I know where you stand, all we need is a one-sentence discussion. You do your job, and I'll do mine."

"Fine! But try to do your job correctly—and not get me killed."

Faith started to answer but then thought better of it. *I can't win battles with an egotistical jerk.* She stood and walked away.

Chapter 2

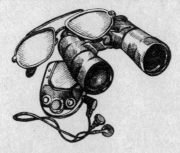

Faith climbed the staircase that led to the spotters' perch atop the Blue Ridge grandstand at Martinsville Speedway and felt awed by the sight of more than ninety thousand excited NASCAR fans waiting for the race to begin. A collage of memories from her brief driving career flashed through her mind—fans seeking autographs, fans wishing her success, fans urging her not to leave NASCAR after her accident.

"I'm sorry I let you down," she murmured.

Faith scanned her surroundings. The spotters were located high above the front straightaway, but Martinsville's small size meant that they had a perfect view of the entire half-mile long, paperclip-shaped track. She had brought binoculars with her, but she doubted she'd use them.

Faith knew that Martinsville was one of the oldest tracks in the NASCAR circuit, built before NASCAR was organized. It had a unique look and feel, to which she also attributed its compact dimensions. NASCAR racing is a colorful sport, but

Martinsville Speedway seemed to squeeze the floods of different colors together more than any other raceway. The brightly painted cars. The drivers' garish jumpsuits. The fan's colorful jackets and hats. The dark asphalt pavement in the two straightaways. The lighter concrete pavement in the four sharp turns. The glorious blue sky of a Virginia Sunday in early spring. They merged together to create a kaleidoscopic image that was worth seeing on its own.

She signed in with the NASCAR official stationed on the spotters' stand. Racing rules required that every driver have a spotter, so unless she announced her presence, NASCAR wouldn't allow Tony to race.

Not that today's 500-lap race looked especially promising for Tony. He had qualified in the thirty-fifth position—the eighth car from the end of the forty-three-car field. Starting toward the back at Martinsville virtually guaranteed that a driver would have a bad day, because passing is extremely difficult on a short, relatively narrow track.

She glanced at the official's clipboard and saw that Clint McCabe's spotter, a taciturn retired Busch Series driver named Ken Cassini, had already checked in. Clint had qualified in the eighth position, which gave him an excellent chance of finishing among the top ten.

Faith felt a tap on her shoulder. She spun around and found herself facing a broad-shouldered man a full head taller than she was. He was at least sixty years old, with lively blue eyes and a leathery complexion that proved he'd spent many of his years outdoors.

"Are you Faith Wright?" he asked.

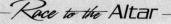

She hesitated before she said, "Yes, I am. Have we met before?"

"Once or twice, but probably too many years ago for you to remember me. I knew your dad well. Dan Wright was the best crew chief I ever worked with."

Faith abruptly remembered. "It's all coming back!" She gripped his hand. "You're Slinky Harris."

"In the flesh." He beamed at her. "It's great to see you again. Are you here for. . .uh, *good*?"

Faith swallowed a laugh. Word of her new job at Grant Racing had probably reached every corner of the tightly knit NASCAR community. The other spotters must want to know more about their unexpected colleague's return.

"No, not for good," she said. "I finished my master's degree in engineering last semester, and I won't return to school until the fall. Emmett Grant offered me a job to fill the gap, and I accepted."

"I'm glad you did. It's great seeing you again."

"Can I ask you a question, Slinky?"

"Ask away."

"How do the guys feel about me?" She tilted her head toward the other spotters gathering on the grandstand roof.

Slinky stopped smiling. "Well, since you want to know, I'll tell you the truth. A handful on one side think you should have stayed away from NASCAR forever, while a handful on the other side think you've been punished enough for what happened and deserve to be welcomed home. Then, the majority of folks in the middle seem to be more practical. They have complete faith in Emmett Grant's judgment. If he says you should be a spotter—that's enough for them."

Before Faith could respond, an energetic voice, broadcasting from the speedway's loudspeakers, announced the invocation and national anthem. She and Slinky moved closer to the railing at the edge of the spotters' perch and stood to attention. While she listened to the prayer, she looked for the two bright green Grant Racing cars in the starting lineup. She quickly identified both, along with their drivers. Faith murmured a brief prayer of her own: "Please God, give me the ability to encourage and help Tony today."

When the guest singer—a country music legend Faith could take or leave—finished vocalizing "The Star-Spangled Banner," she got ready. The race would begin in less than five minutes. She adjusted her baseball cap and sunglasses, slipped the radio headset snugly over her ears, and moved the boom microphone closer to her lips. Then she found her assigned spotting position on the roof. Her location didn't offer as spectacular a view as the front-row panorama enjoyed by the spotters for the top-ten cars, but she'd still be able to help Tony run a better race—if only he would cooperate.

"Gentlemen, start your engines!"

The crowd responded with an enormous cheer as the familiar command echoed through the Martinsville Speedway. Faith felt a surge of adrenaline. How could anyone not be excited by the grind and growl, of forty-three highly tuned V-8 engines? Their combined power—more than 32,000 horsepower—was enough to propel a supertanker. The roar they made would make radio communications almost impossible if not for the noise-canceling capabilities of the headphones that fully surrounded her ears.

The race progressed pretty much as she expected. The field of cars traveled together in one long train, but at slower average speeds than most NASCAR races, with lots of braking in the sharp turns and noisy acceleration on the short straightaways. Faith counted dozens of minor bumps that bent fenders and other body metal, but none of the cars spun out or smashed into the wall.

Tony managed to move up to the twenty-ninth position, but after that, he seemed to run out of passing opportunities. Five hundred laps at Martinsville total only 263 miles. A driver couldn't "wait for later" to improve his place in line.

Faith had heard Tony complain to the car chief that his Dodge was too "loose"—that he had to fight to stay in the groove on every turn because the back end of the car kept losing traction. The same problem had spoiled Tony's qualification runs. Now it kept Tony from unleashing his usual aggressive driving. She guessed that he felt tired from continuously wrestling with the steering wheel—and more than a little bit annoyed at his bad luck.

She gave him advice as often as she could, but true to his promise, he didn't respond to any of her messages over the radio. On at least two of these occasions, she'd suggested maneuvers that might have let Tony move ahead in the field. Faith finally decided that she didn't mind Tony's rebuff. She was doing her job effectively, regardless. Helping to prevent crashes was Job Number One for a spotter. But a driver also needed good advice on when—and how—to pass other cars, because NASCAR race cars don't have side mirrors. If Tony didn't want to listen to her—well, that was his call.

Halfway through the race, the car that started in the forty-third slot managed to get behind Tony. Its driver, Kurt Layton, had qualified for the third position, but during practice on Saturday, he'd pushed his Chevy a trifle too hard. The car spun out and crashed into the wall. The damage was far too extensive to repair given the limited facilities available in Martinsville's garage bays. Instead, the team prepared a replacement race car, which meant that Kurt had to start at the end of the field.

Faith watched the two cars jockey awhile and then realized that Tony was trying hard to prevent Kurt from passing. Tony wasn't going anywhere with his car today, but although Layton had a good chance to improve his position, Tony wouldn't let it happen.

Uh-oh. That's not the way the game is played in NASCAR.

She felt someone pulling her left headphone away from her ear. Slinky Harris had moved close to her and was now cupping his hand next to her ear so he could speak over the roar.

"I just had my ribs elbowed by Kurt Layton's spotter," he said. "He saw me with you earlier and wants to know what's going on. Why is Tony Griffith refusing to cooperate with Kurt?"

Faith shouted back, "My guess is that Tony is frustrated! He's annoyed that Kurt is driving a car that can actually maneuver on a short racetrack!"

"You'd better tell Tony to get *un*-annoyed real quick. Kurt's gonna try to pass him, no matter what Tony does. On this track, that's a recipe for a collision."

"He won't listen to anything I say."

"Won't listen? What does that mean?"

"Exactly what it sounds like. Tony ignores everything I say."

"That's nuts! No driver ignores his spotter."

"Trust me. That's what Tony's doing today." She pointed to her microphone. "Do you want to try?"

"You know the rules. One driver, one spotter. Besides, if I talked to Tony, I'd turn the airwaves blue. I can't afford to pay a hefty fine to NASCAR for using excessively colorful language."

She sighed. "Then I'd better try again."

"You do that—before Tony causes the kind of car crash that makes the evening news." Slinky dropped the left headphone back over Faith's ear.

She took a step closer to the fence and began transmitting.

"Kurt Layton intends to pass you. Suggest you cooperate."

No answer. She saw Kurt's Chevy surge forward. Tony made a quick jiggle that forced Kurt to pull back a few feet.

"Tony—suggest you go high on the next turn to let Kurt pass you."

No answer. Kurt began to probe, first driving high, then low, seeking an opportunity to slip past Tony. But Tony matched his every move.

"Tony. Cooperate with Kurt. You know how NASCAR racing works."

Still no answer.

"Blast you, Tony Griffith! Your pretending that I'm not talking to you is getting ridiculous. I know you can hear me. *Respond!*"

Tony finally answered. "Man, I wish I could turn this radio off. You're as useful as a cup holder in a racing car."

Faith saw Tony's Dodge move a few feet high as he entered

Turn 3. He must have lost concentration for the instant it took to invent his snide comment. Kurt immediately exploited Tony's mistake and forced his way past on the low side, leaving dented metal and doughnut shapes of wheel-scratched paint on Tony's car.

She expected Tony to let loose with a barrage of cursing, but he didn't. Instead, he complained about her. "Thank you for telling the competition how to pass me. I'm sure they were listening on our frequency when you advised me to go high."

She started to reply, but decided not to. Why bother wasting her breath arguing with an obvious numbskull?

She continued providing advice for the rest of the race, Tony continued to ignore her, and then she began reporting Kurt Layton's progress as he continued to pass other cars. Kurt finished the race in ninth position—a remarkable driving performance, given where he started. Tony received the thirty-second swish of the checkered flag.

"That's exactly where you belong," Faith muttered, as she packed her gear. "Way, _way_ out of the top ten."

Tony wanted to find a Jacuzzi somewhere, take a long soak, and then relax in the back of his motor coach while his driver handled the short two-hour drive from Martinsville back to Concord, North Carolina. But he couldn't. Not yet. He had several hours of hard work ahead of him.

There were autographs to sign for the fans, interviews with reporters, and most important of all, photo shoots, handshake meetings, and a dinner with the different sponsors who paid the bills. He would be on duty until nearly 10:00 p.m. before he flew back home with Emmett Grant on the company helicopter.

Win or lose, his after-race schedule didn't change much. A lot of it wasn't much fun, but it was the price he and every other driver paid to be able to race high-performance stock cars in NASCAR's premier circuit. Tony knew that, all in all, he had nothing to complain about. He earned lots of money, lived in a great house, and had thousands of loyal fans.

So stop moaning and start smiling.

He was walking toward his first scheduled autograph session when Ken Cassini came trotting up to him. "The boss wants to see you now."

"I'm on my way to sign autographs."

"He knows that. He says it won't take more than five minutes to chew you out."

"Uh-oh."

"A really big *uh-oh*." Ken frowned. "Emmett is waiting for you in the ladies' motor coach. I've never seen the boss more upset."

"The business with Kurt Layton, I suppose?"

"Don't ask me." Ken raised his right hand in the "Stop" gesture a school crossing guard might use. "I'm merely a humble spotter. I have no idea why Emmett wants to skin you alive."

Tony gave Ken a friendly pat on the back. "You can have my office and my parking spot if Emmett fires me."

"If?" Ken grimaced. "Boy, are you an optimist."

Tony began to jog to the private parking lot where the team motor coaches were parked. *The boss must really have a burr under his saddle,* he thought as he ran. *Emmett Grant never puts team business ahead of meeting and greeting fans.*

He rapped on the door of the big, beige motor coach used by Grant Racing's three senior female staffers, but he didn't wait for an answer before he turned the handle and went inside. He found Emmett Grant sitting in a large, leather-upholstered captain's chair, swiveling back and forth slowly, a furious scowl on his face. Jessie McKnight, the team's car chief, stood behind Emmett, leaning against a birch-paneled wall. She looked even more imposing than usual—her arms crossed, her hazel eyes blazing—and at least as irritated as her boss.

Emmett raised his arm and pointed. "Tony, stand over there."

Tony looked in the direction of Emmett's outstretched finger and saw Faith Wright in the motor home's kitchen area. She stood cross-armed, too, but her body language signaled that her pose was defensive rather than offensive. Her expression looked more unhappy than angry.

Emmett didn't wait for Tony to reach Faith before he started to speak.

"I'll begin with our new spotter. Faith, you should have known better. You caused a good deal of excitement on our radio channel. I'm sure that the fans—and the competition—really loved hearing Grant Racing air its dirty laundry in public."

Tony glanced at Faith. She responded to Emmett with an embarrassed shrug.

Emmett continued. "Everything was okay until you complained that Tony was ignoring you." He pointed his finger at her again. "That was a foolish thing to do. And unnecessary. Keep calling the shots. Keep dishing out advice. Tony can't turn

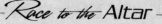

off his radio; he can't lower the volume in his helmet headset. He *has* to hear everything you say." He added, "Do you understand me?"

"Completely," she said softly. "It won't happen again."

Tony bit back a smile. The boss was definitely right, but there was no need to delight in Faith's comeuppance. She seemed to have learned her lesson.

"Now," Emmett said, "let's turn our attention to our hotshot driver, the root cause of all our problems."

Tony realized that Emmett was gazing at him with the single-mindedness of a laser beam. He didn't enjoy the sensation.

Emmett continued, "I would love to know what you had in mind out there today. Is there a reason why you ignored the age-old gentleman's agreement to give the right of way to a car that has a chance to finish much higher than you do?"

"I was working just as hard as Kurt Layton to improve my position. I saw no need to make it easy for him to pass me."

"Even though you could barely keep your car on the track?"

"My car was loose, but it was still drivable."

"And so you made a decision to block Kurt Layton?"

"I did."

"On your own, apparently."

"Well. . ." Tony wavered. He abruptly understood where Emmett's questions were leading.

Emmett bounced out of his captain's chair, reached Tony in three long strides, and poked his finger into Tony's chest.

"Your spotter gave you sound advice, but you chose to ignore it. That kind of brainless arrogance can be deadly when cars are moving inches apart at 170 miles an hour." Emmett slammed his right hand against his left palm. "You were lucky today. The net result of your stupidity came to a few thousand dollars' worth of bodywork damage. Naturally, we plan to recover the cost of repairs out of your earnings."

"Amen!" Jessie McKnight chimed in from across the room. Tony glanced at her and saw she was nodding vigorously.

Tony glared back at Emmett but said nothing. The boss was famous for his dramatic outbursts, but he rarely imposed irrational penalties. Everyone knew that racing at Martinsville was tough on bodywork; teams wouldn't charge their drivers for routine damage.

"One other thing," Emmett said. "You aren't racing next Sunday. Take a week off."

Tony stiffened. This was serious—a heavy-duty punishment. "I'm way behind in NASCAR points this year. I do well at Texas Motor Speedway."

"Forget it! The way you're driving right now, you won't score any points. You're a liability, a driver who's likely to wreck my cars."

"Amen and amen!" Jesse said.

"I'm a good driver," Tony said, "and you *both* know it."

Emmett replied with a curt shake of his head. "What I know about Tony Griffith is that you're a driver with great promise, but for reasons I can't fathom, you're not driving up to your potential."

"That's not fair."

"Stop arguing with me." Emmett looked back and forth at Tony and Faith. "The both of you—get out of here. Go somewhere and learn to play nice with each other."

Faith moved to the door immediately, but Emmett tugged at Tony's sleeve. "If you want to drive in Phoenix two Sundays from now, you start shaping up today. Understand?"

"Completely," Tony said, and then he followed Faith out of the motor coach, stunned by what the boss had done. He wondered if Faith would gloat. She certainly had the right to say "I told you so." He slammed the coach's door shut harder than was necessary to engage the latch.

"Well, what do we do now?" she asked.

"I have to sign autographs. You're welcome to come along."

"I'd rather eat broken glass."

Tony laughed. "I enjoy meeting the fans, but it's probably not fun for other team people to watch. Tell you what—we can talk about our relationship tomorrow, back in Concord."

"Ah. So we're going to have a relationship, after all."

He hoped that his grin didn't look too sheepish. "I'm a quick learner. Despite what Emmett Grant thinks about me, I won't repeat what happened today."

"Me, neither."

Faith smiled at him in a way that lit up her face.

Tony felt astonished. This woman was more than "extremely attractive," she was downright beautiful.

It doesn't make any difference—you're almost engaged to Kathy Mullins of Medford, Oregon.

"I really wasn't ignoring you." Tony took a sip of his coffee. "I may not have been much of a conversationalist yesterday, but I paid attention to everything you told me about the track, the cars in my vicinity, and the people trying to pass me."

Faith smiled. That wasn't the way she remembered what happened on Sunday, but maybe Tony had a conveniently selective memory. None of that mattered, because now—on Monday afternoon—they were talking like true colleagues.

Tony went on. "Emmett Grant thinks that I didn't respect the other spotters he assigned to me. He expected me to follow every piece of advice they gave me. That's where Emmett and I part company. I'm responsible for my own destiny. I can't turn over the responsibility for my success to another person."

"Is that why you didn't follow my advice about Kurt Layton?"

"You bet it was. I made a decision early in the race not to let Kurt pass without a fight. Why should I roll over and play dead for another driver? I was making good progress despite my car's badly tuned suspension. . .and I kept making progress after Kurt slipped by."

"*Slow* progress," Faith teased.

"Yeah, well, you try driving a NASCAR race car around the Martinsville paperclip when the rear springs and shocks are set up wrong for the track."

"How could that happen?"

"You may find this hard to believe, but there are guys working in the garage who don't like me."

"You *do* have relationship problems." Her expression became serious. "But I can't imagine any of the team going out of their way to sabotage your car."

"That's the real problem—they won't go out of their way. Oh, they go through the motions and do their jobs, but they don't care enough to make sure that my car is perfect. They go

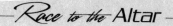

the extra mile for Clint McCabe, but not for me. It's been that way for more than a year." He downed the last of his coffee and crushed his cup. "I'm in the mood for another cappuccino. Can I get you one?"

Faith understood that Tony really had asked her to stay and talk a bit longer. They had arrived at the trendy coffee shop on Union Street in downtown Concord at three o'clock and had talked about Tony's dry streak. He attributed his lack of winning to issues outside of his control, chiefly problems with his car. But he also admitted that he'd ticked off several key people within the Grant Racing organization, a confession that surprised Faith.

She looked at Tony standing at the counter, placing their orders. Nothing about him today seemed arrogant. Quite the contrary. He'd been soft-spoken, self-deprecating, almost humble. And wholly attentive. But which was the real Tony Griffith—the boorish stock car driver or the handsome, well-mannered, nice guy?

I hope it's the latter.

Faith pushed the thought away. It made no sense to think about Tony in those terms. On the one hand, he had a girlfriend; on the other hand, she intended to return to grad school in a few months. They had carved out different futures and would live in two different worlds.

Tony returned with two steaming cups inside insulating sleeves. "I added an extra sprinkle of cinnamon to yours."

"Yum. Thanks."

"What were we talking about before I left?"

"You. But maybe we should tackle the seven-ton elephant

in the room." She paused and shot him a glance. "My past."

Tony nodded. "The story I hear is that you were driving your first race at Dover International Speedway. You qualified in the middle of the field and had managed to advance to the seventeenth position. You were driving aggressively. The accident occurred around Lap 200—"

"Lap 207," she corrected.

"A few seconds before you arrived at Turn 2, you told your spotter that you intended to pass the sixteenth car on the inside—in other words, that you intended to *go low*. He began shouting at you, 'Go high! Go high!'"

"But I didn't go high."

"No. You went low and hit the eighteenth car, which had come up next to you on your inside, where you couldn't see it."

"I don't remember much after that."

"You spun into the wall, knocked yourself out, and totaled your car. The other car flipped several times, then landed hard on its roof in the infield. The driver spent three months in the hospital."

"Don't leave out the 'worst part' of the story, as you called it the other day."

"You claimed that your spotter never told you to go high—even though your crew and several hundred fans with radio scanners heard him yelling at you."

She let herself sigh. "As crazy as it sounds, I never heard his warning. My radio was completely silent after I told my spotter I intended to go low."

"Completely silent?" He peered strangely at her. "Well, if you say so. . ."

She laughed. "It's almost comical. People who hear my side of the story invariably get inane looks on their faces. I can hear them thinking, 'Faith Wright must be loony.' How can she possibly insist that the spotter never told her to go high when everyone else heard him shouting?'"

"Do I have an inane look on my face?" Tony asked.

"Utterly inane." She toasted Tony with her coffee cup. "But I can't blame you. I have no idea how my version of what happened could be true—although it *is* true. I was driving the car that day. I know what I heard and what I didn't hear."

"For what it's worth, I'll do my best to believe you."

"Hmm. I'm not quite sure what that means, but I appreciate the thought."

Without thinking, Faith reached out and squeezed Tony's hand.

Chapter 3

Tony drove Faith back to the vintage house she'd rented on Old Charlotte Road in Concord, feeling bewildered by the story she had told him. It seemed impossible to believe her; what she said couldn't be true. But why would she be dishonest about a three-year-old accident?

Why would Faith insist that she'd never heard her spotter say, "Go high"?

Everyone assumed Faith was lying at the time, because... well, because she must be lying. Upwards of a thousand people had heard the warning that she claimed never came.

According to Jimbo Davis, most of the NASCAR higher-ups concluded that Faith had exercised bad judgment, but they blamed her slipup on her lack of experience. After all, she'd driven only about a dozen major races. Rookies often made foolish mistakes. It took years of seat time behind the wheel to become an accomplished NASCAR driver—not that years of driving automatically eliminated fatal car collisions.

"I could have caused the same kind of crash yesterday," Tony

muttered, as he pointed his red Corvette toward his home in The Sanctuary, a private community on Lake Wylie, west of Charlotte. If he'd zigged rather than zagged at Martinsville, he might have sent Kurt Layton's car flying. And flipped his own car into the wall. The idea made him shudder.

Tony knew that he'd exaggerated Faith's "wrongdoing" when he gave her a hard time on her first day with Grant Racing. But he'd needed a good reason to complain about the spotter that Emmett Grant had unceremoniously dumped on his doorstep. Now that he'd come to know Faith a little better—and, yes, begun to like her as a person—he had to admit that many veteran drivers, faced with the same circumstances, might also decide to overrule their spotter's advice.

That doesn't answer the key question. Why would Faith lie about what happened?

Tony made a snap decision. He flipped open his cell phone and pushed the button that dialed Jimbo Davis.

"I need to talk to you, Jimbo," he said. "Where are you?"

"I'm still at the Grant Racing building. Where are you?"

"Halfway home—but I'll meet you in your office in twenty minutes."

"No way. Meet me at Bubba's Pizza, across the street. Bring plenty of money. I'm in the mood for a Bubba's Deluxe."

"Order one for me, too. I'll drive fast and be there in fifteen minutes."

⌐

"The obvious question is," Jimbo said, with a mouthful of pizza, "do you believe Faith Wright?"

"I want to believe her," Tony said.

"Not good enough. Of course you want to believe her. She's a great-looking woman with a fine personality—a real charmer." He picked up a fresh slice of pizza. "I'll ask you again. Do you believe her? Truly believe her?" He plucked a piece of anchovy off the slice. "If you were on the jury, would you vote not guilty?"

Tony had been staring at the faux marble table. He raised his eyes to meet Jimbo's. "It's not that simple. When she told her story, when she looked me square in the face, I believed every word she said. Nobody's that good a liar."

Jimbo nodded. "I know what you mean. I've chatted with her once or twice—I don't think she's a deceitful person."

"But her story doesn't make sense. You know it, I know it, and so does she. Hundreds of other honest people say she's not telling the truth. How can that many witnesses be wrong?"

Jimbo thought for a moment. "Who says they're right?"

"Give me a break, Jimbo. Most of the people listening to Faith's frequency that day were her fans. They wouldn't lie to hurt her. If anything, they'd want to protect her. They must be telling the truth."

"I didn't say anyone told a lie, my friend. You believe hundreds of witnesses can't be wrong. I disagree." He ate the pointy end of his pizza slice and then said, "What if those nearly one thousand fans didn't hear the same broadcast Faith heard?"

"Let me get this straight." Tony paused a moment. "No—I can't even begin to figure out what you said. We're talking about a simple radio link. The spotter talks, the driver listens, the fans use their scanners to eavesdrop. Everybody hears the same thing."

"Not necessarily."

"Sheesh! I can't imagine what's churning in that warped mind of yours."

"In that case, it's time to tell you another story. Once upon a time there was an evil magician who wanted to end the career of a promising NASCAR driver. . . ."

Tony reached for his telephone and, for the fifth time that Tuesday morning, decided not to call Faith. He knew he had to call her, had to bring her to Jimbo so that he could retell his incredible story. But not quite yet. Not until he came up with the perfect words to say.

A funny thing happened last night, Faith. Jimbo explained to me over a slice of pizza that you were probably the victim of a conspiracy.

Right! That would work.

Tony stared at the phone, uncertain how to handle such a delicate situation. If he—or Jimbo—said the wrong thing, Faith would surely explode, maybe even want to rake up the past and file a complaint with NASCAR. Who could blame her? Faith's promising career as a NASCAR driver probably ended because of a vicious scheme aimed squarely at her.

You have to tell her. She deserves to know.

Tony took a calming breath, reached for the receiver, and dialed Faith's extension inside Grant Racing.

"How are you this morning?" she asked.

"Ah. . .uh. . .I'm fine. And you?"

"I'm fine, too." She added, "What can I do for you?"

"We have to talk. I mean you, me, and Jimbo Davis have to talk."

"About. . . ?

Tony wished he were better at thinking on his feet. Two minutes from now, the perfect thing to say would pop into his mind.

"To tell you the truth, I've been wrestling with myself. I have something important to tell you, but I'm not sure how."

"Something bad or something good?"

"Something. . .bizarre."

"Tell me."

He hesitated.

"Keep talking—I love bizarre." She sounded tickled by his choice of word.

Tony took another long, slow breath to settle himself. "Last night, Jimbo and I had a long chat about your crash at Dover International Speedway."

"I see."

"No, you don't see. Jimbo thinks it may not have been an accident."

"What do you mean, not an accident?" Faith's voice changed with each syllable she spoke, as uncertainty and concern expelled the amusement Tony had heard earlier.

"I'd do a terrible job of retelling Jimbo's theory. You need to hear it from the source. That's why we need to meet with him, now."

"Oh my. I've put the crash at Dover behind. . ." She stopped in midsentence.

"Faith?" To his surprise, Tony realized that he now cared a great deal about the way she felt.

"Yes."

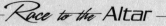

"Please trust me. You need to hear what Jimbo told me. I'll pick you up in five minutes."

"Make it ten."

"It's a date!" Tony winced when he thought about what he'd said. But then he put down his phone and thought about it some more.

That's not such a bad idea.

"The boss insisted that I take this fancy office next door to his," Jimbo said with a self-conscious grin. "I told him again and again that I'd be happier with a desk in the corner of the garage, but he wouldn't listen to me."

Faith smiled along with Jimbo, but she could tell he was proud of his large office and its fancy stainless-steel-and-glass furnishings. She also understood his sudden need to make small talk. He looked as uncomfortable as she felt at the prospect of discussing her accident. And as for Tony, he might have been the proverbial boy caught stealing cookies. His eyes darted hither and yon, focusing on different items in Jimbo's office. Faith could see a gleaming film of perspiration on his brow.

What ridiculous theory have they cooked up between them?

Jimbo's happy expression faded. "If it were my decision, we wouldn't be having this conversation. I left it up to Tony to decide whether or not to tell you what we talked about last night. I assume he knows you better than I do."

Faith needed all her self-control not to laugh out loud. The very idea of Tony Griffith making an effort to understand a woman struck her as absurd. True, he could be personable in a coffee shop for a few hours. But lurking beneath the Nice Tony facade was the egotistical race car driver who cared only about himself. She felt grateful that Tony had loosened up enough with her to build a cordial driver/spotter working relationship, but that didn't mean he knew what made her tick.

Jimbo looked at her expectantly. Faith guessed he wanted her to affirm her desire that he go forward with his explanation.

"Please tell me the idea you worked out," she said, feeling more than a little curious.

Jimbo nodded. "Tony posed an interesting challenge as we ate pizza. He told me your story and then asked if there is a way that everyone can be right about what they heard in the seconds before your crash—you and the people who listened in on their scanners." Jimbo frowned. "I told Tony that the answer was yes. I'll be happy to tell you everything I told him."

Faith nodded, sure that if she spoke, her voice would squeak. This was not what she expected. Jimbo seemed perfectly serious—as if he had actually uncovered what had occurred three years ago.

Jimbo went on. "I don't know if it actually happened this way, but I'll tell you how it could be done." He began to sketch a rough illustration on a white pad on his desk. "The first trick is that someone had to rig up a private radio link between the spotter and the radio in your helmet."

He looked at Faith intently. "Do you understand what I mean? Your spotter had two radios. One—the special radio—connected directly to you. The other—the routine radio—let him broadcast like every other spotter at the track."

"I suppose so." Faith peered at the sketch. "I could talk to the spotter; the spotter could talk to me over the special radio. Except—the fans heard me talking, too, during the race."

"That's the second trick. He wired the two radios together. That Sunday, everything you heard—or said—over your radio was relayed through your spotter's radio." Jimbo drew wavy lines on his illustration, Faith guessed, to represent radio signals.

"Most of the time, the spotter's radio carried all the usual chitchat between driver, spotter, and crew chief. But at the perfect point in the race, the spotter turned off the special radio, so that you couldn't hear him say, 'Go high!' However, everyone else at the track heard him shouting."

Tony spoke to Faith. "By 'the perfect point in the race,' Jimbo means the instant when the eighteenth car started to pass you."

Faith nodded again, this time to camouflage the pang of nausea in the pit of her stomach. Was it really possible? Could it be that simple?

She managed to speak. "But how could my spotter be sure that not hearing his warning would cause me to crash?"

"He probably wasn't sure—at least not the first time he did it. But he probably pulled the same stunt several times during the race, until at the critical instant another driver who assumed you knew he was passing made a move. *Bang!*"

Faith's mind began to whirl. "That's exactly what happened at Dover. He didn't give me much advice that day. I assumed that it was because we hadn't worked together before. Anyway, on Lap 207, when I approached Turn 2, I told my spotter I intended to go low. I expected him to correct me if it was a dangerous move. But he didn't say anything." She gave a quick shake of her head.

"Correction. I didn't hear him say anything."

Jimbo leaned forward. "Why didn't you have your regular spotter that Sunday?"

"He went to a parents' weekend at his daughter's college. Another guy from the racing team filled in."

Jimbo nodded and heaved a sigh. "Yeah, it all fits together. A spotter you know well wouldn't want to get you killed— or dishonored. They waited until your regular spotter was gone."

A fresh stab of nausea made her swallow hard. Of course it was "they." It had to be. A single person could hardly execute the elaborate scheme Jimbo had described. First there was the spotter. Then someone in the car crew had to fiddle with the radio in her helmet. And perhaps someone else in the front office had to make sure that the "cooperative" spotter was assigned to Faith that day.

Faith ignored the sour taste that had filled her mouth. "Who would do something like that to me?"

Jimbo touched her shoulder gently. "The more important question is, why would the people you work with choose you as a target?"

"Okay—*why?*"

"Obviously, you were a significant threat to someone else on your team. He believed that your success might lead to his failure."

"Do you mean one of the other drivers?"

Jimbo stared at his desktop and said nothing. Faith took his silence as a yes to her question.

Tony broke the quiet in the office by leaping out of his

chair and knocking it over. "That's criminal! We have to tell NASCAR. We'll ask them to launch an investigation. The spotter and whoever organized the conspiracy should be banned from racing—for life."

"What do you want NASCAR to investigate?" Jimbo said. "The accident happened three years ago. We have no proof, only our confidence that Faith is telling the truth coupled with a wacky theory that no one of sound mind is likely to believe." He added a disparaging shrug. "Besides, people are happy with the notion that Faith made a rookie mistake. It's the simplest explanation, the one most folks want to be true. Accidents happen. End of story."

"There must be some way to prove what really caused the crash," Tony said. "It's not fair that Faith should go through life with a tainted reputation."

Jimbo chuckled. "It seems to me that Faith has managed to build a pretty fine reputation for herself since the accident. Why don't we ask the lady how she feels? I'd like to know whether she wants to raise a ruckus."

Faith glanced at Tony. He seemed embarrassed by Jimbo's mild scolding. He also looked—what was the right word to describe it?—*guilty* about something. Neither emotion, she realized, were likely to be expressed as openly by a truly egocentric person. Is it possible that she had misjudged Tony?

Jimbo made a sweeping gesture with his right arm. "Ms. Wright, Tony and I are waiting to be enlightened as to your intentions."

Faith clasped her hands in her lap and knit her fingers together. "Every time I think about what happened to me three years ago," she said, softly, "I feel like throwing up. Those were some of the most terrible days of my life. The absolute worst part was learning that the driver of the other car would never drive in a NASCAR race again."

She paused while Tony righted his chair, moved it closer to her, and sat down.

"I was angry—furious is a better word—that no one would believe my side of the story. I knew that I hadn't heard a warning over my radio, no matter what everyone else heard."

Faith peered at Jimbo's attentive face. "I always suspected that someone else caused my accident, but I had no way to convince anyone. I felt bitter; I used to dream of revenge. But then my life. . .ah, changed. I moved on and decided to forgive whoever was responsible."

"Well done!" Jimbo said. "As Proverbs 19:11 so wisely observes, 'A man's wisdom gives him patience; it is to his glory to overlook an offense.'"

Faith smiled. "It wasn't quite that easy. It's difficult to ignore an offense that changes your life, but I've been working on it for the past three years. Anyway, to answer your question, no, I don't want to make a ruckus."

"That much wisdom in a former NASCAR driver deserves a mighty hug," Jimbo said. "May I?"

"Absolutely."

As they hugged, she looked over Jimbo's shoulder and saw an expression of utter astonishment on Tony's face. He clearly didn't grasp how she could forgive the spotter who caused her so much pain.

Maybe I'll get the chance to explain it to him.

Tony struggled to keep up with Faith as they walked the long corridor back to their own offices. She kept charging ahead, a woman on a mission. Or maybe she simply wanted to get away from him?

Who could blame her? His performance at Jimbo's office was not his finest hour. She'd remained unruffled while he'd become furious enough to call for an investigation.

What's gotten into me today?

"Are you in a hurry," he asked her, "or merely anxious to escape from lunatic stock car drivers?"

She laughed as she stopped short. "I feel energized. I know it's crazy, but I'm in a mood to go bungee jumping or rock climbing or skydiving."

"Well, if you want to—I suppose. . ."

"Relax. I'm not going to actually do any of those things."

"Whew!" He tried for a wry expression. "I thought you were going to ask me to go along with you. I hate heights."

She ignored his flippant reply, apparently eager to explain her buoyant mood.

"What just happened is amazing. It's impossible to prove that Jimbo was right, but I *know* deep down that he figured out my so-called accident." She touched Tony's hand. "Thank you. I appreciate what Jimbo—and *you*—did."

Her face was glowing. Tony didn't want to stare, but she seemed even more beautiful than before.

"I have to ask you a question." He took a moment to choose the right words. "What you said in Jimbo's office doesn't make much sense to me. How can you not be bothered by the fact that no one else will know the truth? Most people in NASCAR will keep thinking you made a rookie mistake. A few will even assume that you intentionally knocked that car off the track because you didn't want to let him to pass." Tony took a breath. "I guess what I'm asking is, how can you forgive people who ruined everything you worked so hard to achieve?"

She peered into his eyes. "Do you *really* want to know?"

Tony had another glib comment ready, but the sincerity he saw on Faith's face changed his mind. "Yes. I really want to know."

"Two months after the accident, I became a Christian."

She must have read the puzzlement on his face, because she continued. "Christians are called to forgive. It's a foundation stone of Christianity—to forgive us our trespasses as we forgive those who trespass against us."

"I know. Sort of. I'm a Christian, too." He glanced around the corridor. *Good—no one else in sight.* The conversation had gone in a direction he hadn't anticipated. He felt awkward talking about religion, especially when his other staffers might overhear.

"But how can you forgive people you don't know, who haven't apologized to you or been punished for what they did?"

"It wasn't easy, but I'm glad I made the effort. Three years ago, I wasted tons of energy being bitter. Forgiving my unknown trespassers let me move on with my life." She smiled. "Now you know the rest of the story."

Tony glanced at his watch. "It's close to lunchtime and it's a lovely day. Why don't we go out and find a cozy place to continue our conversation? This hallway is beginning to feel oppressive."

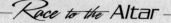

Once again, Faith seemed confused. She blinked a few times, as if not sure how to respond to his straightforward invitation. What had he said wrong?

"No pressure," he said, quickly. "I'll give you a rain check if you're too busy to have lunch with me today."

"I'm not busy, but. . ."

"But?"

Faith brows moved together. It wasn't exactly a frown, but Tony got the idea she wasn't happy.

"Look," she said, "it's no big deal when two business friends—one male, one female—have lunch together in the company cafeteria. That probably happens a million times a day. But you just invited me to a cozy restaurant. Wouldn't your girlfriend out west be a tad concerned about that?"

"Ah." Tony could feel his face go pale. He hadn't seen the question coming. "You must mean Kathy Mullins of Medford, Oregon."

"No one told me her name, only that you're serious about each other and that you intend to get married someday."

Tony found himself staring at the beige carpeting in the corridor. "Have you ever been to Medford, Oregon?

"Nope."

"Well, if you go to the Medford branch of the Jackson County Public Library on Main Street and ask for the reference librarian, you'll soon be standing face-to-face with Katherine Mullins."

"A librarian? How interesting." Faith's voice sounded brittle.

"She's sixty years old—and my aunt."

"Your aunt!" Faith's half frown became a full-blown scowl. "You invented a nonexistent soon-to-be fiancée?"

"Purely in self-defense." He leaned closer to her so he could lower his voice. "When I joined Grant Racing, every un-married female in this building hit on me at least once. The gals around here are positively predatory."

Faith giggled. "I imagine from your perspective they might seem that way. You are a topic of great interest among the Grant Racing women."

"Yeah, well, a faraway girlfriend was the easy way out, so I took it. I didn't want to insult anyone I work with by repeatedly saying 'No, thank you.'"

Faith took a giant step backwards. "From here, you look like a hale and hearty male. I don't get it. Why would you want to distance yourself from every woman in the building? You have lots in common with Grant Racing gals, plenty to talk about. Instead of lying, wouldn't it have been simpler to choose one or two and go out once or twice? For all you know, your soul mate works in this building."

"Much too risky. As Dad always told me, *never* get involved with a woman at work."

She gave a half nod. "Perhaps your father was right. Office romances can be tricky."

"Nowhere more so than on a NASCAR racing team. A rac-ing driver has to be on constant guard."

"Really? On guard from what?"

"A driver never knows who he can trust."

"That seems a bit. . .the only word I can think of is *paranoid*."

"Not at all. It's merely good common sense. Your experience on your former racing team proves the point. You made the mistake of trusting your spotter—and look what happened."

"My regular spotter was a great guy."

"Sure, so you let your guard down." He shook his head. "That's something I'll *never* do. I won't give anyone the opportunity to take advantage of me. That's why I hang out in the garage. It's the only way I can be absolutely sure that my car is set up right."

"Come on! You can't believe that one of our mechanics would intentionally sabotage your car. That's plain silly."

"Why not? Your replacement spotter intentionally sabotaged you." He shrugged. "NASCAR racing is a big-money sport. You have to expect it to attract a few not-so-nice people."

"Maybe it does—but where does your kind of thinking stop? You can't doubt everyone who works at Grant Racing."

"Let's just say that I have a healthy skepticism about everyone I run into in this building."

Tony realized, a moment too late, the full significance of what he had said. He watched Faith's face darken, her eyes begin to tear.

"You are the biggest, most self-absorbed nincompoop I've ever met. You can take your cozy restaurant and...and..." She spun around and strode away.

"Wait!" he called, feebly. "You know that I wasn't talking about you. I trust you completely."

As she turned the corner, he said, "Stupid! Stupid! Stupid! When will you learn to keep your big mouth shut?"

Chapter 4

"Phoenix International Speedway can be a tough track for spotting," Ken Cassini said to Faith. "Because of where the spotters are located, we have a strange view of the track. The cars seem to bunch together on the straightaways. Many spotters find it difficult to pick out a specific race car—and even harder to spot cars trying to pass."

Faith nodded. Ken was right. The spotter's perch was atop the grandstand built between Turn 1 and Turn 2. Consequently, the spotters had down-the-road views of the track's long, front straightaway and its unusually shaped backstretch, with the famous sharp bend in the middle.

She'd had no problems spotting Tony's bright green Dodge during the practice sessions on Friday, chiefly because the other cars were spread out around the track and the drivers made frequent pit stops for adjustments. But this final practice, during "Happy Hour" on Saturday afternoon, would be different. All forty-three qualifying cars would be on the track, driving at full speed, in racelike conditions. Ken continued, "Last year, Clint

McCabe had a bad crash during Happy Hour. He clipped another driver's fender a few yards shy of Turn 3, spun out, and hit the wall. The four turns aren't banked especially high here, so it's easy to lose traction and start sliding. Clint finished thirty-sixth on race day, because he had to start in the back of the field and because our backup car wasn't adjusted properly for Phoenix." Ken rolled his eyes. "Naturally, being a typical driver, he blamed me for the smash-up."

Faith began to nod, thinking that Tony Griffith might also try to shift the blame for a mishap to her. She abruptly glanced away from Ken, feeling embarrassed by her spontaneous reaction.

That's not fair of you. Don't always assume the worst about Tony.

Faith raised her binoculars, looked at the Estrella Mountains behind the raceway, and recalled the past ten days since her pointless tiff with Tony back in Concord. He'd carried out a steadfast campaign to convince her that Tony Griffith was a nice guy after all. He seemed sincere, genuinely committed to improving their strained relationship. Moreover, he must have apologized a hundred times for implying that he didn't trust her.

Much to her surprise, Faith had begun to think of Tony as a friend. But their growing friendship didn't eliminate the niggles in the back of her mind. As the old saying goes, you only get one chance to make a first impression. Tony's bad manners—and even worse attitude—during her first week at Grant Racing made it difficult for Faith to give him the benefit of the doubt. Even though she felt less uncertain about Tony with every passing day, she still worried that he might suddenly revert to acting like a complete dunce. Consequently, she over-reacted to every minor slip of the tongue he made—and often prejudged his behavior.

I have to work on that. I have to try as hard as he's trying.

"Are you ready to spot?" Ken asked. "Happy Hour is about to start, and you look a million miles away."

"I'm fine," she said quickly. She slipped on her headset, readjusted her binoculars, and scanned the track's bright blue painted outside walls.

"Good," Ken said. "This is one track where Tony deserves your total attention, even during a practice session."

Faith nodded. She intended to do the best job she could as a spotter, but would Tony truly listen to her advice in a critical situation? The Friday practice sessions hadn't given her any op-portunity to offer suggestions. Tony had used the two practices as test runs to make sure that his car was no longer "seriously loose," as he'd put it.

"What do you intend to do?" she'd asked him at breakfast on Friday.

"I want to make sure that my car is fine-tuned for Phoenix, so I thought I'd start high on the track and then take the curves lower in each successive lap."

"How fast will you go?"

"Pretty slow in the beginning. Maybe an average lap speed of 120 miles per hour at first—until I'm confident about the car again."

"Sounds like a plan," she said, hoping she'd kept the amaze-ment she felt out of her voice. Had he asked, she would have proposed the same take-it-slow approach to practice. He was acting sensibly on the track for the first time since she'd met him.

Tony seemed in complete control of the car during the first Friday practice sessions. "How's the car doing?" she'd asked, after a few laps.

"It's super in the curves," he'd answered. "The suspension's definitely not loose today. The engine also feels stronger than it ever has." He added, "How do I look from your vantage point?"

"Fast and steady. I can't think of any suggestions to make."

"Well," he said, "I'm sorry to bore you. Try to stay awake up there."

Faith began to laugh. An instant later, Tony joined in.

The rest of Friday had passed just as uneventfully. Would Saturday's practice be the same? Would Tony's good behavior continue during Happy Hour, when the stakes—and the stress level—were much higher? Most important of all, would he continue to take her seriously as a teammate?

Faith hoped so. It was much more fun spotting for the new and improved Tony Griffith.

She moved to the rail of the spotter's stand and watched the cars begin to accelerate along the track. Tony was in the middle of the field. He had qualified in twenty-first position—his best starting slot this year. "Your boy did pretty well during the qualification laps," Ken Cassini had said. "I assume that's mostly because the mechanics worked the kinks out of his car. But I don't think he'll do better than nineteenth or twentieth during the race. He never seems to engage a winning team around him. That's what it takes to finish high."

Faith had merely smiled. Anything was possible during a 312-lap race—even Tony slipping past Clint McCabe, who had qualified a respectable tenth.

"Are you there, partner?" Tony's voice filled her headphones.

Partner? The old Tony would never have said that.

"I'm here."

"The car's working fine, and so am I."

She peered intently through her binoculars while Tony accelerated, maneuvered around several other cars, and gradually improved his place in the pack. He maintained his new position for the next two laps.

"Hey, madam spotter," he said, unexpectedly. "I'm in the mood for some *boogity-boogity-boogity*. What do you think?"

"I concur—but don't ding the bodywork."

"Yes, mommy."

Faith watched Tony pass two more cars and then come up behind a red Chevy, whose driver seemed determined not to let Tony slip by. "Boys will be boys, even during practice," she murmured to herself.

Tony was driving in the center of the lane, waiting for an opportunity to pass the Chevy. A yellow Ford came up behind Tony. She knew Tony would see him in his rearview mirror.

As the cars moved through the bend in the backstretch, both the Chevy in front of Tony and the Ford to his rear jigged slightly to the right. Faith immediately shouted, "Clear low!" Tony accelerated, passed the Chevy on the left, and shot down the back straightaway toward Turn 3.

A flash of something flat lying on the track in front of

Tony caught her eye. "Go high! Go high!" she shouted into her microphone.

"Why? I'm not even—," Tony began.

"*Go* high!"

The something on the track seemed to rise up as Tony approached it. Faith watched it strike the Dodge's bumper, slide over the windshield, hang there for an instant, and finally fly over the roof. The car veered toward the outside wall, but Tony managed to keep from hitting the blue blocks. Other cars passed him on his left as he let the Dodge slow down.

"Thank God," Faith said, softly.

"Amen." Tony sounded shaken. "What was that thing?"

"A piece of insulation, I think. Maybe part of a heat shield."

"It blinded me for what seemed forever. I was driving on autopilot."

"I know. Are you okay?"

"Yeah—and I'm pretty sure the car wasn't damaged. But I feel stupid. I should have listened to you without question."

"True—but it takes time to unlearn bad habits."

She watched the bright green Dodge accelerate again and waited for the sarcastic reply, the snide remark. But none came.

Oh my! He really has changed.

~

Tony walked beside Faith along the path that snaked through the competitors' motor coach parking area in the raceway's infield. She looked happier than he'd ever seen her—and more relaxed, despite his close call on the track. She didn't even seem mad at him for ignoring her timely warning. He felt curious about what she was thinking but decided not to ask.

Why risk upsetting her good mood?

Tony enjoyed being close to Faith. Even more, he looked forward to her company. His feelings about her grew stronger with each passing day. But what would she do if he told her how he felt? She would probably laugh at him or else get mad and run away. He didn't want either to happen.

There was a third possibility, of course—that she might feel the same way about him.

Not very likely. I've seen how she acts around me.

Tony sighed, too quietly for Faith to hear. For a thousand different reasons, she was obviously not attracted to him. His only safe course of action was to consider carefully every word before he spoke and do nothing to drive her away.

"Hold up, guys!" Jimbo Davis called. "Emmett Grant wants to talk to you before you go off to dinner."

Tony whirled to face him. "Rats! I suppose he wants to yell at me for not listening to my spotter during Happy Hour."

"Believe it or not, he wants to congratulate you for being sensible during the practice sessions." Jimbo smiled at Faith. "And he wants to give you a big hug." He opened his arms. "For that matter so do I."

After Jimbo hugged Faith, Tony said, "I did the driving. Don't I get a hug, too?"

"Nope, you get a Bible verse. 'Pride only breeds quarrels, but wisdom is found in those who take advice.' Proverbs 13:10." He clapped Tony's shoulder. "Today you demonstrated your wisdom."

"He certainly did," Faith said. "I really enjoyed spotting for Tony."

"Which brings up a related question," Jimbo said to her. "Did you ever tell Tony what you did for him back in Concord?"

"Uh. . ." She glanced at the ground, clearly embarrassed. "Not exactly. . ."

"That means you didn't tell him anything. I think he should know."

Tony jumped in. "What did you do for me?"

"Nothing, really," she said, her eyes still aimed at her feet. "Jimbo likes to exaggerate."

"Not so," Jimbo said to Tony. "This little lady met privately with the mechanics and asked them to do an extra good job setting up your car this week. She promised everyone that you trust them to do high quality work and that you'll try not to be a suspicious, overbearing pinhead in the future."

"Did you really do that?" Tony said to Faith.

She grinned sheepishly. "I talked to Larry Connors about your car—but I never called you a pinhead."

"I threw that stuff in to make a point," Jimbo said.

"What point?" Tony asked.

"The time has come for you to do your job and let the mechanics do theirs. In other words, try not to be a suspicious, overbearing pinhead any more."

"Aw, thanks."

"You're welcome." He gave Tony a gentle shove. "Now, go see the boss. He hates to be kept waiting."

"Shall we?" Tony extended his arm. Faith took it and said, "Let's."

He felt unusually buoyant as they headed for Emmett's motor coach.

⤳

"It's weird. . . ," Tony said. "I've been to Phoenix ten or fifteen times and never made it to Scottsdale before.

"Well, here you are," Faith said. "What do you think of it?"

"Resort-y, to coin one word. And cactus-y to coin another."

"This part of Scottsdale certainly is that." She laughed. "After all, we are strolling through a cactus garden at one of the town's biggest and plushest resorts."

"That's because you're the one who wanted to eat *gourmet* Mexican food." He wanted, at that moment, to put his arm around her shoulders, but he urged himself not to. *She'll get furious at me if I do.* "Did you enjoy dinner?"

"It was completely fabulous—although I'm so full I can barely walk."

Tony stopped near a tall Saguaro cactus and lifted his arms to mimic the plant's raised branches.

Another couple walked past them. Tony heard the woman giggle at his impromptu pose.

"Did our dinner cost as much as I think it did?" Faith said.

"Even more—but who cares? Emmett's picking up the tab. It's our reward for playing nice together."

She faced toward Phoenix, cupped her hands around her mouth, and mock shouted, "Thank you, Emmett, for being so generous!"

"I prefer, 'Thank you, Emmett, for hiring Faith Wright as my spotter.'"

When she didn't reply, Tony wondered if, yet again, he'd said the wrong thing to Faith.

She finally spoke. "Wow! I'm glad it's nighttime."

"Why?"

"So you can't see what your charming compliment did to me. My face has turned bright red." She strode ahead several paces.

"That's impossible." Tony caught up with her. "Everyone knows that NASCAR drivers are too tough to blush. We're emotionless driving machines."

"Back when I was driving, I sometimes wished that was true." She seemed to be choosing her words carefully. "But it's really the other way around. The drivers I know best overflow with emotion. We care about winning, we care about the fans, and we take every minor problem personally."

Tony nodded, although he doubted she could see his head moving. The decorative lights in the garden illuminated the cacti, but not much light spilled onto the path that threaded past the plantings. He decided to switch to a new, potentially risky topic.

"Faith, when I was practicing today, knowing you were watching me through your binoculars, I began to imagine how you must feel looking but not driving. Do you wish you were behind the wheel again?"

She stopped at a small stone bench and sat down. "It's strange you should say that. I've been asking myself the same question."

"And?"

"Three years ago, I felt certain that my NASCAR days were over. But thanks to you and Jimbo, I've begun to see things differently."

Tony sat down on the other end of the bench, perhaps two feet away from Faith. "I knew it! You _do_ want to drive again."

"Possibly in the future, but not right now. I'm determined to earn my doctorate in engineering and then. . ." She stopped in midsentence.

"Keep going! Don't leave me in suspense."

"I really don't know what the 'and then' will be. We'll have to see what happens. Maybe I'll try my hand at driving again, or perhaps I'll decide to develop future race cars. I may even choose to become a university professor. I really do enjoy teaching." She paused for a few seconds and then continued. "One of these days, I'll find out what God wants me to do when I grow up."

"God?" Tony spoke louder than he meant to. He counted to three and tried again, this time with a calmer voice. "What does God have to do with it?"

"Everything," Faith said. "One of the best things about being a Christian is that I'm learning how to discern God's will for my life. That's made living my life a whole lot easier during the past three years."

"God's will. . . ," he echoed, softly. "You're serious, aren't you?"

"Yes, I am."

"And the notion of God's will doesn't scare you?"

"Not at all."

"Well, it sure scares me. What if God doesn't want me to be a winning driver?"

Faith snorted. Tony could tell she was fighting not to laugh. "Well, if God's against you," she said, between snickers, "I don't

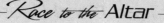

think you stand much of a chance of doing well in NASCAR. Do you?"

Tony felt foolish, but he said nothing until the three other people meandering past their bench were out of earshot. "Okay, I see your point, but I've always relied on what the Bible says— 'Heaven helps those who help themselves.'"

"Those words are *not* in the Bible."

"Whoa!" Tony sat up straight. "Are you sure?"

"Absolutely, positively. And more to the point, things don't seem to work that way. When you go off on your own, you'll often fail—no matter how much effort you apply. What I've come to believe with all my heart is that heaven helps those who act in God's will."

"I admit it's an interesting idea."

"Oh, boy!" Faith leaped to her feet. "I just figured you out. I know why you find it so hard to trust the people you work with."

"And the answer is. . ."

"If you don't allow God to take charge of your life, you *have* to rely on yourself completely. It's the only sensible thing to do in a world full of sinful people. After all, other people will always let you down, one way or another. They may lie or cheat, and they put ol' Number One first." She made a sweeping gesture that Tony saw in silhouette. "They sometimes even do sloppy work on a race car suspension."

"You're hollering at the wrong guy." Tony held up his hands in mock surrender. "Look, I've always believed in God. I say grace before meals. I even attend the NASCAR chapel services on Sundays. I know that God controls the universe. So what am I not doing right?"

Faith bent forward so that her face was close to his. "I'm not talking about the whole universe, only one man who lives in it—Tony Griffith." Tony's eyes had adjusted to the dark and there was enough light to see that her expression had become serious. "I know that I'm right about you. Do you know why?"

"Tell me."

"I used to think and act exactly like you. It wasn't until I turned my life over to God that I was able to trust other people—and forgive them." She gave a bubbly laugh. "The idea is so simple, it took me a year to believe it. I hope you're a quicker learner than I was."

"Of course I am. That goes without saying."

She put her tongue between her lips and blew a loud raspberry. She added, "Very funny."

"A strange idea just popped into my head," he said. "You're saying that moving forward on your own without God is like driving a car that's not adjusted for the track conditions. You'll probably be too loose or too tight. You won't be able to maintain control, and you'll run into new problems on every lap."

"A perfect analogy!" she said, happily. "But stay in God's will, and you'll drive in the groove—lap after lap after lap."

"And how do I make all this happen?"

"It's easy. Just ask God to take charge of your life."

"I'll think about it."

"Good. I don't want to see you spin out and hit the wall. *Ever.*"

Tony could hear a new tone in her voice—gentler, friendlier, more caring. She eased herself down on the stone bench.

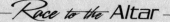

He realized that she was sitting much closer to him than before. If he reached sideways a few inches, his hand would touch her hand. But should he close the gap between them?

His heart began to thump.

Tony wondered what collection of forces had conspired to make him behave as clumsily as a teenager. He'd never acted this shy, this uncertain, around other women. The time and place were perfect. Why not simply lift his arm and put it around Faith? Why not simply draw her close and kiss her?

Because there's nothing "simple" about it. I care about Faith more than I've ever cared about any another woman. I need to know how she feels about me before I kiss her.

Tony knew he was clenching and unclenching his hands. He could hear his heart pounding even louder than before, and he imagined the nervous expression he must have on his face.

Thank goodness it's too dark for Faith to see me. She'd conclude I'm a total dunce.

Another couple, this one holding hands, walked by their bench. The woman spoke. "Lovely evening, isn't it?"

Faith replied, "Yes, it is. Delightful."

Tony was astonished to hear a nervous warble in her voice. Without thinking, Tony asked, "Faith, is anything wrong?"

"This is stupid," Faith said, almost angrily. "I'm a grown woman, but I feel like a fifteen-year-old. My heart is racing, and my breath is ragged. All because I'm sitting next to you."

"How about your hands?" Tony asked.

"My hands?" Her voice became shriller. "Are you making fun of me?"

"No," he said gently. "Trust me. I'm not."

"Well, since you ask, I don't know what to do with my hands. I keep wringing them together."

Tony bit his tongue. *Please God, don't let me laugh, not now.* "I have the same symptoms," he said.

"You do?" She seemed surprised.

"Yup. Pounding heart. Strained breathing. Clenched hands. All because you're sitting next to me."

"Oh my!"

Tony slid next to Faith and put his right arm around her shoulder.

"Now what?" she said.

"Now this." He turned her face gently with his left hand and kissed her. He realized with delight that she kissed him back.

Tony heard footsteps approaching on the path. Apparently, Faith heard them, too. She moved her lips away from his.

"More people are coming this way," she said.

"This is a popular resort."

"It should be, if it has this effect on its guests."

The footsteps receded. "Where were we?" Tony asked.

"Right about here." Faith leaned forward and kissed him again.

He wrapped both arms around Faith and wished that this incredible moment could last forever.

Chapter 5

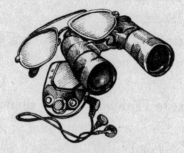

Faith gave a large yawn when she signed in with the NASCAR official overseeing the spotters' stand.

"Late night in Phoenix?" he asked, with a smile.

"Late—and interesting," she said.

"The coffee is over there." He gestured toward a large folding table that held an array of refreshments. She made her way toward it and poured herself a large cup of strong, black coffee.

She took a sip. All things considered, it was probably not a wise idea for a spotter—or a driver—to fall in love the day before a major NASCAR race—especially one that would begin late on Sunday afternoon and finish under the lights.

She and Tony had stayed in the cactus garden, walking and talking, until nearly eleven. Once back in her motor coach at close to midnight, she'd found it difficult to get to sleep. Her alarm clock went off at 6:30 a.m., leaving her feeling muzzy-headed for much of the day. She had thought about taking a nap but had felt too excited to try. Rather, she'd spent much of her free time during the day trying to understand her changed relationship with Tony.

What had happened the night before? She wasn't quite sure. One minute they'd been chatting and the next—kissing, as if the transformation were the most natural thing in the world. And this feeling of rightness had stayed with her throughout the day. She'd sensed no doubts, no fears, no second-guesses—not even a single concern that her new attachment to Tony was moving too quickly.

Tony seemed to feel the same way. She'd seen him at breakfast, briefly again during the thirty-minute chapel service hosted by the Motor Racing Outreach, and once in midafternoon when they'd talked about racing strategy. He'd been charming, attentive, and. . .the only word that seemed to fit was *loving*.

He'd also looked wide-awake during all three encounters—an essential attribute for someone who would soon be driving an eight-hundred-horsepower race car at speeds approaching two hundred miles per hour.

Faith slipped her binoculars out of their case. There would be plenty of time after the race to think about her blossoming relationship with Tony. Right now, she had a vital job to do.

Faith scanned the track. The conditions were perfect this afternoon: temperatures in the high seventies, light winds, dry pavement. She found a folding chair near the back of the spotters' stand and began to review in her mind the specific details of the Phoenix International Raceway that Tony would have to deal with.

"Everyone knows," he'd told her at their strategy session, "the trick at Phoenix is to come out of Turn 4 as fast as you can and then accelerate quickly. That sets you up for a fast run down the front straightaway."

She had traced her finger along the map of the raceway. "Everyone also knows," she'd said, "that there's extra room in Turn 1 and Turn 2 that lets you add power and do some maneuvering."

"Correct. I plan to keep the pressure on in both turns. I'll try to cut to the bottom of Turn 1 if I can, and then move to the right when I exit Turn 2 and enter the back straightaway."

"Be especially careful when you tackle the bend in the back straightaway. It's easy to run your left front tire off the pavement and end up spinning into the right-side wall."

"I'll do my best." He fluttered his eyelashes.

She forced herself not to laugh. "What about Turn 3 and Turn 4?"

"Both of them are tight," he said. "The best way to take them is to run close to the bottom and come out of the corners straight, under power."

She nodded. "Don't let yourself jump sideways, or you'll scrape the wall at Turn 4."

"*O-oh.* That would make both Emmett Grant and Jessie McKnight mad at me."

This time she couldn't stifle a laugh. When she'd recovered, she said, "What about your brakes?"

"My brakes will work extra hard going into Turn 1 and Turn 3."

"Keep that in mind for your car—and remember that other cars will face the same challenge."

"Speaking of challenges at Phoenix. . . ," he'd said with a smile. "Cars can drive through Turn 2 and Turn 4 either high or low. That means there may be two cars—one high, the other low—merging at the start of the front and back straightaways. If two cars meet rather than merge, the high car can get knocked into the wall."

Tony seemed to know the track cold, but then he had driven here before. She hadn't, which meant she might be the weak link during the race.

Please, God, I don't want to let Tony down today.

The before-race preliminaries seemed to speed by. She was almost caught unawares when "Gentlemen, start your engines" blared over the loudspeakers. She took her assigned position near the rail and made sure that her radio was working properly as the cars began the parade lap.

"Let's start with a radio check, Tony."

"The radio's loud and clear. You sound beautifully cheerful, and I'll bet you look cheerfully beau—"

"Never mind what I look like," she interrupted. "Concentrate on the race."

"I'll try, ma'am. I really will." He whistled into his microphone. "Although you're asking an awful lot of me."

⌁

"The lady is right," Tony murmured. "Keep your mind on the race." He slid the shifter into fourth gear and punched the accelerator. Phoenix was a tough place to pass other cars. He wasn't sure he could do it, but it sure would be a hoot if he did.

He'd prayed a simple prayer in chapel that morning. "God, I know You arranged for me to fall in love with Faith Wright last night. She seems to understand You much better than I

do, but I'm determined to learn. I'm not sure yet about Your plans for me, but since You've helped me to become a stock car driver and arranged for me to have a super spotter—well, I get the idea that Your plans have something to do with NASCAR racing. Anyway, what I intend to do today is trust You, listen to Faith, and drive to the best of my abilities. I plan to talk to You a lot more in the days ahead."

Tony had also spent quality time with his pit crew that afternoon, helping plan a pit-stop strategy. This time he'd asked for advice rather than gave it. Pit stops were important at every NASCAR track, but in Phoenix, they often controlled who won and lost because passing was difficult. A few seconds gained—or lost—in the pits could translate into several positions higher—or lower—in the field at the end of the race.

Now that the race had begun, he felt unusually confident, in himself, his car, and the other team members who would support his efforts today.

Tony braked hard as he approached Turn 1. The driver ahead of him waited a fraction of a second too long. He hit the turn too fast, skidded north, and slid against the wall. Tony zipped past him at the end of the turn and moved from twenty-first to twentieth position.

"That was easy," he said to Faith.

"Too easy. Don't count on it happening again."

"Roger that."

Tony drove low out of Turn 2 and flew into the backstretch. The car in nineteenth position—a yellow Ford—seemed to be wobbling from side to side, as if the suspension was too loose for the track. Tony guessed that the driver would slow somewhat at the upcoming curve in the backstretch.

He was right. The Ford slowed and also moved toward the high side of the track.

"Clear low!" Faith shouted.

Tony now knew there was no other car to his left. He held his breath and zipped past the Ford on the inside, with maybe an inch to spare.

"That was...perfect!" Faith said. "I saw you ready to pounce, but I didn't think you'd try it."

"I might not have—except for your encouragement."

"Yeah, well, you did it. I merely watched."

"Not so—you're my eye in the sky."

"But you're holding the wheel."

Jessie McKnight's voice boomed over the radio. "Hey, guys, people are getting nauseous listening to you praise each other. How about passing a few more cars? This is a race."

"Sheesh! A race you say," Tony said. "And here I thought this was a Sunday drive on ol' Interstate 77." He could hear Faith smother a laugh.

"There are two blue Chevys in seventeenth and eighteenth position," Faith said, "both from the Campion Racing Team. Let's see if I can cut a deal." She was back in forty-five seconds. "Okay. I spoke to a Campion spotter. Both drivers know that you've got a faster car today. Draft with them for a couple of laps and then, when the time is right, slingshot past them."

"I've never done a slingshot pass in a NASCAR race."

"That's because you've never cooperated with other drivers."

"Good point."

Tony moved close to the two blue Chevys, which were

traveling one behind the other. Almost immediately, he began to feel the effect of the "draft." Three cars traveling in a line— only a few feet separating the first and second car, then the second and third car—generated less air resistance than three separate cars. By cooperating, the three cars could move faster together than separately.

"Simple in theory," he muttered to himself, "much harder to do for real."

Keeping three cars moving as one, at high speeds and through sharp turns, was tricky work. The slightest mistake would send the second car crashing into the first, or the third car into the second. Keeping lined up took every ounce of Tony's attention.

On the third lap, drafting paid off. The three cars passed the sixteenth car on the front straightaway. Tony was now in eighteenth position and poised to climb two whole slots.

The opportunity came a lap later, as the three cars exited Turn 4.

Faith shouted, "Clear ahead, low!"

Tony didn't hesitate. He dropped back slightly, moved forward again to take advantage of the draft's pulling power, and then broke left as he applied full throttle. His car, boosted by the additional momentum he'd gain, slid past the two Chevys on the left.

"You're in sixteenth position," she screamed, "and there are still 170 laps to go!"

"I don't concur."

"You don't?" Tony had never heard Faith sound so surprised.

"Nope. *We're* in sixteenth position."

"Oh. I suppose *we* are." She began to laugh.

"There's nothing to suppose. I wouldn't be here without you. In fact. . ." He paused, not sure how to continue.

"In fact, what?" she said.

"You are the perfect spotter for me. I can't imagine driving without you when you go back to school."

"I've been thinking about that."

"And?"

"There are some great engineering schools in North Carolina."

"Whoo-ee!" Tony shouted. "Yippee!"

"Yuck!" Jessie said, over the radio. "I may throw up."

"Get used to it," Tony said. "It's the new me."

"Old or new," Jessie said, "it's time for you to pit."

"On my way."

Tony turned into pit road and slipped neatly into his assigned slot.

⌁

Faith watched the pit crew swarm around Tony's car to replace the Dodge's four tires, top off its gas tank, and yank away a layer of plastic film to give Tony a spotlessly clean windshield. They also used a long crank to adjust the car's rear suspension to compensate for the increased slickness of the pavement as the temperature climbed during the race.

The crew seemed to work faster today than ever before. She wished that she'd used her stopwatch to time them. Maybe they'd set a team record.

She murmured a quiet, "Praise God," when Tony roared back onto the track, fifty yards or so beyond Turn 2. He'd fallen back

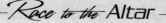

in the field, but he would quickly regain the sixteenth slot when the leading cars pitted. With luck, one or two of the lead cars would have a longer pit stop than Tony, and he would gain another notch or two. But that was hardly a winning strategy. *What can he do,* Faith mused, *to improve his position significantly?*

"Howdy spotter," Tony said. "Any suggestions? I really want to finish in the top ten today."

She swallowed hard and then said, "You know what works at Phoenix. You have to pass going into—and coming out of—the turns. Your Dodge is running great today, which means you can take some risks. You'll have to get around the corners quicker than the other guys."

"*Zowie!* You're turning me loose."

"I am." She chuckled. "Good hunting!"

"Watch my back and my sides for me—here I go."

The laps seemed to fly by for Faith as Tony slowly clawed his way to eleventh in the field. No matter how the day ended, fans would remember this race as one of Tony's stellar performances—the day he became a for-real NASCAR driver. He was yards away from a top-ten finish, when the best he'd done in any other race this year was a so-so twenty-seventh.

Faith gritted her teeth as Tony flew through the backstretch bend and settled behind a black Chevy that held tenth position. The driver—or his spotter—recognized that Tony intended to pass. The car began jigging back and forth to block Tony. A few hundred yards before Turn 3, the Chevy veered slightly above the center of the track to enter Turn 3 and then swung lower coming out of the turn. Faith guessed right that the car would enter Turn 4 low and then go high into the front straightaway.

"Chances are, the driver will do the same thing on this lap," she said to Tony. "Stay right behind him until the last possible instant, then drive through Turn 3 and Turn 4 on the low side. You'll have to brake hard, but you should have plenty of room to blast past him at the end of Turn 4."

"That's a great strategy—*if* my tires don't let go." He added, "The track's getting slick."

"If you slide, he'll slide even farther. He looks a lot looser than you."

"Roger that," Tony said, softly.

Faith watched the green Dodge move closer to the black Chevy. Tony hadn't said the obvious—that she'd better be right about the stickiness of his car, otherwise both the Dodge and the Chevy would make friends with the blue wall at the top of Turn 4.

Once again, the Chevy moved high to enter Turn 3, swung low as he exited the turn, and then moved high as he drove around Turn 4.

Now!

"Clear! Clear! Dear!" she shouted into her microphone, then held her breath as Tony accelerated. The Dodge jittered on the pavement, but the tires held, and Tony moved past the Chevy into tenth position.

"Thank you, darling!" Tony yelled.

"Did you call me darling?"

"Sure—you called me dear."

"I didn't!"

"You most assuredly did—honey, sweetums, sugar pie."

"Okay, okay. I believe you." She tried to keep the amusement she felt out of her voice. "Concentrate on the race."

"Anything you say—lover girl."

"Knock it off, you two," Jessie said.

"Why? I want the whole world to know how I feel about Faith Wright."

Faith cringed. Tony wasn't exaggerating by much. Thousands of fans in the grandstands listened to scanners tuned to Tony's frequency and had heard their recent conversation.

When this race is over, I'll kill him.

She watched Tony drive another lap. At least he seemed determined to maintain his position in the field. Faith glanced at the track's lap counter. If Tony could hold tenth place for only thirty-seven more laps, he would have his first top-ten finish.

"If" turned into certainty as the race went on. Two cars ahead of Tony dropped out with blown engines; a third skidded into the wall on Turn 3 and was too badly damaged to continue. And, to everyone's surprise, Tony was able to pass two other cars that held higher positions. He drove under the checkered flag fifth in the field—an almost miraculous triumph, considering that he'd qualified in twenty-first position.

"I take back everything I said earlier!" Ken Cassini shouted above the end-of-race roar from the stands. "Tony showed his stuff today. So did you."

Faith gave Ken a hug to reward his generosity. She knew that Clint McCabe had finished in nineteenth position—a serious disappointment for a driver who'd started tenth. Ken must feel equally frustrated by McCabe's performance.

"Hey!" one of the other spotters shouted. "Take a look at

the TV set. The camera is following Tony Griffith, and he's headed here."

Faith and Ken moved toward the large-screen TV set up next to the refreshments table. It carried the usual NASCAR race broadcast for the benefit of the handful of non-spotters who were invited to watch the race from the spotter's perch.

"It's Tony," Ken said.

Faith groaned softly. She felt her eyes grow large as steering wheels when the commentator said, "What started as an exchange of affectionate words between driver and spotter seems to have become more. . .ah, *heartfelt*. Tony Griffith looks in a powerful hurry to reach the spotter's stand. The fans are taking a great interest in what may be a love story in the making."

"He's here!" someone shouted. Faith turned just as Tony, a vast smile on his face, bounded onto the spotter's stand, followed by a camerawoman toting a large TV camera on her shoulder. She was huffing and puffing.

Faith forgot about the fans. She ran to Tony and let him put his arms around her.

"You are—weird," she said, merrily.

"Did I ever tell you that I love you?"

"Well. . ."

"Actually, I don't think I did. Let me make it official. I love you."

Faith needed a moment to realize that the roar from the grandstands had grown louder.

"Oh no!" she said to Tony. "My microphone is still live."

While she fumbled with her headset, she felt Tony slide his arm around her waist and pull her toward him. He kissed her gently, but with an intensity that made her toes curl.

"Oh my!" she said, breathlessly. Behind her, the TV continued to blare: "Well friends, you saw it first right here. A genuine eight-hundred-horsepower NASCAR kiss delivered by Tony Griffith to Faith Wright—a kiss seen by millions of NASCAR fans everywhere."

"Millions of fans everywhere...," she murmured.

The commentator went on: "It looks like Tony has found his groove...and true love...and a fabulous spotter. Talk about a lucky day for a NASCAR driver!"

Out of the corner of her eye, Faith spotted the camerawoman zeroing-in for a close-up.

"Oh, who cares?" she shouted.

She wrapped her arms around Tony's neck and kissed him as intensely as he had kissed her.

RON BENREY

Ron is the author of seven published nonfiction books and has cowritten, with his wife Janet, seven Christian cozy mysteries. Before turning to fiction, he built a career as a business writer specializing in speechwriting and marketing communications. Ron holds degrees in engineering, management, and law. He is an avid sailor and enjoys watching NASCAR races.

The Remaking of Moe McKenna

by Gloria Clover

Dedication

To Scott Peterman,
who introduced me to Sunday afternoon NASCAR.

My thanks to Bill and Matt Snyder and Martha McGrath
for helping me with the NASCAR details,
and to Pennsylvania State Trooper Jim Starcher.

*" I will give you a new heart and put a new spirit in you;
I will remove from you your heart of stone
and give you a heart of flesh.' "*
EZEKIEL 36:26

Chapter 1

Pocono Raceway, Pennsylvania

D on't be that way, Moe." Slick Charlie moved to pin her between the stack of tires and the car jack. "One kiss, babe, for the hardworking man."

Martha "Moe" McKenna raised her chin and held her smile even though she knew she was out of her league. She was beginning to understand that Charlie got his nickname from more than being the guy who serviced the underside of the race cars. "I would, Charlie." Except she was afraid he'd want it to go further. If not now, then later. She held up her left hand and wiggled her bare fingers in front of his face. "But I'm holding out for a ring."

He sucked air and straightened ever so slightly.

Moe found it easier to smile. "I'm a forever kind of girl. And though I think you're awfully cute"—*Cute in the fashion of a Jack Russell terrier,* she thought—"I think you're still a sowing-wild-oats kind of guy."

Charlie beamed at this description and straightened even more, giving her much needed breathing, if not moving, space.

When she slid away from the tool that was poking her from behind, Charlie wrapped an arm around her waist.

Moe knew better than to get caught in a partially packed semitrailer, but when Charlie had offered her a chance to sit in Boedy Sutherland's number 52 race car, she'd blown off caution. In the two months she'd been traveling the NASCAR circuit, this was the closest she'd been to an actual stock car and the work the crew did in the pits after a race. Often, track guards were gracious to her requests. And Boedy's own crew had taken to getting her places the average fan couldn't go, but Moe should have thought twice before following a man into an enclosed space.

The worst part was that if Charlie hadn't tried to force the request, Moe would have given him a quick kiss of gratitude.

"Forever girl," Moe mumbled to his chin. She latched onto his fingers, which gripped her waist, and attempted to pry them off, one at a time.

"Sassy tail," Charlie said. "You're no more a forever girl than I'm Mark Martin. You're all about the moment. Like me." He crowded her backward.

Moe fought the tension looming in her chest. She had to stay calm, or she was done for. She didn't want romance in the back of a half-packed semitrailer. "Not on the jack, Charlie. Not here."

Any amount of time she could buy would give her a better chance to escape. Soon one of the other crewmembers would bring equipment from the pits.

Charlie dove for his kiss, and Moe twisted her face to the left. His lips brushed the skin below her dangling earring and above the tie of her halter top.

Panic surged through her, and she lost herself to its frantic call. Her body stiffened. Her arms straightened, pushing his chest and arching herself over the equipment that was once again poking into her backside.

"Slick!"

The command, the harshness, the recognition of the voice all swept into her. Slick Charlie scurried backward. Relief grabbed for a spot in her heart but washed away in the muddy despair that swirled through her. Why Boedy? Why wasn't life ever fair? Why did she always have such bad luck?

Boedy could cause more pain and loss to her dignity with a few choice words than all of Charlie's disrespect had done.

"It's just Moe."

Charlie's comment helped her find her backbone. Just Moe, her foot. She was a person. She should be treated with—

"Get out of here."

Charlie obeyed the cold command without comment, and Moe moved to follow him. She skirted Boedy as far as the crammed semitrailer allowed. She didn't have far to go, but she'd have to pass him to be free. He snagged her upper arm before she made it out of the open end of the trailer.

She shuddered.

He dropped her arm and stepped back a pace, effectively blocking her escape. "Moe," he said and then sighed. "Are you all right?"

She gave a quick nod.

"Look at me."

The command was back, and Moe found herself obeying without conscious thought. The guy was the biggest bully she'd ever met. Arrogant. Bossy. Complex. One of the most fearless NASCAR drivers she had ever laid eyes on. He enthralled her.

She withstood the scrutiny of his hard, blue gaze and straightened her shoulders.

Whatever he saw, or thought he saw, started a tic in his left jaw. She eased back two paces, making sure he would have to lunge for her before he laid a hand on her again.

"This cannot continue, Moe." His words were distinct, sharp, and left no room for misinterpretation. "You have to go."

"Please!" The plea slipped from her mouth before she thought through her defense. "Give me one more chance."

"I've given you too many chances," he ground out, fingers clenching into fists. "What was going to happen here?" He motioned toward the stack of tires. "Thank God, we don't know, but now I'll have to deal with it."

"Nothing happened."

"So you say. But how's Charlie doing? What junk is going through his head? Where does he get rid of the frustration? The shame?"

"He said I was just Moe." She hated the hurt that slipped into her voice.

"I heard him." Speaking hadn't relieved the tic in his jaw. "So was it said to save face? Or did he mean it? Or would he have reined himself in when he realized you were leading him on?"

"I wasn't."

"Sassy tail!"

Moe gasped.

"You think I don't hear what they call you? You think I don't see the extra wiggle you put in your step when you hear it? What would you call it, if it isn't leading the guys on?"

"Being fun," Moe whispered miserably.

"And what are you wearing?"

Moe realized Boedy was too angry to hear anything she said in her defense and looked down. White jeans and a red cotton halter top. It was August in Long Pond, Pennsylvania, home of the Pocono Raceway. Her clothing was suitable for—

"You're wearing a matador's red cape to every red-blooded male in the pits—and the red is not flashing 'Stop.' It's screaming, '*Go, go, go!*'"

"All right," she muttered sullenly. He was always on her case about what she wore. It was as if he didn't want her to be pretty.

"I can't let you destroy my team."

"I'm not."

"You are." He rubbed his hand around the back of his neck. "Russ and Bobby Ray argued over who would get you past security so that you could stand beside them during the national anthem."

Luckily Moe swallowed the "Really?" that had made it to the tip of her tongue.

"Hought begged me to keep you off camera. His wife has seen you so many times with him, she's asking questions."

Hought, the crew chief, was happily married and Moe's friend. Nothing more.

"I'm not—"

Again he interrupted her. "I know you don't mean it, Moe. You just don't think. It's like today. However you happened to end up in here with Charlie, I know it wasn't your intent to have at it with him on the car jack."

Blood rushed into Moe's face.

"But if you aren't going to think for yourself, then you're going to have to listen to someone who knows."

"Knows what?" she asked, unsure where the conversation was going now that he seemed to have shed the heat of his anger toward her.

"Race protocol. Men. What to wear. Where to go."

"Who did you have in mind?" Nervous, Moe shivered in the stagnant, fuel-charged air of the semitrailer.

"Anyone, Moe. If you want to stick with my team, you're going to have to pick one of the guys and obey him. No more playing the field. No more sassy tail. You've been dogging us for two months. You know the guys. It's pathetic to say, but you gotta know you can have your pick. So pick one."

"I don't want a lover." Her heart sank at the thought of what he was asking of her. "I just want to be a part of the team. I want to be here in the rush." Moe's college roommate had scraped together the funds to backpack across Europe this summer; Moe had headed for the NASCAR circuit.

He sighed deeply and shook his head. "No. You're a loose cannon. You're going to have to leave."

Just the thought of losing her dream gave her unexpected courage. "You can't make me leave."

"I can and I will." He said it with the same tone of command that he'd used on Charlie.

"You don't have that much power."

"I do."

It had to be bravado. She wasn't his employee, and he was just a driver. A good driver. Oh, and the oldest son of racing legend Kent Sutherland. Of course, the Sutherlands, into their fourth generation of race car drivers, were the family name in NASCAR following only the Earnhardts and Pettys in awards, applause, and fan worship.

"But, Boedy—"

His fist smashed backward into an engine crate. "You don't get it."

Moe jumped, but he didn't even flinch as he continued to drill her. "This wasn't just damage to your pride. Though I'm beginning to doubt much damage there. This is messing with the team. With their performance. Their focus."

Even though she was only an observer to the NASCAR world, she understood how important it was for the team members to be a unified body. She nodded her agreement, but Boedy didn't pause to draw a breath.

"Even if we could both walk out of here and pretend nothing happened, is that the best for Charlie? And what about tomorrow? Or next week? You are bad news, Moe McKenna, and I don't have the resources to deal with you any longer."

Yep. She felt the tears welling. She'd been shredded more thoroughly than if he'd put her in a food processor. She wished she didn't care. She tried not to. That was always what got her into trouble. She wanted people to like her. She wanted them to find her attractive and fun. Was it really her clothes that made men like her more than women did? And why didn't Boedy like her at all? She'd wanted him to notice her, but not like this.

Circumstances didn't matter. This was her dream. He was her hope. He was the one who could make it all happen.

"I pick you, Boedy." She said it softly to the floor. Then she repeated it louder. "Boedy Sutherland, I pick you." She raised her gaze to his. "I'll do whatever you tell me to do. I'll wear whatever you want me to wear. But I get to stay, be a part of your team, do something useful."

For the first time since she'd known him, Moe watched him gasp like a landed fish.

"You, you what?" He clamped his lips together tighter than the space between three cars on the Watkins Glen track.

"You said," she whispered meekly.

He stepped backward into the sun, away from her.

Moe came forward, pausing at the top of the trailer's ramp. She blinked and glanced around. No one was near. The stands had emptied. The crew members must be cleaning their pit before they closed up the semis. Suddenly she wondered why Boedy was here. Usually after a great race like today, he headed out with his family. Dinner. Laughter. A full recap of the race highlights.

Moe knew, because more than once she had followed them to their restaurant of choice and then weaseled a seat close enough to eavesdrop and enjoy the lively, Sutherland camaraderie.

Usually such a fix could get her through until the next race. Sometimes, however, listening to the love bandied around the table would create an ache that Moe didn't know how to assuage. Her desire to be a part of that beauty ate at her and wore her down. Some days she was ready to admit defeat. She'd never be accepted or loved in such a fashion.

But then, out of nowhere, a resilience would form, and she would regroup. If Boedy was her destiny, she wanted to give him time to realize it. A summer. Two months ago, that had seemed like plenty of time to catch his eye and win his favor. This morning, when he'd walked by her without even his usual brusque greeting, it had seemed hopeless. Now—she grinned her thousand-watt smile—now she was going places.

He wiped the back of his hand across his forehead. "Moe, I don't have time—"

"You said," she repeated more firmly. He had. She was right in this.

"Not me. Any of the other guys would be pleased to—"

"You won't expect me to sleep with you in exchange for watching over me." She knew she had him there. She knew how he was. . . . His beliefs and commitments ran deep. She hadn't figured it all out yet, but she knew this much and said so. "You won't be fooled into thinking I'm leading you on."

He stood taller and glared at her.

She knew he wasn't angry with her, that he'd never hurt her, and that he was trying to intimidate her into backing down. She wouldn't. This was the best shot she'd had all summer.

"One more month." She was whispering again, and she wasn't sure why. Were they hashing out the details of a secret pact? "That's all I'm asking for. I'll be so good, you'll miss me when I'm gone."

To her surprise, he dipped his chin in silent acquiescence.

Chapter 2

Thurst's an awesome idea!" Boedy Sutherland's sister-in-law, Kolette, dropped her fork into her fettuccini and grabbed her husband's upper arm. "Mason, we could help."

Unwilling to meet his baby brother's mocking gaze across the restaurant table, Boedy stared down at his own plate—the house special, spaghetti and meatballs. Why had he even mentioned Moe to his family? If Kolette was interested in taking the woman under her wing, Boedy could only imagine what his sister, Dale, would decide needed to be done.

Dale's fingers tapped beside her butter knife. "Am I thinking of the right girl? Bleached blond? Tall and skinny? Smile like a halogen headlight?"

"Yeah," Boedy muttered to his uneaten spaghetti. He breathed in vinegar from the leftover salads and hoped the dimmed lighting would hide his discomfort, because it certainly wasn't suppressing his family's enthusiasm for loud conversation.

Thankfully, the half-moon-shaped table where they were

seated was set back from the main trafficked area.

"She seems so fun. You're right, Koly, this will be awesome." Dale's finger tapping moved to her chin. "Imagine how much God can do in her heart if she's as yielded as Boedy said she is."

"I didn't say yielded."

"Willing to wear what you tell her to wear?" Kolette's excited voice drilled into him.

Boedy finally lifted his gaze. He didn't want a dissertation. He'd only wanted the name of a clothing store.

Kolette finished, "That's yielded, my friend."

"Or desperate," Boedy's mother inserted. "Do you remember the half-grown raccoon you brought home when you were fourteen?" She directed this question to Boedy, and he unconsciously felt the ridge of scars on the two fingers of his left hand that had taken the brunt of the raccoon's fear. "Wild things don't like to be penned, changed. Even when it is for their own good. I know that raccoon wouldn't have made it through the winter if you hadn't doctored it, but. . ."

Her voice dwindled away, and Kent Sutherland cleared his throat. "Let's not forget this is one of God's children we're talking about."

"Exactly, Dad!" Dale now had her fingers drumming the tabletop. "She needs to be cared for and loved."

"Not smothered," Mason said.

"Not pampered," Boedy added.

"Guided," Kolette said, then giggled. "It'll be awesome. Leave her to us."

For the second time in as many hours, Boedy found himself nodding in agreement to something he didn't agree with.

After they finished dinner, Boedy didn't head back with his family to their home-away-from-home, a Prevost XL-45 Royale motor coach. He had one more thing that needed his attention before he called it a night. He took Dale's smaller sports car rather than the family SUV. Parking was always in short supply, especially at the smaller tracks, and he didn't want to have to traipse on foot across the infield if Charlie wasn't at the Sutherland Racing Team's main sponsor's tent.

He hoped *she* wouldn't be there. Yet part of him knew that it might be easier if she was.

The infield partying was in full swing. Sponsors' and vendors' tents offered free drinks and food to entice the crowd inside to buy their products. He entered the Micro Funding Corp's tent. The powers-that-be put the company logo on everything from his car, to caps, to soda bottles, to all the toys the sponsor carted to each race to draw people to its tent. He spotted Bobby Ray and Russ at the pool table. Three more guys from his team were sharing a pitcher and playing cards at a folding table. Where was Slick?

Charlie came into view from the far right and headed straight for Bobby Ray, who leaned over the pool table. His voice carried to Boedy where he stood just under the canvas. "Man, are you two still at it? What's it going to take to sink that eight?"

"Hold your horses, Slick. Your turn's coming."

Boedy released his breath. Various folks—racing team crews and fans—indulged in frivolous pastimes. *She* wasn't here. *Thank You, Lord.* Now he could do what needed to be done without terrifying her.

He headed to the pool table and nodded to his friends.

"Hey, Boedy." Bobby Ray shifted his cue stick to his other hand to shake Boedy's. "Don't see you after a race too often."

"Just a matter of business that needs to be addressed with Charlie here before we start the new week."

Boedy turned from Bobby Ray to Charlie and sent him a fiery glare.

"Look, man, about Moe. . . You know I didn't mean—" Charlie's mouth started to move faster than a car with four new tires on the straightaway. "I just got a little carried—"

Boedy cut off the explanation with a nice, solid punch to Slick Charlie's gut.

"*Oof.*" Charlie doubled over.

Bobby Ray hollered and stepped back, while Russ stepped forward, palms out. "If this is personal, maybe you better take it off-site."

Boedy fought down an unexpected rush of satisfaction at having delivered a well-planted punch. He'd merely tried to send a message in a language Charlie understood, not carry out a vendetta. This wasn't about him or avenging Moe; this was about Charlie—the Charlie who now groaned and straightened slowly. "Yeah, man, I guess I had that one coming."

Russ's gaze traveled back and forth between the two of them. "You got any more coming?"

Other people in the tent swiveled on stools and folding chairs to watch.

Boedy held Charlie's gaze. He didn't see any anger or bitterness. Good. "You got anything in you, Slick, that we need to take elsewhere?"

Charlie took a deep breath. "Not—uh—not unless you need more flesh for your satisfaction. I've been plenty stupid for one day."

It was all the apology Boedy needed, but he hoped Charlie would do better by Moe in the future. "Good." He offered his hand to Charlie, and they exchanged a firm handshake. "Now there's something else you need to understand." Boedy raised his voice. "All of you need to hear this." He wouldn't let himself swallow. He said it with four generations of confidence bred into him. "Moe McKenna's mine."

There was so much more that he could have said. She wasn't in the field any longer. They must all treat her with respect. He never wanted to hear the phrase *sassy tail* again. But when it was all said and done, his team knew him. He didn't need to say more. He'd said it in a way his men would understand.

He let his gaze circle the gathering, stopping on a particular man until he understood Boedy's sincerity and depth of commitment, and then he moved on. When his gaze reached the tent's entrance, he again paused, this time in frustration. Two women struck a sensuous pose of surprise and amazement. The older woman broke from her frozen stance first.

"Boedy Sutherland, as I live and breathe," she drawled, pursing her red lips into what she probably intended to be an invitation.

The second woman now snapped out of her stupor. "I'm sorry." She stepped backward. "I shouldn't have come." She twirled and raced away.

Boedy stared at the empty space that, moments ago, had held Moe McKenna.

She hadn't understood. She really hadn't understood. Boedy was a man of his word. She'd known it, but she hadn't grasped it. Not deep down where belief makes a difference in how you behave.

Now she might have ruined everything. Her heart thudded madly at the mental picture of Boedy facing an entire tent full of people. Granted, not all of them would have heard his words, and perhaps even less cared what he had to say. But Moe had heard.

"Moe McKenna's mine."

She shuddered, catching herself against the open tailgate of a stranger's Ford pickup. Oh, why was she so easily swayed by peer pressure?

After her run-in with Charlie and her secret pact with Boedy, Moe had bumped into another NASCAR fan, Vanna, in the parking lot of their motel. Since so many of the race car groupies were on a budget, they often ended up at the same low-rate motels and hung out together.

Though Boedy had agreed to be Moe's what—? Her advisor? Her escort? Her prison guard? Moe didn't know what that meant for the rest of the evening or for the coming week. Was she supposed to check in with him when they reached Watkins Glen International. . .and leave him alone until then?

Vanna had taken one look at her and laughingly suggested she needed infield revelry. Moe knew she never *needed* the after-race partying, that it didn't get her any closer to Boedy or even the racing team, really, but she'd let herself be talked into dressing for the night. She hadn't thought it could hurt anything.

Straightening away from the tailgate, she swallowed hard and tried to focus. First things first. She needed to get back to her motel, but Vanna had driven. She turned to see if there was any chance that Vanna had followed her out of the tent, but no. Moe hadn't expected it. Vanna wasn't really a friend, just another girl who liked fast cars and the men who raced them.

Surrounded by the Pocono Mountains, Moe knew she'd never find a bus stop. She kicked at a piece of gravel, and it skittered under a blue-gold Pontiac G6 convertible. Dale Sutherland's car. Moe did a double take to make certain Boedy's sister wasn't in the car watching her little dance of indecisiveness, then looked back at the tent, hoping Vanna would come. Instead, her gaze fell on Boedy, striding straight toward her.

Rats.

She reversed three steps in rapid succession and backed into the Pontiac with enough force to set off its security alarm. The honking froze Moe, and she wondered if she could die before the ruckus alerted everyone in the tent.

Boedy did a "The force is with you" *Star Wars* move, obviously holding the remote key fob in his palm, and the noise stopped.

Moe wanted to crawl under the car. "I'm sorry."

He'd reached her by then and tugged her off the bumper, steering her toward the side of the convertible. "Dale's kind of particular about not sitting on her car, Moe. Just something you should know."

She heard another *click* as the door locks released, and then he opened the passenger door. "In you go."

Her feet wouldn't move, and she looked up at him. Wasn't he angry?

She withstood his head-to-toe scrutiny and heard him sigh. She could never please him. And she wasn't even wearing a halter top. The blouse she had chosen was a filmy green that brought out that color in her hazel eyes. It was even long-sleeved—though admittedly, the cloth had been cut in strategic places to give tantalizing views of the flesh beneath. It was creative and flashy, and it made her feel that way to wear it. Usually.

"What's wrong, Moe?"

Moe didn't think she'd ever before stood so close, for so long, to Boedy Sutherland. Thinking was too hard, so she smiled at him.

He shook his head, a lopsided grin developing slowly. "You're killing me. Will you get in the car?"

She nodded but didn't move.

"Sometime tonight, do you think?"

Nope. That was her problem: She didn't think. At least not when she could look and feel and soak in his presence. What was the one thing that she liked the absolute most about Boedy? The clearness of his blue eyes and how they seemed to slice right to the center of a situation? The brown hair that curled around his ears and into his shirt collar and onto his forehead? Or the wide forehead itself, square chin with a hint of dimple? The curve of his lower lip? The—

Boedy grabbed her, one hand on her shoulder, the other on the top of her head, and he tucked her down into the leather seat. Thankfully Moe's tingling feet seemed to follow on their own.

He closed the passenger door.

Moe took a deep breath. She needed to pull herself together before she destroyed what little respect he might have left for her. Boedy wouldn't be interested in a love-struck moron.

He slid into the driver's seat. As he inserted the key into the ignition, his arm brushed hers.

Tingles zoomed to her toes once more.

His gentle, warm touch, Moe decided. That's what she liked the most about Boedy Sutherland.

Chapter 3

Boedy took one look at Moe's motel and decided—not on his watch. Wasn't going to happen. Didn't matter that she'd already spent three nights in the place. If he left her there, something bad would occur.

That seemed to be God's modus operandi with him to date. God was good about protecting him, but once a warning had been given—to slow down or speak up or even leave the raccoon alone—the divine protection disappeared in proportion to his human disobedience. Dale tended to disagree with his assessment, so Boedy wasn't prepared to make a sweeping statement on God's character. That had just been his experience.

And a warning was being given about this motel.

"Let's get your things," he prompted Moe as they faced each other at the convertible's bumper.

"But I've already paid for the night."

Wind scurried a fast-food bag across the parking lot.

"Good. Then we can leave your car and come back for it in the morning."

"But why? Where do you want me to sleep?"

He was finding that actions worked better than words when motivating Miss McKenna. He placed a hand at the small of her back and *helped* her toward her motel room door. He followed her in, froze at the smallness of the bed-dominated room, and backed up two steps to place him back on the motel sidewalk. He held the door open with his foot.

"I'm sorry." Moe sounded almost shy, and her voice drew his attention to her well-painted face. "I'm not usually such a slob, but Vanna was hurrying me."

Boedy hadn't noticed the disarray of clothing until Moe brought it to his attention. "Throw it in a bag, and let's get out of here."

"But why?" At his silence, her spiky blond head tilted farther to one side. "I don't expect you to adopt me, Boedy. Granted, I'm not sure what to expect, but taking charge of my sleeping arrangements. . ."

Her questioning frustrated him because he knew she was right, and he didn't know what to do with her. So he did what he'd learned at an early age: brazen it out. "This is never going to work if you can't even listen to me about something as simple as packing your clothes. Would you rather stay away from my team?"

With a dark scowl, she began to gather clothing from the bedspread.

Then Boedy remembered her fear that if she gave a man her obedience about racing protocol, it would lead to the man's assumption that he had the right to her, uh, sleeping arrangements.

"Oh, no, Moe. I didn't mean that you'd be sleeping with me."

She jerked straight and eyed him in amazement.

Had he read everything wrong? He hoped he wasn't blushing. "I, ah, I wasn't answering you, because I don't know what I'm going to do with you yet. I do know I can't leave you in this rat hole."

"I haven't seen a single rat." Then she grinned to let him know she was messing with him. Like he hadn't known that for two months. She bent to retrieve a black duffel bag from the corner of the room and plopped it on the bed. "Boedy, you were stuttering. Did you know that? And you're hovering in the doorway. Are you afraid I'm going to jump you?" She flashed him that intolerable smile. "I know you aren't interested in me like that."

If only. But wanting and having were laps apart on his scorecard. He stepped into the doorway and leaned a shoulder against the metal jamb. Who was this crazy girl? How did she get under his defenses so easily? He never let the, uh—he searched for his mother's kind word—the *fans* get into his private life, into his thoughts. Yet here was one who had been underfoot and in his mind for the past two months.

But she was a kid. Probably barely out of high school. For the first time he wondered if her parents knew where she was, and he felt kind of sick that he hadn't asked before. "Moe—"

She came out of the bathroom with another bag that she shoved into the duffel. "It's all right. Really." She spoke to the bedspread as she finished packing. "I know you're not into race trash, that I'm not in your league."

Where had that come from? The harshness of his indrawn breath caused him to choke and cough. Did she think they were in some sort of caste system? He was thinking off-limits

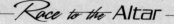

because of her age and his faith. What was she thinking? When he straightened, she stood directly in front of him, possessions in hand.

"Are you okay?"

He should have been the one asking that question, but he nodded. He knew he needed to address what she'd just said, what she believed about herself, but he didn't know how. He could tell her that Jesus loved her, but somehow the words seemed overused. Actually, he was the spiritual chicken in his family when it came to witnessing. He preferred people see who he lived for rather than just talk the talk. Yep, all that would be better left to Dale and Koly. Girl talk. He would bring it to their attention.

"Are you ready?"

At her nod, he took her bag and stepped back so that she could precede him into the humid Pennsylvania night. A few stars shone through the cloud cover. He missed North Carolina and the smell of honeysuckle.

He was reminded that he missed a lot of things when he spent too much time with Moe McKenna. The leading hole in his life was the fact that no one looked at him the way his mom looked at his dad. Moe's looks had come the closest, and he couldn't trust what his heart wanted to believe. Moe didn't know him. What he was seeing had to be some twisted form of fan worship. She didn't know about his faith or his fears. She certainly didn't know how he felt about her—because even he hadn't reached any conclusions on that sore subject.

He dropped her duffel into the trunk and resettled her in the passenger seat. Crawling behind the wheel, he realized he now needed to make a decision about what to do with her. No more waffling. Besides, there weren't that many options. He wasn't doing things halfway. If he was going to be responsible for her, he needed to be responsible for her.

He put the car into reverse and backed away from the cheap motel.

Moe rode in silence. They'd traveled a few miles before she realized they were heading toward the raceway. She wasn't sure of his plan, but she knew enough not to ask. But that didn't feel right either. Why would he expect her to go blindly along with whatever he asked of her and at the same time reprimand her for not thinking for herself?

"Where's the balance?" she asked. . .again without thinking through the consequences.

"Hmm?" Boedy glanced her way as he braked at the intersection.

Moe straightened her shoulders against the soft ebony seat. "Where's the balance between thinking for myself and listening to what you tell me to do? Like now. I'm supposed to trust you to take me wherever you want, without my car, to who knows where, just because you don't like where I chose to stay."

The glow from the dashboard revealed the look of consternation on his face. He wasn't as confident as he wanted her to believe. On one hand it tickled her, but on the other, her stomach tightened with trepidation. What were they getting into?

"I'm sorry, Moe." He reached over and patted her knee

awkwardly, then returned his hand to the wheel. "I didn't mean to scare you more. I just. . ." He paused, glanced at her, and made a left turn. "I didn't have a good feeling about that place. We made a pact, right?"

Moe only half heard the inflection that made her realize he'd asked her a question. All the rest of her attention was on ignoring the warm current zinging from her knee to her heart. Man, that hardly seemed fair at all. He casually could tap her—

"Did you change your mind?" His voice was sharp. "Do you want to head home tomorrow?"

"Home? What?" *Think, Moe.* "No! I'm good with the pact." She shifted to give him a hard stare. "And quit trying to use that as a weapon. I wasn't trying to be a pain, Boedy. I was wondering how much you wanted me to follow you in blind faith."

His cocky grin returned. "All the way, lady."

Moe smiled because she knew he expected it, but her heart sank a little. She wasn't sure why. Flirting with Boedy should have filled her with elation.

"I'm kidding, Moe."

She shrugged in passive defense, but she hoped it looked carefree.

"I'm taking you back to my family's motor coach. I could put you up in a better hotel, but after a big race like tonight, there's no guarantee we'll find an empty room. Besides, this way you'll get to meet the girls. They'll help you with. . ." Again he paused and sent a quick look in her direction. "The stuff I mentioned."

"Okay," she agreed while her mind ran rampant. Boedy was

taking her back to his family. The girls? She knew he didn't have any children. Maybe he referred to his sister as—

"But I guess that brings us back to your question." His voice interrupted her thoughts once more. "Moe, I do want you to obey me. Like tonight about packing your bag and leaving the motel. I don't want to fight with you over stuff like that. But I guess if I were in your shoes, I wouldn't want to follow me on 'blind faith' either. I'm okay with your asking questions and learning why. But when we're on the track and when we're around the team, I don't want you to question me or talk back."

He paused, but she didn't know what to say to that, so she stared out the windshield. Part of her felt as if she should be ruffled by his assumptions, but mostly she did trust him. She'd willingly made the pact; it would be unnecessary to question him on every decision.

His voice softened. "I'll explain myself when I can. You can ask me about stuff later if you don't see why I told you to do something specific. Will that work?"

Her heart lifted. Did he care? Like a friend? Wanting her to fit into his world? Like a boyfriend? Her eyes widened at the thought, but it sure sounded as if he intended to bring her into his circle. Completely. Not just on race day. For a moment, Moe thought she was going to hyperventilate. She shoved her knuckles against her lips and forced herself to breathe deeply through her nose.

"Do your parents know where you are?"

She blinked. Tried to make the jump in subject. "I think." Her mom didn't keep up with NASCAR. Her dad hadn't been impressed with her decision to be a summer race car groupie, but since her parents' divorce when she turned eight, she hadn't felt a great hunger to impress her dad.

"Well." Boedy cleared his throat. "I better ask you this now, because I'm sure it'll be one of the first things Mom asks. Are you over eighteen?"

Over eighteen! Moe pressed her knuckles harder, but she couldn't stop the grin from forming. "Poor Boedy." She dropped her hands back into her lap and grinned at him openly. "I'm getting a taste of how brave you were to agree to that pact, aren't I? I'm twenty-three. I'm not a runaway. I'm not pregnant. I'm not a convict, and though some might disagree, I don't think I'm insane. I just like fast cars."

By the time she'd finished her spiel, he'd parked the Pontiac in the designated parking spot in the camping area of the Pocono Speedway, and now he shifted in the seat to look into her eyes.

Her smile faded at the intensity she found in his gaze under the parking lot lights. She had hoped to put him at ease.

"I can't knock that," he murmured. "I do, too."

She had no idea what he was talking about, so she forced a new smile.

"Yeah, ah"—he pushed open his car door and sprang to his feet—"let's get you settled in."

She met him at the trunk as he pulled her duffel from its depths.

"It looks like everyone's turned in for the night already." He sounded disappointed. "You can bunk with my sister, Dale." He directed her toward a huge Prevost motor coach and then motioned toward a smaller fifth-wheel camper connected to a dual-wheeled truck in the neighboring slot. "I'll stay there with my brother and sister-in-law for the time being. That's what I do when Grandpa Sutherland spends time with us on the road."

"Won't we wake them?"

"Probably." His tone said it couldn't be helped.

He set her bag on the ground and opened the coach's door. "Up you go."

He directed her movements once again with his warm, gentle hand. Her lower back tingled, and she found herself in the soft glow of a nightlight filling the living space of the motor coach. The interior of the bus seemed even larger than the outside.

Boedy motioned toward the back. "My parents' bedroom is through the bathroom area. Don't hesitate to ask if you need anything." His voice remained soft but clear. "The toilet has a separate door. Shower on the opposite side. Towels are in the closet." Then he turned her toward the front. "The sofas—as you can see—open into single beds. It's a bit crowded, but it's comfortable. Dale, you awake?"

Moe waited behind him when he entered the small space and set her duffel on the floor. "Dale, wake up and say hi to Moe."

A lump in the left bed shifted and said plainly, "Go away."

Boedy chuckled. "She's sleeping. You'll meet her in the morning. You need anything else for the night?"

Moe was clueless what she needed. She was just now processing that he was leaving her with his sleeping family and wasn't in the least concerned about it. "Boedy, they don't even know me."

"Sure they do. Besides, they'll figure it out. Oh, and sorry

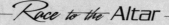

about the bed." He motioned toward the ill-made right bed. "Even if I knew where fresh sheets were, we'd definitely wake Dale changing them."

Moe shrugged. "It doesn't matter." She was more concerned about his family. "I think I should sleep in the car."

Boedy shook his head and reached out with one large hand to ruffle the top of her spiked hair. "I would think you're insane," he teased, then deftly pulled her forward with a tug on her neck and, with a neat turn, put himself out into open kitchen space. "G'night, Moe."

Slack-jawed, she stood in the soft light as he disappeared from her view.

Before she could pull herself together, she heard him talking at the other end of the coach. She strained her ears then gulped.

He'd just told his parents Moe McKenna was sleeping in his bed.

Chapter 4

In the motor coach bathroom, Moe washed the makeup from her face and changed into her pajamas as quietly as possible. She slipped into the right bed and stretched out her tense muscles. She was never going to be able to sleep in Boedy's bed. Especially with a woman she'd never officially met sleeping so near her. What had Boedy been thinking? How was this better than the "rat hole" where she had been her own person and had her own space?

She sighed. With her next indrawn breath, the scent of Boedy flooded her senses. She breathed deeply and a smile curved her lips. She rolled onto her stomach and buried her face in his pillow. *Intelligent Designer, or Force, or Fate. . .whatever name You choose tonight, I want to say thanks for the best day ever.*

<hr />

Moe woke with a start, unsure why. Jerking up, she lost the warm covers in a pool around her waist. Then she remembered and sank back onto the mattress in realization.

"Sorry." A dark-haired girl Moe recognized as Dale Sutherland wrinkled her nose and held up a handful of clothing. "I didn't mean to wake you. I was heading to the shower."

Moe didn't know whether to get up, shake the girl's hand, or pull the blankets over her head. She pushed to an elbow. "Hi."

A grin dominated the girl's oval face as she scurried to the bed and plopped down on the mattress beside Moe. "Hi. You're Moe McKenna."

Did she look so lost that the kid thought she needed to be reminded? "And you're Dale Sutherland."

"I am." She giggled. "He actually brought you. This is going to be so much fun."

Moe momentarily wondered if she should be terrified, but the blue eyes staring into hers seemed sane.

"Oh, you're beautiful," Dale said. "I don't think you'll need much taming."

Moe blinked and self-consciously fingered her "wild" hair.

"But"—Dale's fingers began to drum a syncopated rhythm on her thigh—"first things first. I don't want you to think that we're this weird, perverse family because Boedy and I share sleeping space. I'm only here for the summer and occasional weekends. Obviously we're too old to share a room, but Mason went and married my best friend, Koly, this spring, and that messed up the sleeping arrangements. So Boedy and I have been making the best of it through this summer. It's probably my last chance to spend the summer with the entire family because I'll graduate next year, and well, I haven't decided exactly what I'm going to do, but I doubt I'll have the summers off to travel the race circuit."

Moe nodded for lack of a better response. She didn't have a brother, and she hadn't given any thought to inappropriateness—other than the inappropriateness of her being here.

"The last two summers, Koly slept here with me and the boys shared the fifth wheel. Then, at Easter, when she and Mason eloped. . ." She paused, shook her head as though the world had briefly ended, and grinned. "Well, you get the picture. Are you awake? Are you ready to get up?"

Moe nodded, then heard the distinct sound of the shower running.

Dale groaned. "Dad beat me again."

Moe instantly liked her frankness and decided she could return it. "I'd like to get up, but I don't have a robe."

Dale jumped to her feet and grabbed a dark blue shirt from the end of Boedy's bed. She held it by the collar before handing it to Moe. "This will work."

As she slipped into the sleeves, Moe once again found herself surrounded by Boedy's spicy scent.

＝

Breakfast consisted of fried mush and sausage links, introductions to Boedy's parents, and a G-rated report of Moe's evening activities. She wasn't sure how much Boedy wanted his parents to know, and she didn't relish repeating his statement, "Moe McKenna is mine." Wary, delicious shivers still quivered through her at the thought.

Seated across from Boedy's dad, Kent Sutherland, Moe was amazed at how down-to-earth the superstar ex-driver was. She shouldn't have been surprised. She was eating fried mush

drenched in syrup with the man, but still—Kent Sutherland.

On catching her eye, he sent her a lopsided grin that immediately reminded her of Boedy. "You're a true fan, aren't you, Moe McKenna?"

She dipped her chin in sudden embarrassment. "Yeah."

"Have you ever been in a race car?"

Her gaze flew to his in wonder and hope. "No, sir."

"I'll have to take you—"

"Kent!" But Boedy's mother laughed as she squeezed his arm.

Dale piped up. "Poor Daddy. He's always looking for an excuse to get back in a race car."

"Retirement is for the birds," he muttered and then winked at Moe.

The retirement had been forced on him over six years ago, according to the gossip magazines Moe had read, after some nerve damage during a race crash. But retirement from racing hadn't led to retirement from NASCAR. Kent partnered with his grandfather, Benjamin Sutherland, who had come into NASCAR on the ground floor as a young man and was now in his eighties. When Kent's two sons came of age, the Sutherlands had formed a formidable racing team. Various sponsors were only too happy to back such a name in NASCAR, and Boedy and Mason began making a reputation in their own right.

"Boedy will take you—"

"I could!" Dale interrupted her dad. "We could go before practice gets intense—"

Her father reinterrupted. "Poor Dale. She's always looking for an excuse to get into a race car."

"Do you drive?" Moe asked hesitantly. She hadn't read,

heard, or seen anything about Dale Sutherland joining the family business.

"Is my name Sutherland?"

"Dale!" For all her warm smile and motherly baking, Mrs. Sutherland employed her tongue like a cracking whip. "Don't be rude."

Then, before Moe could assure her that she hadn't taken offense, the motor coach door swung open. Kolette, then Mason Sutherland, popped through the opening.

"Is Grandpa here?" Mason asked by way of greeting.

Kolette called, "Good morning! It's Moe! That explains Boedy on the pullout this morning. I didn't think you'd really come. How cool is this?" She hugged Dale's neck without any obvious expectations of her rising from her seat; then Kolette slid onto the chair vacated by her mother-in-law, dropped a kiss on her father-in-law's cheek, closer to his sideburn, and stretched her arm across the table toward Moe. "Hi. I'm Koly."

Moe couldn't stop her grin any more than she could the flood of immediate acceptance she felt in the other woman's presence. "Pleased to meet you, Koly."

"Wow!" Koly gripped her hand and grinned back. "That is the best smile. No wonder Boedy's all befuddled and ornery."

Dale nodded. "She's nice and beautiful, too. He's obviously the one with the problem. I think—"

"Girls!" The whip cracked once more. "Restrain yourselves. At least until Boedy is present to defend himself. Moe, more sausage?" She set a plate in the center of the table.

Kent excused himself, and Mason took his place.

Dale and Koly talked nonstop about clothes and race gear

and Moe's size. "She's so much taller than us," Dale admitted with a sigh.

Moe tried to think and process. She wasn't sure what they were insinuating or what they expected of her, but somehow she knew Boedy was at the root of it. Where was he? She wished he'd come and explain.

Mason caught her eye and mouthed, "It will be okay."

And suddenly it was. Whatever the girls had planned, Moe knew that they had her best interests at heart. They were so open and spontaneous, she didn't have to second-guess their motives. She'd also figured out why Boedy called them "the girls." Perhaps they weren't teenagers, but a person couldn't tell from their enthusiasm and energy.

Moe decided she liked Boedy's brother, as well. His hair and eyes were darker than Boedy's and lighter than Dale's. As the middle child, he seemed well-adjusted and content in his own skin—like his older brother.

For the first time, Moe wondered if their confidence really came from their NASCAR successes. Somehow that seemed to hold no weight in this family of successful people.

Then Dale said something silly, and Koly giggled and grabbed Moe's arm.

Warmth gushed into Moe's heart. Never in her life had she experienced such simple joy in the moment. If she had as a child, she couldn't remember the time. But being in the midst of these family members—with their interrupting and their opinions and their acceptance—was everything she wanted. . . and her heart swelled with the knowledge that Boedy was offering them to her for an entire month.

When Boedy slipped into the coach ten minutes later, he stood silently, listening to the family chatter around him. They were having a nonsensical discussion about who in the Sutherland family was the most physically demonstrative. He guessed from Moe's nonplused expression that he'd been awarded the honor.

He half smiled at her surprise. He'd thought for a long time last night about her comment that she was out of his league. He hadn't liked it, and he finally realized why. His hands were completely tied until she came to grips with her own worth and purpose. He liked being in the driver's seat. He'd never been too keen on going slow. But with Moe, there wasn't a thing he could do until God did an overhaul on her heart.

Sure, even now the girls were making plans for a shopping spree. . .as he'd asked of them. . .but that wasn't what Moe needed.

Chapter 5

Less than two hours later, Moe once again found herself in Dale's convertible with Boedy Sutherland at the wheel.

The leisurely, albeit boisterous, breakfast had given way to a not-so-surprisingly streamlined postrace departure system. Everything fell into place until Moe mentioned her car. Boedy assured her that he hadn't forgotten. The rest of the family would get on the road in the motor coach and the pickup while he and Moe did a side trip to retrieve her car. They'd catch up with the rest of the family on the interstate.

The plan had seemed flawless until they neared the motel. Someone's dark blue Camaro had come off the worst in an encounter with the marquee. At one end of the parking lot a police car sat with its roof light rotating in red and blue silence. Yellow police tape covered the doors of three motel rooms. Boedy slowed the car, and Moe straightened in her comfortable seat.

"This doesn't look good," Boedy murmured.

"What's happened?" Her first thought was for Vanna, but then Moe realized that the yellow tape covered her old motel room and the next two doors to the right. Vanna's room had been on the upper floor.

Her second thought was to realize her 190,000-mile clunker wasn't in the parking space in front of her hotel room.

Boedy pulled to a stop and cut the engine. "You stay here until I see what's going on."

Moe watched him cross the parking lot toward the police cruiser. At a quick rap on the glass beside her head, she nearly jumped out of skin. Then she recognized Vanna beyond the tapping. She pushed open the car door, and Vanna's words poured over her.

"Moe, am I ever glad to see you! I hoped you'd left with Sutherland when I didn't see you again last night. But I came in too late to check on you. Then the gunshots about seven and the squealing tires and, oh, what a mess. Police sirens and everything. Then the cops started going door-to-door, asking for witnesses. When no one could rouse you, the manager opened your room. Your stuff was gone. Your car, too, but I could have sworn it was in the lot when I came in last night. So I wondered if you'd been kidnapped or what."

When Vanna paused to suck air, Moe slid to her feet and asked, "What happened?"

"Where have you been?" Vanna demanded instead. Then she squinted as if seeing the car Moe had exited for the first time. "Sutherland."

"Boedy took me to stay with his family." Moe didn't want anything crass read into the situation. "When he dropped me off, he didn't like the looks of this place."

"Who would?" Vanna dismissed. Then she added, "Domestic violence is what the police are calling it. An angry husband took an automatic rifle to his wife's love nest." Vanna motioned toward the taped fronts of the three motel rooms. "Unfortunately—or fortunately for the wife—he was too angry or high to have decent aim. He took out the windows in three rooms."

Hers being one of them, Moe realized as weight sank in her stomach. "Was anyone hurt?"

Vanna wiggled her hand carelessly. "Scared. Minor wounds from the glass. EMTs didn't even take anyone to the hospital."

"That's good. Do you have to stay?"

"No way. I didn't see anything. I'll be out of here by noon. Just wish I could have gotten more sleep."

Yeah, that sounded like the old Vanna. She rolled with the waves and complained about every one, tide in or tide out. After the sweet taste of the Sutherlands this morning, Moe shuddered at the life she—and Vanna—had been living. She hungered for so much more.

"What's this about my car?" Pushing away her disturbing thoughts, Moe eyed the emptying parking lot.

"I don't see it." Vanna did the hand jiggle again as if it were little concern of hers. And by rights, Moe admitted, it wasn't. Vanna grinned wickedly. "I should have known even you couldn't pass up an opportunity like Sutherland."

Moe told herself to ignore the insinuation. There were more pressing issues. "We left my car last night. That's why we're here."

Moe scanned the parking lot one more time to make sure

she hadn't parked somewhere else and forgotten. Instead of her car, she saw Boedy and a gray uniformed police officer approaching.

Vanna gave a little squeak and then muttered, "I'll catch you in Watkins Glen, girl. Don't do anything I wouldn't do."

Moe nodded and focused on the policeman who Boedy introduced to her.

"Martha McKenna?" the middle-aged officer queried. At her silent nod, he continued, "Do you know Theodore Mason?"

Moe shook her head and whispered, "No, sir." She didn't know whether it was the uniform or the stern expressions that seemed prerequisite for the job, but she found Pennsylvania State Police officers intimidating.

"Do you drive a brown 1980 Ford Pinto?"

She nodded. "Yes, sir. But it doesn't seem to be where I left it."

Boedy slid a half step closer. "Moe, it seems there was a shooting at the O.K. Motel this morning."

She couldn't even summon a smile at his overstating the obvious. "Vanna said no one was hurt." She turned questioning eyes on the policeman.

He nodded. "I need to get a statement from you, just to verify what Mr. Sutherland has already told me. Tell me where you were this morning."

"Of course."

In the process of answering the officer's questions, Moe learned that a man had fired on his wife and her lover and then totaled his Camaro on the marquee pole. He'd hot-wired Moe's Pinto to escape the scene but crashed three miles up the road. Still high, he'd been apprehended with the rifle on the seat beside him. That was the good news. The bad news was, he'd totaled her car, and the police had impounded it for evidence. She could collect her things—Moe was certain she hadn't left anything of value in the car—and call her insurance company, but she'd probably never drive the Pinto again.

Moe had little emotion for the loss of her relic. It had served her well, but it hadn't had much life left in it. She concluded her statement for the officer and left him with her contact information and Boedy's cell phone number if they should need to speak to her again.

Dazed, she allowed Boedy to settle her back into the passenger's seat of Dale's sporty G6. The soft leather soothed her, but the variance in their two lives pinched at her. What was she doing with Boedy? What was she going to do without her car?

They rode in silence until Boedy took the entrance to Interstate 80.

Suddenly Moe was doubly glad that the Sutherlands weren't flying home before flying to their next destination as they usually did, leaving the coach and camper in the hands of their drivers. Boedy had explained earlier that Watkins Glen, mere hours from the Poconos, was too close not to avail themselves of quality family time. If Boedy had been racing for the airport, he would have found it easy to ditch her in the process. Now, without a vehicle, even an old one, she was completely at his mercy.

"Now what?" Moe asked softly.

"Now we'll catch up with my family." Boedy offered her a

lopsided grin. "And we'll have each other's company while we do it."

〜

"Boedy, you may have saved my life last night."

From the surprised look on Moe's face, Boedy guessed the realization had just set in. "I'm glad no one was hurt," he offered in response.

"How did you know?"

He sent her another quick look. "Know what?"

"How did you know that I needed to get out of there last night?"

"Moe, had you looked at the place?" He let his tone insinuate that it had been obvious that no one should have spent the night there. "I told you I didn't have a good feeling about your staying." But that wasn't a fair explanation either. The Holy Spirit deserved credit. "The truth is, it was more than a feeling."

Moe watched him with wide-eyed gullibility. Had that always been the difference between her and the Vanna-types? The accepting trust in her gaze?

He cleared his throat, glad to keep his focus on the road before him.

"How could you have known some guy was going to shoot up the motel?"

"I didn't know that. God wasn't that clear."

"God?" Moe sounded dubious, not cynical.

"Sure. You've heard of Him, right?" Boedy wanted to keep the conversation light.

"I believe in God!"

Surprise shot through him, but it was quickly checked. The reality was a lot of people "believed in God" without having a clue about His character or power. "Are you a Christian?" The question clogged in his throat. Likewise, a lot of people claimed to be Christian without accepting Christ as Lord.

The woman in question now jerked against her seat restraint. "Contrary to what you think, Boedy Sutherland, I don't sleep around and hang out in bars or kill people. I pay my debts and my taxes, and maybe I don't go to church every Sunday, but I have a Bible, and I know we didn't spontaneously burst out of primeval goo."

He let the tirade wash over him. He heard her hurt and confusion. And her embarrassment. "Moe." He reached out and finally managed to capture one of her wringing hands in his. "You don't become a Christian by default just because you live in America. Nor does having the unblemished record of not killing a person make you one."

"I know." Her tone suggested the opposite.

"Lots of people use the term loosely, but it originally referred to a disciple or student, a follower of Christ."

Her hand stilled beneath his.

"I guess the best way to put it is that a Christian is a person who trusts Jesus Christ with his or her life—both the here-and-now living one and the eternal after-we-die-in-this-body one."

Her other hand, warm and firm, settled on top of his.

"But the truth is that you have to know some facts about Jesus before you can trust Him. Saving faith isn't blind."

"Like trusting you?"

"I guess. The more you know me and learn that I'll keep my

word and that I'll take care of you to the best of my ability, the more you'll be able to trust me and want to do what I ask you to do." He waited for her response, but she merely tightened her grip. "That's how it is with Jesus, too. But until you know Him, any trust that you have in Him is superficial or forced at best."

"Does He talk to you, like the two of us are talking?" She shifted but didn't let go of his hand. "I mean, I know we can't see Him, and that He's not going to sit in the car with us or anything. I mean, how did you know—know that I shouldn't stay in the motel last night?"

Boedy thought through his words carefully, well aware that he was treading on matters of eternity. "With me, God doesn't talk so much as He impresses. But sometimes those impressions transfer into words or phrases. Last night I was hearing 'Get out' over and over in my head. I thought it was because the place was grubby. Trust me, it wasn't like God said, 'Take Moe away from here, or she'll be killed by a stray bullet.'"

"Wow." Moe sighed, then patted his hand in sudden energy. "I'm glad you listen to God."

So was Boedy. A part of him wished that it was always that clear and simple, even as he acknowledged to himself that it wouldn't have been clear or simple if he hadn't been in the habit of listening and obeying God's still small voice.

Lord, he prayed silently. *Moe's seeking. Meet her where she is. She needs You. Help the girls—help us all—to share You in a way she can grasp.*

Chapter 6

"Trust me," Dale Sutherland said as she tossed another pair of Capri pants over the door of the changing stall. "The beginning of the week is slow. We aren't missing anything. They aren't missing us. Try these on."

"Speak for yourself!" Kolette called from the stall to Moe's right. "Mason is missing me. I wouldn't be surprised if Boedy was missing Moe."

The latter comment was muffled as Kolette tugged clothing over her head, but Moe knew what had been said because the girls had been hinting or blatantly commenting on Boedy's interest in her for the past two days.

She couldn't take them seriously, however, because they didn't know about the secret pact.

After an entire morning of trying on clothing, they'd settled on seven outfits between them. Koly found one "marvelous" blouse that brought out the beauty of her natural skin color. The rest were for Moe. One calf-length dress in deep red. Inch and a half heels. A pair of capris, white cotton pants, blue jeans—a size larger than she normally wore, and yet, somehow, a more attractive cut than any of her other jeans—and two pair of walking shorts. Nor could she figure out what it was about the tops that gave her more class than her own clothing. They didn't all have sleeves or buttons, but even to Moe's unpracticed eye, she could see that the clothing her new friends were dressing her in was more than a step above her usual brands.

As Dale handed over cash for this last purchase, Mrs. Sutherland appeared in the boutique doorway. "I've made us hair appointments for one fifteen. Let's get some lunch."

Moe once again found herself caught up in the Sutherland exuberance for life. She couldn't remember the last time she had gone shopping with her own mother—with anyone for that matter. But these three women made the experience all about the person, not the clothing. Moe would grab something off the rack that caught her eye. . .and buy it if the price was right. But Mrs. Sutherland showed her that every piece of clothing was beautiful in its own right; however, to be purchased, it had to fit Moe. Fit, it turned out, meant more than being her right size. How the cloth draped. How the colors melted with her skin tones. If the outfit projected the image she wanted to project.

Until today, Moe had always gone for the "fun-loving" image.

"No, no," Dale had insisted when she'd mentioned this. "Your smile and your clear eyes already suggest fun. You're not going to lose that."

"Your clothing sort of narrows the type of fun you're looking for," Koly added.

Moe hadn't understood a word of what they were trying to tell her. And that was before they started talking about God.

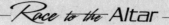

Half the words they strung together—relationship, submission, guidance, Spirit, repentance—didn't make any sense. Even when she thought she knew what the words meant, they used them in ways that made her pretty sure she didn't. But she wanted to learn, so she kept smiling and nodding and eventually asking questions of her own.

That conversation carried them into the hair salon.

Dale abruptly changed the subject. "I think she needs to go back to her roots. I like the spiked look. It suits her high cheekbones. But bleached blond just seems so brash, and Moe isn't really brash."

Moe blinked in surprise.

Koly rolled her eyes. "You might have let the hairdresser suggest it, Dale."

"You don't like blond?" Moe hadn't expected that. She thought they'd be trying to talk her into letting her hair grow out. She looked to Mrs. Sutherland for confirmation.

"How long have you been blond?" Mrs. Sutherland reached up to rub a few strands of hair between her fingers.

Moe's lips twisted in self-deprecation. "Since May. When I decided to be a race car groupie."

Dale snorted and Koly giggled, but Mrs. Sutherland merely smiled. "Then I think the blond can go. . .as you are not a 'race car groupie.'"

Moe wondered about that long after her hair had been deep-conditioned, darkened, and trimmed. Who was she, now that she'd been welcomed into the Sutherland family? She wasn't family. She was a guest, sort of. But again, the family didn't know about her pact with Boedy. They were only welcoming her, befriending her, helping her to fit into their world, because Boedy had asked them to. Or was it because Jesus asked them to?

One thing she was certain of by the end of the tiring day was that she respected and very much enjoyed the women of Boedy's family. They accepted her as she was. Which seemed insane when the entire day had been spent making her question her self-perception and nearly every belief on which she'd based her decision making. They didn't ask her to change or tell her she must; they simply presented a different way and gave her options. In doing so, they somehow didn't make her feel less—than them, than what she could be—they made her feel more. As if she were becoming the person she was always meant to be.

The outfits, the hairstyle, the makeup, the impromptu lesson on how to carry her body, and that talk about who Christ created her to be, all melted into a warm glow deep in the center of her being.

"One more thing!" Koly called as they headed toward the mall's exit. She waved them back to the perfume counter.

"Sweet," Dale agreed. "How could we forget the all-important nose?"

"I'm not that big on perfume," Moe admitted. She didn't want them to waste their money, and though they had been adamant that this day was their gift to her, Moe knew she would need to pay them back.

"I know which scent," Koly insisted. "There's no point in spraying you with a lot of stuff that will give us all a headache." She murmured something to the clerk.

The lady nodded and returned almost immediately with a small bottle. "On the wrists. Behind your ears. Some women do a drop down the cleavage or behind the knees."

Koly motioned for Moe to hold out her hand. She dabbed the scent on her wrist. "Wave it in front of your nose. Slowly."

Moe complied. The faint fragrance settled into her, calming, tantalizing, promising. "What is it?" she asked.

Dale sighed. "Umm."

Mrs. Sutherland whispered, "Oh, that's honeysuckle. Precious."

With a wide grin, Koly nodded to the clerk. "We'll take it." With her package in hand, she turned back to Moe and looped her arm through hers. "Girl, Boedy thinks we're fixing you up for the track, but I'll have you know, we're fixing you up for Boedy."

Finishing in the top five was always cool. Finishing in the top five with Mason one car behind him was even better. Watkins Glen was good to them.

The week had flown by, and Boedy had seen considerably less of Moe McKenna than he'd expected—than he usually did, if the truth be known. She wasn't underfoot. She wasn't hanging at the pits. She wasn't even at the racetrack most of the week.

She slept in his bed and danced in his dreams, but she'd quit haunting his team. And his team had been in the zone for this race. Life was excellent.

He should have been ecstatic instead of antsy.

The weekly Sutherland Sunday dinner—tonight at a steak house—had grown to include not only Moe, but also Boedy's crew chief, Hought, and his wife, Glenda, who had flown up for the race.

The evening started with Glenda elbowing her husband in the ribs and exclaiming, "Why didn't you just tell me she was Boedy's girl?"

Dale snorted; Koly giggled. And Boedy realized it was the most natural thing in the world to rest his arm across the back of Moe's chair.

Moe flashed her sun-rivaling smile. "Ma'am, your husband has been a great friend to me these past months. He's explained a lot about the cars and racing in general."

Hought sat as silent as a plucked tomato.

"He does like to do that," Glenda agreed.

Boedy watched his mom swoop in and take charge of the conversation, and then just as neatly drop it back into Moe's lap. "How did you like your first race from inside the track?"

"It was fun." Moe leaned forward, pretending to fan herself with her napkin. "The entire week has been awesome. I wanted so much to. . ."

Boedy quit hearing her words. He wiggled his nose. He sniffed again, but the scent was gone.

"Mason, is it tough being in Boedy's shadow?"

Mason grinned. "I won't be there forever. Boedy has seven years professional driving under his belt. I'm a rookie. Besides that. . ."

Boedy tuned out his brother's response. The fleeting scent of honeysuckle sent him back to North Carolina and a hunger for a family of his own. He focused on the intent face of the lady beside him. She fit so well. Not only under his arm but also with his family. She held her own in the opinioned conversations, and she volleyed easily in the informational conversations like the one now circulating around the table.

He enjoyed her company, especially in the evenings. Often he'd catch her watching his mother with such intensity that once he'd asked her why. She'd blushed and admitted that she'd never lived with a couple in love before. Somehow he'd kept himself from hugging her tight.

On top of all that, her new look was fabulous. He'd made only one faux pas—that he knew of—by commenting, after the girls' first shopping spree, that Moe looked great without makeup. The professional had gone with subtler colors than Moe's usual blues and greens, and Boedy had been fooled into thinking she was au naturel.

But Moe didn't take offense. Too enthralled by her new world, she was a wide-eyed kid watching the animals board the ark two by two.

Her enthusiasm stirred him, but left him on edge, as well. Not quite satisfied.

Boedy realized he wanted some one-on-one time with Moe McKenna.

"One week down and three to go," Moe quipped. "How am I doing?"

Boedy had invited her to join him for a walk back at the campgrounds to watch the sunset, but Moe seemed determined to keep her distance and the conversation light.

He intended to humor her. "So well I'm going to miss you when you're gone," he teased.

She laughed. "Yeah, right. Seriously. Do you like the new clothes?"

"Very spiffy."

She arched her brows and tilted her head. "I guess they're still fun but not vampish."

"*You* are fun." He grabbed her hand. "Clothes don't change who you are."

"Just how people treat you."

Boedy heard the underlying sadness. He tugged her a little closer. "How have people been treating you?"

She smiled. Nowadays it was easy for him to spot the sporadic fake ones. "Perfectly," she assured him.

"Hmm." The back of her hand was soft beneath his thumb. "Have the girls been too bossy?"

"Absolutely not!"

"Is the family smothering? I know you're used to being independent. I can put you up in a hotel if you don't—"

"Boedy, I love your family."

He didn't think that sort of declaration should have been clogged with tears. He stopped their slow walk and snagged her other hand, drawing her around to face him. "What's wrong, Moe? Race life not all you'd hoped it would be?"

She shrugged, then mumbled, looking at her feet, "I'm having a hard time remembering the pact."

"The pact?" Where had that come from? "Moe, you've been marvelous. The team was clicking today. You stayed with Mom

and Dale like I asked you to. You've been keeping your end of the pact."

"But I had to keep reminding myself that's *why* I was with them." Finally she looked up at him, and fresh tears flooded her eyes.

"Ah, well." He hated to see her cry. "Maybe we could look at it as a starting-off point. How would that work?" He was rambling, paying little heed to his words, but very aware of her bright eyes and slow smile.

"Do you mean it?"

"Do you know me to say stuff I don't mean?"

She shook her head, and her smile brightened another notch. "Thank you."

Glad that the emotional scene was past, he leaned down to kiss her forehead and breathed in the scent of honeysuckle. His nose detoured into her temple. "Hmm."

She stiffened. "Boedy, you're sniffing me."

He couldn't disagree. He took another whiff. "You smell like I should be stretched out on a hammock."

She stepped back from him, but both her look and tone were coy. "I smell like a hammock?"

He ignored her flirtation. "You smell like home."

Chapter 7

Four days later, as Moe lounged on a bleacher seat, waiting for Boedy, she realized she had never met a family that talked about God and to God in simple, everyday conversations as much as the Sutherlands did. When Grandpa Sutherland, who was actually Kent Sutherland's grandfather, came on the scene in Michigan, he might have brought the person of Jesus Christ with him as companion for as often as He was the center of conversation.

But still, Moe couldn't seem to get a hold of Him—of God. She'd learned some of the names He preferred, such as Father, Lord, Almighty, and she talked to Him now, especially at night as she was going back over the day in her mind. Yet something was missing. Koly had explained to her about God's holiness and man's sin, and though Koly had made a face as if she expected Moe to disagree, Moe hadn't. She could admit to being a sinner, not only to breaking aspects of all the Ten Commandments but mostly of wanting to control her own destiny, to be her own person without anyone, including a God—whom she'd always known in her heart existed—telling her the best way to live. No, confessing her sin wasn't hard.

Believing that Jesus, who was God from the beginning, put on skin and lived on Earth without ever sinning Himself, that He came to live the Truth and died to conquer death and sin—that got a bit harder to grasp in her brain. But it wasn't hard to believe. God was God. He could fix things however He wanted to.

Which was the part that was tougher to swallow. That God had wanted to. God wanted to fix the mess of man by sacrificing Himself and serving that which He'd created. Wild. Seemingly insane. And then, even crazier, Koly insisted that God did it for Moe—that if no one else in all the world would have believed Jesus was the way, the truth, and the life, and if Moe was the only one who would believe it, Jesus would still have set aside His glory and been crucified. . .for Moe.

She wasn't *that* special. In fact, it kind of made Moe wonder if Koly knew what she was talking about. God didn't even know her like that, did He? It wasn't as if she'd been seeking Him all of her life. In the beginning *Jesus* was a fight word between her parents. And then, in her college days, He was good for a rousing debate between her faith-diverse friends. But she hadn't even owned a Bible until the beginning of this summer when she realized how important it was to Boedy. She'd read it on and off over the summer, and some of the stories were interesting, and she saw that God got involved in some people's lives. But in hers?

No. She wasn't special enough to warrant God's attention.

That was where she got bogged down, when Koly continued to talk about God's mercy and grace, and being baptized into new life and living in the Spirit.

Why would God do that for her?

"Hey, Moe, come on!" Boedy called her out of her thoughts and back to the racetrack in front of her. "We have a small window of opportunity here, remember?" His easy smile weakened the harshness of his words, and her heart responded to his confidence. "Unless you've changed your mind?"

"No way!"

Boedy had gotten the use of a car with a passenger seat and permission to take her on the track this evening. A few other drivers might be testing cars, but in general, the track would be theirs. Boedy said it would be one of the safer opportunities he'd have to give her that much-desired spin. She was a bit amazed she had been able to think of anything else—even God—when she was so close to achieving her summer's goal.

Moe noted he carried a dark green helmet as he dropped into step beside her. His hand spanned the small of her back. He turned her toward the pits, and the butterflies tickling her stomach fluttered toward her throat.

"There's not much to this once we get you strapped in." He motioned toward a multicolored car, his lopsided grin accompanying his shrug. "Looks like this poor thing is used for more than test rides."

Moe grinned back at him, but realized, now that the moment of truth had arrived, that she was a bit tense and stiff. She looked at the car, bereft of the great paint jobs the sponsored cars touted. What if the ride wasn't what she'd dreamed of?

He squeezed her shoulder. "Let's see how the helmet fits first."

Moe pulled it on. Snug. Hot. Heavier than she'd imagined. She crinkled her nose.

Boedy placed a hand on each side of the helmet, then wiggled. Moe felt her head move with the helmet, and he nodded in approval. "Great. Loaning you her helmet was the only way I could get Dale to believe I should drive rather than her."

Moe knew he was joking. She offered another stiff grin.

Boedy helped her into the car and snapped all the safety harnesses into place. It seemed her helmeted head was in the way of everything, bumping into the car frame, the seat, things that shouldn't have been in the way. She decided to sit exceptionally still. When Boedy began to back away, Moe grabbed his hand. "Isn't there anything I should know?"

He was already wearing his driving gloves, and she missed the warmth of his skin, though his thumb rubbed against the back of her hand as if he were used to holding it every day. "Stay in your own space. I don't care if you yell or scream or laugh. It's too loud to hold a conversation, and I didn't bring any mics. So once we start, enjoy the ride."

Strapped tight, Moe couldn't imagine how she could get into his space. She was more concerned about how she could get him to stop if she wanted out. It would be horrifying if she were sick. She'd never given it any thought until Dale and Mason started telling tales about other people they'd taken for rides. Grown men in tears. Puking.

She'd wanted to be in a fast car for so long that she couldn't imagine that her body would betray her, but she'd been reading a lot of Proverbs, and one that had stuck in her mind was about pride going before a fall. She didn't want to fall in Boedy's eyes.

Please, God, don't let me be sick.

Somehow she thought she could control the rest of her actions. She'd never ask Boedy to stop, so she didn't need to know how.

Boedy slid down behind the wheel and in rapid habit clicked the various straps of his own five-point safety harness. "Are you ready?" At her abrupt nod, he started the car.

Before he'd even put it in gear, Moe felt the power, the thrum beneath her outstretched legs and feet. As soon as the car rolled forward, she became aware of how low to the ground she was sitting, how enclosed she was in the contoured seat and car frame, roll bar, fiberglass. . .and Boedy.

He gave her a thumbs-up before he pulled onto the track.

Michigan International Speedway was a two mile D-shaped oval. She'd heard the stats earlier. Eighteen degree banking in the seventy-three-foot wide sweeping turns. SAFER walls. She'd laughed about that, but Hought had been the one to explain the acronym: Steel and Foam Energy Reduction walls.

Boedy accelerated steadily through the first turn and beyond. Moe felt pushed back into her seat, her head seeming to rattle around on its own accord. She'd been warned about the jerkiness, the bumps, the noise, but still it seemed more than she'd anticipated, more than it should be for how smooth race cars looked from the outside. The car continued to gain speed.

She felt the quick brake check before the third turn where Boedy once more accelerated. Inertia grabbed her. Disconcerted, she felt the car turn without her. But, of course, she was strapped in and made the turn. How fast were they going?

The muscles in her neck bunched as she struggled to hold

her head in place. A strange dizziness gripped her, and she swallowed hard.

As they came back into Turn 1, likely traveling as fast as Boedy intended to take her, Moe saw the wall approaching at an incredible speed. Why wasn't he turning? Why wasn't he—

Her muscles clenched for the crash, and the car sped out of the turn, back into the straightaway. Moe blinked and then started to laugh. Wow. It was incredible. The laugh didn't last long as they hit another turn and she was pressed back into her seat, head tilting with the weight of the helmet and force. Again the blurry wall zoomed at her, and then it was gone.

Race car driving was a blast. Amazing. Maybe someday she'd have Boedy teach her how to drive—

She clamped down the thought immediately. Enjoy the moment. She might never be in another race car her entire life. This would be enough. This one time with Boedy Sutherland.

She started to reach out to him before she remembered his one request: "Stay in your own space." She translated that to mean "Don't touch me."

What an idiot she would be if she'd reached over and grabbed his arm. Yet she'd almost done exactly that. Still felt compelled to do exactly that.

Touch Boedy. Feel his life. Curl her fingers around his biceps. Rest her palm on his knee. Anything to feel the human contact. To reaffirm that they were in this together. That he wanted her here.

She didn't have time to rationalize the urges or even to think through her thoughts. Her fingers were reaching out to him. She was no longer aware of the speed, the looming walls, the bumping, or the engine's thrum. She needed to touch Boedy.

But it was the one thing he'd told her not to do. And she couldn't keep herself from doing it. Her fingers stretched toward Boedy.

Please, Jesus, I need help.

Moe breathed through her nose. Blinked. Swallowed. Then realized her hands rested in her lap.

Peace.

The track zoomed by at an implausible speed. What had just happened? She'd never experienced anything like that in her entire life. Neither the unfamiliar, uncontrollable loss of her own will, or the desperate plea for help to the only One who could help her.

She didn't know what to make of it all, so she decided not to think about it yet.

She tilted her head enough that she could see Boedy's profile, and she watched him drive. It was as beautiful as the ride itself. He loved to drive fast. Any fool could see how it filled him with delight and purpose. She lost track of the turns and laps.

Boedy said something, but she didn't catch it.

Suddenly, Moe realized he was slowing the car and bringing them back down pit row. The ride was over too quickly. She wanted to go again. She told herself to be content.

Boedy parked the car. The silence was deafening. She swallowed. Heat swamped her, and she struggled out of her helmet. Boedy helped her out of the harness, back onto solid—slow—ground. It took a few steps to find her land legs. Moe flung herself at Boedy.

She wrapped her arms around his middle and squeezed him as tight as she could. "That was the best. Thank you, thank you, thank you."

He laughed, and his arms came around her lightly. "You're welcome, Moe. I'm glad you enjoyed it."

She knew that was her cue to release him, but she squeezed him again and tilted her head back to grin up at him. "You're the best. The absolute best."

Chapter 8

Boedy swallowed hard and raised his chin. She was killing him. At the same time, he felt able to leap tall buildings in a single bound. What was it about this woman? She was easy to love in so many ways, and terrifying in others. She knew enough about men to be dangerous, and yet every time she cashed in on that knowledge, Boedy could see right through it. Then, at times like these, she simply laid him low. Clueless to what her innocent words did to his heart.

She released his waist and stepped backward. "Boedy." Suddenly she sounded shy. "The strangest thing happened in the car."

He felt an irresistible urge to keep the conversation light. "You weren't feeling sick, were you?" He ruffled her hair, respiking it where the helmet had matted it to her scalp. That was a safe touch, and with her, he was all about low risks.

She shook her head solemnly, and the weight in his stomach expanded. "Out of nowhere, I had this need to grab your arm."

Boedy blinked. *Huh?* Though he hadn't known what he had expected her to say, that wasn't what he'd been expecting her to say.

"That's all I could think about. My fingers reaching out and grabbing your arm...and...and...you told me not to, but I wanted to, but I didn't want to. Still, I was going to, but I asked Jesus to stop me."

Moe looked up at him expectantly, and Boedy didn't have a clue. He needed to take a lesson from the new kid's book. *Lord, I could use some insight here.*

"Have you ever had that happen to you?"

Stalling, Boedy shook his head. "Not that I remember." He didn't even understand what had happened to her. "Why would you want to grab my arm?"

"I didn't want to! It was the one thing you told me not to do!"

The lightbulb clicked on. "Oh, yes." Boedy captured her hand and directed her toward a bleacher seat. They sat. "Put in that context, yes, I've had that happen to me many times. It's called temptation."

"Temptation?" Moe echoed. "Isn't that...?"

"Wanting to do something you've been asked not to do. Don't touch the hot stove. Don't drink under age. Don't eat the fruit from the tree in the center of the garden. Temptation."

She tapped her lower lip.

He forced his thoughts from Moe's lip to Dale's habitual tapping. He wondered if Moe had spent too much time with Dale and was picking up some of his sister's habits. It was better than where his thoughts wanted to go.

She quit tapping her lip and grinned. "I get it."

He was glad someone did. "Are you thirsty?" He was, from the drive and the heat.

"Sure."

But he could tell she was thinking of deeper matters. Perhaps he should prompt the conversation instead of run from it. "What do you want out of life, Moe McKenna?"

Her gaze flicked away and then came back to his. "I never thought I wanted anything special. The normal stuff. A job to pay the bills. A few decent friends. Someday a husband and kids." She glanced away, sighed, and then came back to him. "But before I settled into that normal life, I wanted one summer of dreams. I wanted to be a part of this." She gestured toward the track. "I wanted what you just gave me. A fast ride. But now—"

Boedy watched her throat muscles contract and release.

"I want your God, Boedy. I want to know this Jesus who talked to storms and dead people. I want Him like I've never wanted anything in my entire life."

He watched the tears well in her eyes and drip onto her cheeks. He opened his arms and gathered her close. "That's sweet, Moe, 'cause He wants you the same way."

She shook her head and began to cry in earnest. "I hurt in places I didn't even know I had."

"I know." Boedy rubbed her back. "I know. It's a hard thing to see yourself through the holy One's eyes. But He's going to remake you—new from the inside out."

"I want that."

⌇

Moe's "I want that" carried them into a three-hour discussion

where she barely shifted on the hard bleacher seat. She soaked up the stories he shared about his own faith walk, his struggles and temptations, and shared a few of her own. She listened as he once more explained about what Jesus did for her and what He expected from her. She would give Him her hard, rock heart in exchange for a new heart. And she would gladly give Him her new heart, too, every day of her life as long as He wanted her.

"But, Boedy," she finally found the nerve to say, "I can't believe I'm that special. Koly said Jesus would have died just for me. That's crazy."

Boedy was quiet for so long that she thought he wasn't going to respond to her indirect question. "God's love...," he said finally. "It's hard to grasp, for sure. But maybe what is important for you to know is that God's character is love. That's who He is, Moe. It's not seasonal apparel for God, something He puts on and takes off when it suits Him. God loves. God loves. Always. Koly was right when she said Jesus would have died for only you. But that's hard to grasp because you need His forgiveness and healing, and you know you aren't worthy. From where you're standing it does look like Jesus' dying is all about saving you. But once you're saved, you'll see that Jesus' death and resurrection was about bringing praise to God."

Moe tried not to look as confused as she felt.

"I guess it doesn't matter at this point anyway. God saves because He wants to, because that's His nature to love and pursue and redeem. It has absolutely nothing to do with you being loveable—good, worthy, or able to do anything for Him. It has everything to do with who God is, all by Himself. Better than we can imagine."

Somehow knowing that God's love was completely independent of her gave Moe hope. He knew what she was like and He didn't care. Except He did care—enough to die.

Boedy continued to explain that faith was choosing to believe, and though she didn't think it could be so easy, as they continued to talk, Moe found she did believe. Jesus loved her.

Often the conversation carried them into side waters, and Moe learned more about the inner workings of Boedy Sutherland than she'd ever dreamed she would know. Boedy had actually dated Koly a few times before Mason had claimed her. Daniel Sutherland, Kent's father, had died in a race car crash more than fifteen years before Boedy was born. Boedy had seen pictures of his grandfather and once watched a news clip of the fiery pileup that had taken one life and ended a few careers. It was a stark reminder to live every day for the Lord, because a person didn't know when it might be his last.

Although Boedy didn't have any fear about driving professionally, he shared that spurts of anxiety would try to surface when Mason raced. Irrationally, risk was okay for him, but not for his baby brother. He confessed he became concerned for Koly and his own future wife—how they would handle the tension, week in and week out.

Moe asked, "How does your mom survive it all?"

"She says there are no accidents in Jesus."

"Then I imagine Koly will do fine." Moe couldn't bring herself to think about Boedy's future wife.

They talked about dying to self and being reborn. About God's grace and her need to submit to His authority. This time it made more sense.

Moe spent at least ten minutes confessing all the things that she had done wrong in her lifetime. At first she thought Boedy was going to stop her, but he bowed his head and held her hand, his thumb rubbing across her knuckles on occasion. She was sure there were other ways she'd sinned in her life, but her words dried up, and Boedy closed her spontaneous prayer with thanks to Jesus.

Close to dark, Dale found them still in the stands and insisted that they come back to the motor coach for dinner. All she wanted to talk about was Moe's first ride, and Moe obliged, but her gaze kept seeking Boedy's.

The next Sunday morning, Moe soaked in the experience of the early service. She was seated between Boedy and his dad. Dale and Mrs. Sutherland were on one side, Koly and Mason on the other. Moe was truly surrounded by love. So when the preacher concluded his closing invitation with the words of the Ethiopian eunuch, "Look, here is water. Why shouldn't I be baptized?" Moe felt the responding need in her own empty heart.

With a small moan, she pushed her way through the surrounding love of Boedy's family, out into the aisle, toward the front, and the water, and the new life and the sacrificial love of Jesus Christ.

She confessed Jesus as Lord before a body of strangers who didn't feel like strangers. She embraced the blood of Jesus, which washed away her sins, and exchanged her heart for a new one. Moe McKenna was remade more thoroughly and permanently than any shopping spree, language lessons, or day spa could ever do.

She arose a redeemed child of the living God.

With the afternoon sun warming his head and Moe's shoulder brushing his arm, Boedy closed his eyes and let the beautiful power of the "Star-Spangled Banner" sweep through him. His cup overflowed with blessings. God's grace was amazing.

Boedy breathed Michigan race air and loved the fumes tickling his throat. He loved starting on the pole. He loved the cloudless sky and the fighters flying overhead. Today, he didn't even mind prerace interviews. God's grace was amazing.

Though he hadn't thought it through in such simple terms before, now he realized why he'd felt his hands were tied in pursuing a dating relationship with Moe. A guy doesn't go after the same girl his best friend is pursuing. And his best friend, Jesus, had definitely been pursuing Moe. Now, however, Boedy felt as though he'd been given a green light as far as Moe was concerned. It seemed as if Jesus were saying, "Okay, she's given Me her heart. I am number one in her life. Now you're free to take your appropriate place in her earthly journey."

It was whimsical, but that was his spirit's impression—that now it was okay to pursue Moe McKenna.

Of course, he knew he would need to go slow. In the overall scheme of a lifetime, they hardly knew one another. But he had another week before the pact was up to convince her to stick around and see, just see, where their relationship might go. He had a solid idea of where he wanted it to go. . .but he would take things slow.

Chapter 9

"Martha?" Koly giggled. "Your given name is Martha?"

Moe shrugged. Nothing was taking away the beauty of this day. Boedy was leading his seventh lap. She was seated in an awesome terrace suite, and today was the first day of her new life. "It is." She jokingly patted at her spiked hair, but she didn't take her gaze from the cars circling the track. "Don't I look like a Martha to you?"

Koly giggled again.

Dale tapped her fingers against her soda can. "Moe suits you pretty well."

Mrs. Sutherland wrapped an arm around Moe. "Before this conversation goes any further, I'll have you know that my grandmother was named Martha. In Hebrew Martha, like Mary, means *bitter* with the connotation of *sorrow*. In Aramaic, Martha means *lady*, an elegant woman."

That drew Moe's gaze away from Boedy's car. "No way!"

Mrs. Sutherland smiled into her eyes. "Indeed, Miss Moe McKenna. You've been called a lady all your life. Now I think you'll start to believe it."

Moe smiled and returned her gaze to the track, but in the back of her mind, she wondered if her parents had known the meaning of the name they had given her. Deep within her heart, she knew that God had.

A blown tire had knocked Mason out of the race on Lap 156. Everyone was disappointed for him, and Koly had left for the pits to comfort her husband, though she acknowledged that now he would be focused on Boedy's driving.

Around Lap 310 Dale spilled her soda down her front and left to make a quick change of clothes.

And on Lap 332 Moe started to think about going down to the pits. True, Boedy asked her to stay with his mom and the girls during the race, but she wanted to be in the pits. The new seating was phenomenal, but she should be in the pits. Something was going on down there.

Though Boedy had fallen out of the lead, he stayed close, moving between the sixth, seventh, and eighth positions. He would have one more scheduled pit stop before the race ended, depending, of course, on any yellow flags. Moe knew she didn't want to get in anyone's way. This was obviously a temptation, and she should fight it off.

When that reasoning didn't work, she realized that the last time she had been so successful was because she had asked God for help, not because she had "fought it off." So she whispered a soft prayer, "Please, Lord, I want to obey Boedy. Take away this desire to go to the pits."

She waited for the freaky peace she'd felt in the race car.

It didn't come. Instead, she started to think about Hought. The more she thought about him, the more she knew she needed to find him.

But Boedy had told her to stay with his mother. She glanced at Mrs. Sutherland. Hat shielding her eyes, the older woman was engrossed in the race. Moe shifted.

God, what's wrong with me? What's going on?

Hought echoed in her ears, and with it came the memory of the first night of her pact with Boedy. At the cheap motel, God had prompted him to take her away from there. Boedy had said, "God doesn't talk so much as He impresses me."

God was impressing her with Hought's name.

She shot to her feet. Then hesitated. Was He talking to her? Was He really? Or was it a temptation to do what she had been asked not to do?

The inner urgency prompted her to quit speculating and act. She raced for the stairs.

If Mrs. Sutherland looked or called after her, Moe didn't hear or see. She focused on her steps, on not getting tripped up or waylaid. She was pleased to see the security guard was one who often let her into the pits after races, but today she used a family pass instead of a smile.

She stayed back from the action, but with her heart beating in her throat, she surveyed the Sutherland Racing Team's area. Where was Hought? What was wrong?

Her vision narrowed to freeze-frame. Mason and Koly to the side by the water thermos. Russ organizing tires for the next pit stop. Bobby Ray with the fuel can—her gaze moved on. Kent in the headset, most likely listening to Boedy's spotter. Where was Hought?

Moe's gaze clicked on the crew chief, back behind the action, bending, kneeling, no, crashing to the floor.

Moe raced to his side and dropped to her knees. She covered the hand that Hought clutched to his chest. "Hought! Can you hear me?" His eyes rolled and his jaw slacked. "We need help!" she shouted.

Leaning down to his gaping mouth, Moe was relieved to feel his raspy breath against her cheek. "Keep breathing," she urged. "We'll get help."

Mason dropped to the ground at Hought's other side. Moe could hear Kent's voice, strong, confident, barking orders. Moe shut him out and listened to Mason assure the downed man that help was on the way.

How long? How long when she couldn't do anything but watch him struggle to breathe? Suddenly, the roar of car after car penetrated the hazy scene. The leaders zoomed in for their last pit stop. . .and a medical team loomed above the fallen Hought.

Moe was helped to her feet, brushed aside.

In seconds, Boedy was back on the track, perhaps none the wiser about what was happening backstage in the pit. It took the medical staff a few minutes to stabilize Hought, load him onto a gurney, and roll him toward the waiting ambulance. Then Hought was gone and Mason with him.

Moe started to shake. Standing against one wall, directed there so the professionals could get to Hought, Moe trembled, then slid downward. She didn't need to be crying, so why was

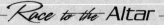

she? She wrapped her arms around her drawn-up knees. Hought had never lost complete consciousness; surely he would be fine. What was her problem? She'd never come apart in a crisis before.

She dropped her forehead to her knees. "Oh, God."

Then she gasped and began to rock. *God.* She'd never even thought to pray. Was it too late?

Boedy's top five win for the second week in a row nearly went unacknowledged as the Sutherland family and crew rallied to their ailing crew chief. Hought suffered a heart attack en route to the community hospital, but he was stabilized, diagnosed, and scheduled for angioplasty.

Boedy's parents exchanged places with Mason at Hought's bedside while Dale and Koly drove to Detroit to pick up Hought's wife who flew in on the earliest available flight. Boedy stayed with the crew members as they went about their usual duties.

Moe didn't know what to do. She felt useless. Unneeded. Surplus.

Especially after Boedy point-blank told her to go back to the coach.

For the first time since the pact, she wished for her car. For a hotel room. For some way to escape the pain. . .or embrace it. Instead, she obeyed and waited in the motor coach, out of the way. Silent. Invisible.

Boedy came in at dusk, barely glanced her way, and headed for the shower. Moe curled into a ball in the corner of the sofa and cried. She still didn't know why. Was it really just this morning she had completely turned her life over to Jesus? Today was supposed to be the best day of her life. Instead she felt abandoned.

⌘

Feeling a bit more human, Boedy pulled on clean workout pants and a black T-shirt. He padded barefoot back into the living area of the motor coach to see if Moe was hungry. He hoped they could find something acceptable in the cupboards because he didn't want to drive into town or go back out into the after-race madness of the infield.

He'd no more than spotted Moe tucked away in the corner of the sofa than Mason came up the front steps and nearly collided with him.

"Here." Mason handed him a box of hot dogs. "They don't taste as good as I thought they would."

Boedy took the box.

Mason turned and headed back down the steps. "I'm going to take a shower."

Boedy snagged a hot dog and had a bite in his mouth before he reached Moe and extended the box. She shook her head. He plopped onto the seat beside her. The hot dogs weren't the greatest, but he ate three.

Reluctantly he pushed back to his feet to see about something to drink. He was bushed tonight. Race and stress and—he eyed the unusually silent Moe—and a special kind of tension. He found a bottle of juice and brought one for Moe, as well.

Dropping back onto the couch beside her, he asked, "Did you find something to eat?"

She shrugged him off.

He drank his juice and then hers.

"Hought's going to make it. You'll see," he offered into the silence.

Moe rubbed at her face with the back of her hand.

"Come here, lady." He opened one arm to receive her into his embrace.

She didn't come.

He lowered his arm and shifted to face her. "Moe? What's wrong?"

"What's right?" burst from her like a bullet.

He blinked. Perhaps she expressed her stress with hostility. "Yes, Hought had a heart attack, but he's still alive. He's receiving the medical attention he needs. Glenda has arrived safely, and the girls will have her to the hospital in no time. Jesus is still Lord, babe."

She scowled at him. "Don't be flip."

He straightened. "I wasn't. It doesn't do any good to freak over might-have-beens and could-be's. I'm sure this will sound cold to you, but middle-aged, overweight men who live on hot dogs and stress have heart attacks. You'll probably be going through this with me someday."

Now her eyebrows as well as her lips scowled at him. "Stop it, Boedy. That isn't even funny."

He was serious, but he wouldn't have minded a smile from her. "What's really eating at you, Moe?"

She shrugged him off once again and then apparently changed her mind. In a sudden blur, she flung herself into his lap. "I'm horrible, Boedy. I didn't even think to pray." She pressed her forehead into his collarbone.

He allowed his hand to smooth the curve of her spine. "Hmm." As usual it took some divine intervention to follow her thought processes. "You mean for Hought? You haven't prayed for Hought?"

"I have now!" She made a fist in his T-shirt, but she didn't raise her head. "But I didn't pray when he fell, when I was the only one who knew he was in trouble. I just—just shouted for help."

With his free hand, he gently pried open her fist and then smoothed her fingers against the cotton material. "You think God doesn't hear shouts for help as easily as whispered prayers?"

"I wasn't talking to—" Moe straightened and frowned. "Oh."

Heaven help him, but he loved to watch her think. He reached up to trace the wrinkled skin between her eyebrows. "Have you ever heard of baby steps? I know you're an all-or-nothing type girl, and Jesus does want your all—but baby steps. You'll learn to pray about everything. And you'll realize that often in the crises, our prayers aren't as coherent or even as conscious as other times. God knows we're made from dust."

Her eyes widened. "Oh. Maybe I wasn't so horrible?"

A corner of his mouth hitched upward. "No. You aren't horrible."

"Are you mocking me?" Her eyebrows crashed together. "Besides, Boedy"—to his relief and disappointment she slid off his lap and began to pace—"you don't know everything. God was talking to me, impressing me with Hought's name. How could I forget to talk back to Him?"

Boedy leaned back into the cushions and stretched out his

legs. With Moe he never quite knew what to expect, but he trusted her to be open and honest about what she was feeling. "God was talking to you, was He?"

"Yes, up in the booth. I had that same horrible urge to go down to the pits, like I had to touch you in the race car." She paused, and he nodded. "So I thought it was temptation. But when I prayed for God to help me, the peace didn't come. Instead, all I could think about was Hought and that he was in trouble. So I went to the pits, and I'm sorry."

She dropped to her knees on the carpet beside him. Boedy jerked straight. "Sorry? For what?"

Her eyes drilled him. Then she blinked and focused on his hands. "For going into the pits when you told me not to," she whispered.

Boedy processed the confession slowly. From the sounds of it, Satan's side had been having a field day with her mind all evening. Accusing her of everything from not being spiritual enough for God, to not being obedient to him, and most likely everything else in between.

He ruffled the hair on the top of her bent head. "You did good, kid. I'm proud of you."

She jerked beneath his touch, and then her wide-eyed gaze fastened on his once more.

"I'm serious, Moe. You were open to the Spirit's prompting. You tested the spirit to verify His message. You obeyed God even when there was a personal cost to pay. Some people, after years of serving the Lord, don't have the faith you exhibited today. I'm proud of you."

She swallowed, and Boedy momentarily let his gaze slip

to the tanned expanse of her throat. "But, Boedy, I broke the pact."

He leaned forward, intending to pull her up onto the sofa beside him. Instead, his hands settled over the roundness of her shoulders, and he paused with his forehead almost touching hers. "You were obeying God, Moe. That's the one time that it's right to disobey your husband."

She pushed upward until their foreheads connected. He could feel the tension in her shoulders, hear it in her whispered announcement. "You aren't my husband, Boedy."

He drew her toward him, his head tilting, his lips brushing hers. "That's just a matter of logistics."

Chapter 10

Moe accepted his kiss. Returned it. Nearly crawled onto his lap before she restrained herself and pulled away.

Stumbling to her feet, she breathed deeply through her nose. She held her breath and relished the tingles radiating from her heart and sparking across her lips. "Wow."

He grinned up at her and slowly pushed to his feet.

Moe held out a hand, palm forward. "Hold on, Boedy. You're rushing me."

"Rushing you!" But both his exclamation and blue eyes held lively humor. "You've been tempting me for nearly three months."

"But I didn't know what I was doing then!" Moe didn't know where that comment had come from, but it was definitely true. Three months ago, she hadn't known one important thing about how to live or who she was. She'd wanted fun. She'd been fun loving. And she'd wanted to be loved.

But she hadn't known how to love. She had thought love

was a blue-eyed boy in a fast car, not a Savior stepping out of a tomb.

Moe covered her face, pressing her palms into her eyes. "Boedy, I'm so confused. Don't tempt me to believe nonsense."

His fingers closed around her wrists. "Moe McKenna, look at me." When she did, he didn't release his hold. "What craziness are you thinking now?"

She shrugged, helpless. "I don't know."

His lips tugged up at one corner.

"I'm thinking you don't know what you're insinuating," she said, hoping to sound firm. "Or I'm interpreting it wrong. And kissing me is because you're tired and Hought is in the hospital and—and—" She stuttered to silence.

"Really?"

His mocking prompt was enough to get her going again. "You've fulfilled my dreams, Boedy, and then given me more than I even knew I wanted or needed—I've met Jesus because of you, because of your family. And you let me share your family, and I've never known such respect and closeness and love. I mean, my sister tries and my mom used to, but it was never like this—wanting the absolute best for everyone else. You all have made me feel special, honored. . .and it's so much more than new clothes. . .than a certain code of behavior. . .it's belonging."

"I'm glad."

"But I don't belong. Don't you see that? I didn't go to the airport or the hospital. You didn't even want me in the pit as an extra set of hands to help. I—"

"You distract me, Moe."

She jerked her hands free and pressed them over her ears,

shaking her head in dismay.

"Moe, I said it was the guys, but it was mostly me. You're beautiful and alluring, and you distract me. If you're in my presence, I want you in my arms, not rolling a tire to the semitrailer."

Moe pressed her palms tighter on her ears, but she heard every low-spoken word. She wanted to believe, too. His intense gaze tempted her to believe.

"And, Moe, don't think for a second that I didn't notice you before the outside overhaul, 'cause it ain't true. Your smile cuts me off at the knees every time you shine it on me."

Moe's hands drifted from her ears to her mouth, covering the "oh" that formed on her lips.

"Granted," he continued softly, "I was concerned about your opinion of yourself. Frustrated by some of your choices, how you seemed to view the world and me. So, try not to hold it against me, but I'm as excited as you are about the engine restoration work the Lord's doing."

Moe grinned behind her hands. Engine restoration work indeed. A complete heart change.

"After today's choices, Moe, I don't see any reason I need to hold back my feelings. Do you want me to hold back?"

Moe swallowed. Did she? Sort of. He was scaring her. And making her the happiest woman ever. Boedy Sutherland had feelings for her that he'd been holding back? Really? She swallowed again, tried to clear her throat. "You're seducing me without even touching me. But I don't want to be seduced."

Pulling ever so slightly from her, Boedy stood a bit taller.

"Boedy, this is horrible. I've loved you forever, and now I'm all confused. Do I love you because of all the things you've done for me—God, family, acceptance—or do I love you for you? Do I love your family because I first loved you, or do I love you even more because they've loved me? I don't want—"

Boedy's laughter cut off her impassioned plea.

She frowned, hands dropping to her hips.

He laughed harder.

"Boedy, stop it. I'm trying to think things through."

He snagged the back of her neck and raised her up on her toes to meet his kiss.

Moe forgot to think.

Eventually, he released her from their kiss and nuzzled her ear. "I wonder if I love you because you smell like honeysuckle, or if I love the smell of honeysuckle because you're wearing it."

"Shut up." However, she did feel a little foolish.

"I love you, Moe McKenna, remade and reborn, and just as you are and who you will grow to be tomorrow."

She sighed and leaned into him. Thinking wasn't all it was cracked up to be.

"If you need time to get things straight in your head, I'll give it to you. Some days racing is a game of patience." He straightened slightly but didn't loosen the arms that encircled her. "And some day, not tonight, I'll explain to you how a husband's love is like Christ's for His church, and with a little revelation from the Lord, you'll see that you're worried about nothing. You can love Jesus, me, my family and yours, and be the fuller for it, still having enough love for others."

"I do love you, Boedy." Everything in her strained to be close to him even as she pushed back from his chest to look up at him.

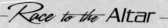

He smiled down at her. "Glad to hear it, lady."

She smiled back. This was the second best day of her life, rolled right into her first best day.

"We'll take it slow," he said, shifting to hold her shoulders. "Give ourselves time. I want to be your lifelong friend as well as your lover. I want to make sure you actually like the race circuit. Not every driver's wife travels with him, you know."

"I'm good with slow." Moe wanted to say that she loved everything about the race circuit, and she couldn't wait to get back into his race car.

"Since when?"

"Since you are?" She asked it as a question because she couldn't remember a time she didn't like speed.

He gave one short bark of laughter and then kissed her again. Murmuring against her lips, he challenged, "Race you to the altar."

GLORIA CLOVER

Gloria lives in western Pennsylvania with her husband, Scott Peterman, who prompted her switch in Sunday television interest from football to NASCAR—both provide excellent backdrops for reading. She writes Christian fiction, prayers, and devotions, and codirects an annual writers' conference. Gloria is a member of American Christian Fiction Writers, St. Davids Christian Writers Association, the Christian PEN, and various local writing groups. She works in women's and youth ministries from her home church of Emmanuel Christian, where God has taught her it is more important to be than to do. To learn more or to write to her, visit her Web site at www.gloriaclover.com.

Over the Wall

by Becky Melby and Cathy Wienke

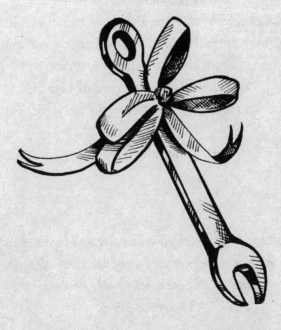

Dedication

To my "*grand* son" Jacob and our "princess child" Mackenzie,
who have given me a glimpse of God's unconditional love
and taught me to live in the gift of the moment.
And my thanks to my family who have
answered all my NASCAR questions:
Chuck Lake, Bill and Stacy Terhune, and my dad.
Cathy

To my amazing grandkids—
Reagan, Sawyer, Sage, Ethan, Peter, and Cole.
My prayer for each one of you is that you will always
"Shine like stars in the universe
as you hold out the Word of Life."
You are certainly stars in my universe.
Love you all,
Grandma Becky

*Trust in the LORD with all your heart and lean not on your
own understanding; in all your ways acknowledge him,
and he will make your paths straight.*
PROVERBS 3:5–6

Chapter 1

Camela Eastman yawned as she reclined the back of the passenger seat and stretched out. She smiled at Joe and spread his firefighter jacket over her Cookie Monster scrubs. Not wanting to keep him waiting, she'd run across the hospital parking lot balancing two suitcases, a dress bag, a boom box, and a sun umbrella. She was clammy from the exertion, and now the air conditioner was giving her a chill.

Joe patted her hand. "Tough night?"

"Two car accidents, an appendicitis, a four-year-old with an eraser shoved up his nose, four heart attacks, and an overdose... Pretty much a typical twelve-hour shift."

"Well, sleep fast. If MapQuest is right, it'll take us three hours and eight minutes. If we don't get snagged in construction, we'll be driving through the Darlington Speedway gates at 10:34 a.m."

Camela snuggled under the jacket that smelled like the Calvin Klein Eternity she'd given Joe for Christmas. She had hoped the name would send a subliminal message. Eternity...forever...I do. . .diamond. . . It hadn't worked. She stared at his profile and felt the same stirring of twitterpation she'd experienced twice a week for three years and seven months. He was gorgeous. She'd tried a lot of other words to describe Joe Jorgensen—handsome, striking, cute—but she always came back to gorgeous. He was beyond handsome and striking and was far too classic to be labeled cute. He'd just turned thirty, two years older than she, but he looked twenty-five. At just over six feet tall, he'd earned his rock-hard physique with hours in the gym and on the job. Coal black hair, jade green eyes, perfectly prominent cheekbones, and a kissable cleft in his chin had garnered him many requests to model for firefighter calendars. Camela admired the fact that he'd only agreed to tasteful shots.

"You're staring." He flashed bright white teeth at her. "Like what you see?"

"Love what I see." She closed her eyes and drifted into her usual fantasy. He was Lancelot and she, the fair Guinevere—

The *ding* of the turn signal woke her. She blinked at the clock. Three hours had passed, but it felt like mere minutes. As Joe took the exit, Camela kicked off her lime green Crocs and put her bare feet on the dashboard. She stretched, pressing her right foot against the windshield. Her toes made five little steam circles on the cold glass. "Wow, was I zonked. Did I snore?"

"Actually, you made kind of a *whoof-ly* sound." He reached across her and opened the glove compartment. Nodding at the windshield, he handed her a package of Windex Wipes.

After cleaning the glass, Camela rolled her window down. When the Lady in Black came into view, she took a deep breath. The South Carolina track got its nickname from the tire marks that blackened the walls. The decades of hot rubber and asphalt combined with the smell of motor oil and exhaust fumes to produce an ambiance like no other place on earth. To Camela Eastman it meant one thing—vacation.

True, it was a working vacation, but somehow the adrenaline rush of being part of a NASCAR medical team never left her drained the way a night in the ER back in Raleigh could. Between Darlington on Mother's Day weekend and the All-Star Challenge at Lowe's Speedway in Charlotte the following week, she and Joe would find some downtime. They'd volunteered at both tracks for the past three years and had made a few good friends in the process.

As they drove through the gate, Camela offered up the same kind of words she said each night as she began her hospital shift. *Lord, use me and teach me this week. Let my love for You shine; let me be a light in darkness. And Lord, if it's Your will and Your time, please open doors for me to talk to Topaz.*

She dug in her purse until she found a tube of lip gloss and a compact of brown eye shadow. Flipping open the visor mirror, she shined her lips and rubbed a dab of eye shadow in the crease above each eye. She'd read somewhere that brown eye shadow made blue eyes bluer. Using her fingers, she fluffed her shoulder-length blond layers until they no longer looked slept on. As she closed the visor, her gaze landed on a woman in hot pink Capri pants carrying a gold hobo purse the size of Texas.

"There's Topaz! Why don't you drop me off here and I'll meet up with you at the barbecue."

Joe parked on the side of the infield road and waved to the dark-haired woman with the ponytail sprouting from the top of her head like whale spume. Topaz Rodriguez ran up to his open window. "Hey, it's G.I. Joe!" She squeezed his arm, her gum snapping between words. "Ready to party?"

Joe's smile was polite. "Hey, yourself. Keep my girl out of trouble, okay?"

"I promise I won't let her do anything I wouldn't do!"

"That's not exactly what I was asking for."

"Don't worry your pretty head about us nurses. Give her a smootchie-woochie and go play with the firemen."

Camela puckered and Joe leaned in for her kiss. As she got out of the car and Joe drove away, Topaz grabbed Camela's left hand. "Well? Where's the ice? You said any day now."

It had been only two weeks since she'd seen Topaz for pre-race medical team training, but in that time, Topaz's hair had changed from red to brown and grown considerably. Camela touched the pretentious ponytail. "Where'd this come from?"

"Extensions. Don't change the subject. Where's the bling ring?"

"I'm still working on it. Friday night; I've got a plan."

"Well, if it doesn't work, you've always got Plan B."

"Plan B?"

"Jackman Garrett." Topaz pointed toward the group of men in lawn chairs sitting in front of a massive Four Winds motor coach. "He's been bugging me all morning about when you're gonna get here—and whether or not you and Joe are official."

Clinging to Topaz, Camela spun her around, using her as a shield. As she peered over her friend's shoulder, she saw him.

Thankfully, his back was to her as he gestured wildly with his right hand. His left held a book. Tommy Garrett was leading a Bible study. Camela's hands dropped to her sides, but a smile escaped through her frustrated sigh. "What am I going to do with that boy?"

"Has he been bugging you?"

"Not technically. We e-mail a couple times a week. We're doing the same online Bible study, and we discuss our answers and catch up on day-to-day stuff." Though she wouldn't admit it out loud, she sometimes wondered if Tommy Garrett knew her better than Joe did. "I can read between his lines. I know he'd like more."

"Maybe you just need to give him a chance."

Camela stared into Topaz's almost-black eyes. "Don't. Please. Where's that coming from, anyway?"

Topaz shrugged. "I don't know...those sweet brown puppy-dog eyes. . . . And he's so nuts about you. I'd die to have a guy that crazy about me."

"I have a guy!"

"But. . . Yeah, you're right. Maybe we can hook Tommy up with somebody this week."

"Yeah...maybe."

The group of men was breaking up. Camela recognized three of them. Two of them smiled and she smiled back. Tommy Garrett didn't smile.

Tommy Garrett beamed. And sighed. And clutched his chest...and fell off his chair.

The four men around him guffawed and clapped. One of them waved with both arms like a drowning maniac. "Nurse!

Nurse! We need a nurse! Code red or blue or something! Quick, he needs CPR. . .and TLC!"

Tommy raised his head. "I need mouth-to-mouth!" His head fell back again.

Camela tried not to laugh. Letting Tommy see her laugh this early on would be like giving cheese to a maze rat when he'd reached a dead end. He wouldn't quit for the rest of the week, even though his head repeatedly slammed the wall. She managed to quell the spasm of laughter. After a moment, Tommy stood up, brushed off his jeans, and walked over to her, hand extended, as decorously as if he hadn't just been lying on the ground, acting like an eight-year-old.

"Hi, Cammie. Good to see you."

"Hi, Tommy." His untamed rust-red hair was longer and curlier than a year ago, and he'd added some bulk to his not-too-tall but already muscular form. Cammie smiled and took his hand. His left arm went around her shoulders, drawing her into a brief hug. When his arm dropped, she felt her face warm. "How's life in the pit?"

"Fast and furious. Did I tell you we won the last pit-stop competition in 12.8?"

"Twice. Now you've told me three times. Nobody jacks a car like you, Tommy."

Ryan Weber and Howie Schmidt, both tire changers, walked toward her, their laughter barely under control. Unlike Tommy, who was also a full-time mechanic on the team, the two usually flew in just for the race.

Cammie shook the hands they extended. "What are you guys doing here two days early?"

"Howie and I bring our wives and kids for the race fest and hauler parade. It's kind of a tradition." Ryan grinned at Tommy. "But Garrett here came early for the fireworks." He winked at Cammie. "I hear they're gonna be partic'lar'y fine this year."

It was only then, staring into Tommy's "puppy-dog eyes," that Cammie realized he was still holding her hand. She pulled away. Still snickering, Ryan and Howie left. Cammie ignored the blush warming her cheeks. "Number 24 ready to win?"

"Absolutely. We're gonna ace this race!"

"Always the poet. Any new songs?"

A smile spread across his freckled face. "Yup. And they're all about you."

Cammie looked away. He'd agreed to respect her relationship with Joe in his e-mails, but she'd forgotten to draw a line about meeting face-to-face.

Nodding toward the pit crew guys hovering around Topaz, Cammie shook her head. "I need to rescue her. We've got a med team meeting in five minutes." She turned back to him and felt a sudden, unexpected sadness. She hid it with a smile. "See you around."

"Yes, you will." He said the words with an air of mystery.

It wasn't until she'd grabbed Topaz by the arm and put twenty yards between her and Tommy that Cammie allowed a laugh. "What am I going to do about him?"

"Just don't lead him on." Topaz's tone was uncharacteristically serious.

"Lead him on? Are you nuts? I've done everything but rent a billboard!" She stopped walking. "I have no intention of ever

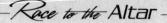

hurting his feelings, okay? I agree, he's a sweetheart and nobody could ask for a more loyal friend. But he's not for me. End of subject, so let's change it. How's the new job?" She kept to neutral topics all the way to the meeting.

They left the infield care center after one. The meeting had gone longer than scheduled. Cammie lifted her nose and sniffed. "I smell Southern-style calories." The air was pungent with hickory smoke and the sweet smell of barbecue sauce as they headed for the lunch line of volunteers and crewmembers. Joe, standing near the black roasting barrels with two empty plates in his hand, glanced at his watch. Camela lifted his arm, draping it across her shoulders. He kissed the top of her head. "Long meeting, huh?"

"They've changed some procedures and there's a whole passel of new volunteers. Sorry you had to wait."

Topaz got in line in front of Camela, and they filled their plates with spare ribs, home fries, corn-on-the-cob, and more. Joe skipped the fries and took a double portion of coleslaw. "Wish they'd have some healthier options at these things." He said it loud enough for the red-aproned woman behind the table to hear.

As they walked toward an empty table, they heard music playing softly. Guitar music. And a familiar voice. Tommy Garrett was sitting on a picnic bench singing "Live Like You Were Dying" in a clear, rich voice, sounding for all the world like Tim McGraw. As the three of them got closer, the music stopped midsong. Tommy nodded to Topaz, then Joe, and fixed his eyes

on Cammie. His hands changed position on the guitar, and he
began to play. She knew the tune. . .the words were his own.

"Lady in scrubs is a—void—ing me
Week to week
Ev—ry—body's here
Not just you and me
Or where I wanna be
I just wanna know the secrets that you hide
I'll never forget your eyes in this sunlight. . . ."

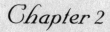

Chapter 2

"Hang it up, Garrett." Ryan Weber lifted his cap and rubbed a hand across his blond buzz, then picked up a lug nut. "The competiton's too stiff."

Tommy lifted a box and set it on the table. "I may not have Calendar Boy's looks, but I've so got him beat in everything else. I've got charm. . .wit. . .sensitivity. . .and Joe Jorgensen has the personality of toast."

Ryan sputtered and dropped the lug nut. "And there ain't a drop of jelly on that boy!" He scrambled after the nut, and his voice rose from under the table. "But you still can't go flirtin' with a girl who's spoken for. Crumbs, flirtin' don't describe it. You acted like a plumb fool yesterday."

Tommy ignored the last part. "Who says she's 'spoken for'? Just because she's been with the same guy for three years doesn't mean it's a done deal."

They stopped talking when a new kid, a gofer everyone was calling *Skinny*, walked up. Though a few inches taller, the boy could have been Tommy at eighteen, toothpick arms and legs, with ears that stuck out too far. Skinny's hair was mouse brown but as unruly as Tommy's had always been. Every freckle on the boy's lanky body proclaimed his lack of confidence. Tommy knew how that felt. He'd been in junior high when he'd overheard one of his uncles say, "With a face like Howdie Doodie, he'd better be funny."

Skinny stuck his hands in his pockets. "I'm lookin' fer the long weight."

"Well, it's not here." Tommy didn't dare look the boy in the eye.

Ryan pointed toward the door. "Try asking the guys unloading the hauler."

Skinny sighed and walked away, and Tommy gave in to laughter. "That one never dies."

"I musta been sent on fifteen goose chases on my first day." Ryan crossed his arms over his barrel chest. "Ended up in the GM's office before I figgered out the long wait."

"Dummy. I had it figured out by noon."

"Yer the smart one, I guess. About the nurse—did ya look at her ring finger?"

"I tried." Tommy cracked the old blade off the end of an Exacto knife. "Haven't gotten close enough to see."

"Can't you just ask Topaz?"

"She wasn't sure. Hey, if they're officially engaged, I'll back off. If not, it's open season. I may not have a chance of beating the competition, but I sure intend to have a blast trying."

"So how you gonna get close enough to see if she's got a rock?"

"That's where you come in. . . ."

Stepping onto the treadmill next to the one Topaz was sweating on, Cammie croaked, "Morning." It was the first word she'd spoken in twelve hours.

"Hi! I didn't wake you, did I? I tried to slip out quietly."

Cammie squinted at the chipper girl in coral spandex. As if the fluorescent lights weren't bad enough. "I heard the shower, but I fell asleep again." She set the controls for a turtle pace and turned again to stare at Topaz. "Why did I hear the shower?"

"The lady at the front desk said they had reservations from eighteen different states and a few from Europe."

As she tried to make sense of Topaz's answer, Cammie stared in the mirrored wall at her own gym attire—the same Winnie the Pooh tank top and baggy blue shorts she'd slept in. "Well then, that explains showering before you exercise."

"You never know who you might meet in a hotel this size."

"Ah. . ."

"Are you and Joe going to Bible study this morning?"

"I was so tired after supper, we didn't talk about it. I suppose we will." *But I'll sit in back, far away from the guy with the puppy-dog eyes.* "Why?"

"I thought. . .I might. . .go with you." Topaz meted out the words as if she were afraid of them. When she got them out, she smiled.

Cammie missed a step and had to grab the rails. "Okay, I know I'm supposed to act all nonchalant here, but *what* did you just say?"

"You heard me." Topaz slowed her pace to keep time with

Cammie. "I know you think I just delete all the God stuff you send me, but I don't. And I've been reading your blog, too."

"Seriously?"

"Seriously."

Thank you, Lord. Don't let me push her too hard. "Can you be ready by ten thirty? All buffed and gelled and exfoliated in less than two hours?"

An icy spray from Topaz's water bottle hit Cammie between the eyes. Topaz smiled smugly. "I just remembered something."

"What?"

"You promised I could do your hair and makeup."

Cammie looked at the Cleopatra eyes, thick black stripes lining top and bottom lashes. . .and this was Topaz's understated gym look. "I did, didn't I?" She thought of a statement she'd heard in a lifestyle-evangelism class: *"One of the best ways to build a relationship with a nonbeliever and earn the right to be heard is to allow the person to do something for you." Even if it means public humiliation?*

She'd met Topaz at the orientation meeting the first time she'd volunteered at Darlington. In so many ways they were complete opposites, and yet something had clicked and an unlikely friendship was born.

Topaz was pointing a fushia-painted nail at her, lowering and raising the finger to include all of Cammie, head to toe. "You need to step it up a notch for G.I. Joe."

"He likes the natural look."

"*You* like the natural look. Guys are different."

Turning back to the mirror, Cammie studied her reflection.

She was a hair over five-foot-three and weighed just under 140. She could afford to lose a few pounds, but, as her father so graciously put it, she was solid, a comment that always made her picture a tub of margarine. She'd been blessed with a decent bone structure and clear skin and couldn't see the point in trying to look air-brushed. But maybe she did need to "step it up" for Joe. "Maybe for tomorrow night."

"You really gonna go through with this plan? Joe's not going to the Busch race?"

"No, he only follows the cup series." She increased her speed. "He's been working extra shifts at the station lately, and he's not the kind of man who can just flip a switch from work mode to romance."

"So a romantic dinner's gonna set the stage and *bingo!* he pops the question?"

Cammie swiped at a strand of hair. "Joe's a planner. I know he's rehearsed a proposal. I just need to give him the opportunity." She looked down at her close-clipped nails. "Okay. I need a makeover. First, we need to shop. I brought a dress, but I'm not sure it's pizzazzy enough. I want something jaw-dropping. Red, maybe."

"Perfect. The color of love. This is gonna be fun."

Cammie pulled out her barrette and swung her hair until it covered the side of her face. "Make me luscious, baby."

They ran into Joe as they were walking out of the fitness room. He bent to kiss her. "You worked up a sweat."

He'd said it like a compliment. He didn't need to know

she was damp from Topaz's water bottle. "Thank you." Cammie lowered her voice so that Topaz, standing a few feet away talking to the guy Joe was rooming with, wouldn't hear. "Guess what? Topaz is going to Bible study with us this morning!"

"Oh, man, I forgot. I promised Dean I'd lift with him after we swim laps. You two have fun, and I'll see you at lunch." He opened the glass door.

As he walked into the fitness room, Cammie stared at his broad shoulders beneath a tight white T-shirt. For some strange reason, she was reminded of missing the school bus by only seconds, watching the back of the bus drive away.

Topaz touched her arm. "Can I say something?"

"I guess."

"I'm not feeling it."

"What?"

"The love. The sparks. Where are the fireworks?"

Cammie glared at her. "Fireworks cause fires. All I ever wanted was a grounded guy who would always be there for me. Joe's always there."

Topaz sighed and gestured toward Joe's back as he leaned his elbows on the front desk. "Whatever floats your boat, but I'm lookin' for a whole lot more than just 'there.'"

<hr>

"So what's on the menu for the fancy-shmancy dinner?" Topaz was toting a massive plastic purse as they walked across the Speedway grounds. "By the way, I borrowed a DVD so I'll have something to do when I'm locked in my room while you're getting proposed to. You still sure about me being there?

It's weird, you know."

"I know. But you're the security system."

"If you've been with this guy for three years and you haven't—"

"We haven't because we always have security systems. We're human, you know. Just because you don't see the fireworks doesn't mean they aren't there." Topaz's comment this morning had irritated her. She and Joe had chemistry. But they also had self-control. Joe could write a book on discipline.

She pointed toward a concession stand. "Coffee." She was still feeling the effects of four twelve-hour shifts. "I'm going gourmet for the dinner, but healthy. Joe's not a meat and pota-toes guy. I found a recipe for asparagus soup. . . ." Tommy and Ryan were walking toward the same concession stand. "It's a. . . cold soup. And spinach salad with strawberries and—"Tommy stopped, looked directly at her. . .and plowed into Ryan.

Ryan's tool box went flying and opened as it hit the ground. Screwdrivers and wrenches bounced and scattered on the grass. Cammie ran to Ryan. "Are you okay?"

He rubbed his right arm. "I'll live." He glared at Tommy, already on his knees picking up tools. "Ya' crazy yahootie, you could say yer sorry."

Tommy barely looked up. "I'm sorry. Go get the coffee, and I'll pick this up."

Topaz grabbed Ryan's shirt. "Wait. I'll come with you. These guys can handle the mess. Hazelnut cappuccino, Cam?"

Cammie nodded, staring down at the top of Tommy's head, and did the only logical thing. She got down on her knees. She had half a dozen wrenches in her hand when she picked up a wrench with a silver ribbon tied in a bow around it. "What's this?"

Tommy looked over at her and lifted his sunglasses to the top of his head. "That is a very special wrench. It's a sizer wrench."

Cammie tried to turn away from the soft brown eyes that seemed to be scanning her very soul line by line. She couldn't move.

"I bet you'd like to know what it's for."

The next thing Cammie knew, Tommy was on his knees directly in front of her, taking the wrench and reaching for her left hand. "This," he whispered, slipping the end of the wrench onto her third finger, "is what it's for." He raised her hand to his lips and kissed her fingertip. "Perfect fit."

"Remember that scene in *The Last Crusade* where Indiana Jones comes to this humongous chasm?" Tommy faced the Bible study group, holding his Bible in one hand as he swept the other in an arc toward his feet. "It was like a hundred times the Grand Canyon, and he can't go back and he can't go on. But then he looks at the guidebook and all of a sudden he has a lightbulb moment. 'It's a leap of faith,' he says.

"With his father whispering, 'You must believe, boy, you must believe,' Indiana looks straight ahead and slowly raises one foot into the empty air in front of him. Thud! His foot lands on solid ground. He looks down to see that he's really standing on a narrow rock bridge, camouflaged because it matches the exact outline of the chasm."

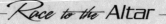

Resting one foot on a folding chair, Tommy put the Bible on his knee. "That's it. That's faith. In the book of Hebrews it says, 'Faith is being sure of what we hope for and certain of what we do not see.'

"When Peter stepped onto the water. . ."

Out of the corner of her eye, Cammie studied Topaz. She was leaning forward in her chair, arms wrapped around her huge pink purse; her eyes were glued to Tommy. Cammie's head was starting to hurt. It was only because of Topaz that she was here in this study. Every fiber in her being wanted to run as far away from Tommy Garrett as she possibly could.

Now that most of the volunteers had arrived, there were about fifteen chairs filled, forming two horseshoes in front of Tommy. Forty-five minutes earlier, in spite of her planted heels and death grip on Topaz's purse, Cammie had somehow been dragged to the middle of the inner half circle. Every time Tommy looked her way, Cammie looked down at her Bible. Twice she'd felt her face get hot, because even with her eyes on the page in front of her, she could tell when his gaze lingered. *Lord, I have to talk to him. This has to stop.*

"To borrow from a song I know you're all familiar with, we need to start each day with"—he reached down for his guitar—"'Jesus, take the whe–eel. . .'" His imitation of Carrie Underwood was uncannily accurate. The room erupted in applause and Tommy bowed. "Okay, seriously, it's not just about crying out to Jesus when you're in an out-of-control spin at 180 miles per hour, it's about giving Him the keys to your pace car, to every minute of your life. It's trusting Him every time your kids walk out the door, it's trusting that He'll help you stretch your paycheck, that He'll change you so your marriage can be saved. It's about taking a leap of faith into the job or the ministry or relationship He's called you to, even if it doesn't make sense to you right now."

Cammie looked toward the open garage door, willing Tommy to finish, knowing she couldn't leave without making a scene. *Lord, show me when to talk to him.* Her prayer melded into Tommy's. "...and You are beyond amazing, Lord. Touch hearts here this week. Show us Your glory and let us leave this place changed. Amen."

Topaz raised her head slowly. "Wow. Cammie, he's making it all clear. Everything you've been telling me...I'm getting it." She appeared on the verge of tears, but her smile was huge.

Cammie was already standing, ready to bolt. It took a moment for the impact of Topaz's words to hit. All she could do was hug her.

"Cammie, listen to me." Topaz grabbed her arm. "You're an idiot."

"Why, thank you. I've had my suspicions."

"For real. You're a complete idiot. He's smart, he's deep, he's funny—"

Cammie put her hand in front of Topaz's mouth. "Weren't you listening this morning? Can't you get it? Tommy's sweet and wonderful and all of that, but he's not ever going to be the one thing I need. He's not ever going to be...*there.*"

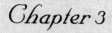

Chapter 3

Thirty-six hours into her vacation, the giddiness finally hit. Cammie twirled in front of Topaz and several other shoppers in the department store. She wore a glitter-covered red halter dress. " 'Lady in red is dancing with me. . . .'" Suddenly she thought of Tommy's revision of the song—*"Lady in scrubs"*—and changed her tune. " 'I feel pretty, oh so pretty. . . .'" She held up both hands, looking at her nails. "Flames! Can you do flames?"

Topaz laughed. "You bet. First we do tips, then we do flames."

"I need earrings. Diamonds maybe?"

"Very subliminal."

Cammie put her hands on her hips. "This is so not me."

"If this doesn't knock his socks off, you gotta move on."

"This'll work. I'm gonna be flypaper, and that boy's gonna be stuck tight!"

After a curtsy to the people who were pretending not to stare at her, she went back to the dressing room. She was hanging the dress on its padded hanger when her phone rang.

"Hi, Mom."

"Hi, baby girl. Everything going good down there?"

"Everything's wonderful."

"You and Joe getting to spend some quality time together?"

Cammie sidestepped the question. "I'm taking your advice about giving him bigger hints. I'm making him dinner in our suite tomorrow night. Candles, music, the whole deal."

Her mother laughed. "History repeats itself. The night I proposed to your father—"

"Whoa! I'm not going to propose, Mom! I'm just going to make it easy for him."

"Well, honey, do what you gotta do. Just don't let Gorgeous Joe slip between the cracks too much longer."

"This'll work. How's Daddy?"

"Antsy. He's over helping Norm take an engine apart. After thirty years on the road, the man can't sit still. Between you and me, I don't think he can keep up this retirement gig much longer; he's missin' his truck."

"How about you? Are you loving having him around?"

There was a significant pause on the other end. "I'm thinking we should do one of those marriage seminars. We're kind of having trouble finding things to talk about. Maybe we just need to bring our cell phones to dinner. . . . We're pretty good at communicating that way." Her mother laughed, but it wasn't convincing.

After saying good-bye, Cammie tried recapturing the free and easy vacation feeling, but her mother's words had tarnished her mood. While paying for the dress, she turned to Topaz.

"How's sushi sound? You're driving. I'll treat."

"Sounds great, but don't you have to get back to Joe? You've hardly seen him all day."

"It's an off day."

"An off day? Like he's in a bad mood you mean?"

"No." Cammie took a deep breath and smiled. "We see each other on the 'on' days and do our own thing on the 'off' days. It keeps things from getting smothering."

Topaz stared at her like she'd just sprouted a second head. "Don't tell me. . . . Joe came up with that one, right?"

"Well, we. . .he. . .yeah. Joe came up with that one."

She couldn't get the song out of her head. Even at the Sushi bar with Japanese music playing. "Lady in Red" was looping in her brain, only she wasn't hearing the original words. She was hearing Tommy's words. *I just wanna know the secrets that you hide; I'll never forget your eyes in this sunlight. . . ."*

Cammie dipped a chunk of salmon sushi into the wasabi dip and popped it into her mouth. The horseradish flavor brought tears to her eyes. Topaz was chattering about a guy she'd met back home in Fayetteville, but Cammie couldn't concentrate. There was something she had to do before tomorrow, something she had to set right so that she could enjoy the rest of her vacation. Topaz stopped talking to take a bite, and Cammie blurted, "I have to call Tommy."

Topaz stopped chewing. . .and grinned. Around a mouthful of rice and seaweed she said, "Finally. That dress won't be wasted after all."

"No! No, no, *no*! I have to tell him to back off. I have to spell it out. For his sake."

<hr>

Keep it light, keep it light. Lord, give me the right words. Back and forth, she talked to God, then herself. Tommy had agreed to meet her in the stands just above Turn 3. Private but public; that was good. Her hands felt clammy; her pulse skipped every dozen beats. *I just want to make him see. We can still be friends. . . .* He was walking toward her, taking his hat off, and running his hand through his hair as he climbed the steps. He smiled and waved. Far above his head, the sign over the grandstand read DARLINGTON—TOO TOUGH TO TAME.

He stopped two feet in front of where she was sitting, staring into her, reading more than she wanted him to see. "This isn't going to be good, is it?" He sat down, keeping his eyes on her.

"Tommy. . .I need you—"

He put his finger on her lips. "That's good. Can't we just leave it there?"

Cammie groaned. "Please. I need. . . Can you please be serious for a minute?"

"I'm only laughing on the outside, Cam." The smile left his lips.

"You're one of the most incredible, talented, attentive, God-focused guys I've ever met. There are a million girls who would die to go out with you." A thought came to her. "Do you pick a different girl at every track?"

He laughed. "How can I be serious if you ask me something like that? The answer is no. I'm not saying I don't go out now

197

and then, but you're the only girl I fall off my chair for."

She was losing sight of the reason she'd asked to meet with him. "Why? Why pick someone who's practically engaged when there are so many available women in the world? Why me?"

"Because of the first time we met. You came in late to study, wearing Scooby-Doo scrubs and purple shoes, and you jumped right in, asking questions, even challenging me. You were passionate and inquisitive, and you didn't give a rip what I thought of you, and I told God right then and there that I could spend the rest of my life with that girl."

She concentrated on simply breathing and avoiding his eyes. "Even if Joe weren't in the picture. . . You travel thirty-eight weeks out of the year. My dad missed my birthdays and softball games and prom. I won't let that happen to our—my kids or my marriage."

"We haven't had a single date, and you're already talking about our kids." Tommy smiled, but it was a sad smile. "People do make it work, Cam." He sighed. "I'd like to spend some time with you; that's all. I'm not proposing here, okay?"

Cammie blushed. He was right. She was turning this into an all-or-nothing thing instead of taking one step at a time. She gave him a sheepish smile, and he continued.

"I wouldn't even consider marrying somebody if I couldn't commit to enough time to make it good; I want to be in my kids' lives. I won't be full time on a crew forever. Someday I'll open my own shop and just show up for the races. And even that's limited. I'm twenty-seven. . . . I'm getting old." His voice shook like an old man's. "My days are numbered." Without warning he stood, holding his hand out to her. "Come with me.

I want you to meet someone."

With no idea where he was heading, she took his hand, calloused and warm, and followed him down the steps. He took her first to the garage, where whispers about "Garrett's woman" echoed off the concrete. Tommy hopped over the two-foot wall in one smooth motion. Holding out both arms to her, he swayed his hips to the left, then the right and tossed his head in a perfect Elvis imitation. "I'm over the wall for you, baby."

Cammie laughed. "You never miss an opportunity, do you?"

"Never."

She stepped up and stood on top of the wall. "So this is what it feels like."

"Next to driving, it's the biggest adrenaline rush in the whole place."

She held her arms out like a conductor. "I love the feel of history. . . . Johnny Mantz, Fireball Roberts, Cale Yarborough, the Pettys—all earned their Darlington Stripes by grazing those walls." She pointed at Tommy's feet. "Any one of them could have stood right where you are now."

"This is the granddaddy of all tracks. So your father brought you here?"

Cammie nodded. "The closest we ever came to a vacation. I saw Bill Elliott win in 1988 and watched Ricky Rudd start in thirteenth and win in '91. That's the one that hooked me for life; I've always rooted for the underdog."

Tommy raised both eyebrows. "Oh, really?"

"Don't read a book into one little comment." She copied the lift of his brows.

He put his hands in the back pockets of his jeans. "You look nice there. Stay." He pulled out his phone and took her picture, then once more held out his arms.

With a shake of her head, she hopped to the ground, but not into his arms. He took her hand again, but she pulled away. As they walked across the track, Tommy bent to pick up a piece of rubber the size of a vitamin capsule. He handed it to her. "Something to remember me by."

"My very own Darlington marble. I'll keep it forever."

"I could start you a collection. Bring you one from every track."

"My friends would be so jealous."

"Better yet, you could collect them in person."

She narrowed her eyes, but couldn't help but smile. He led her to the infield RV park. Row after row of class-A motor homes towered over them. A little girl with blond ringlets ran up to him, and he lifted her to his shoulders. "This is Tib, Ryan's daughter. Tib, shake hands with Cammie."

The girl reached down to Cammie. "I'm almost five. Are you Tommy's girlfriend?"

Cammie laughed. "No. Just a friend."

Tommy held both of Tib's Band-Aid-clad legs against his chest and lifted his index finger to his lips. "It's a secret, Tib, but Cammie's going to marry me. Just don't tell her."

Cammie rolled her eyes.

With a giggle, Tib clapped. "You said I could be your flower girl when you get married. Can I still?" She bent down to look at Tommy's face, then turned and stared at Cammie. "Can I?"

"When Tommy gets married, you'll make a very pretty flower girl."

Grabill Missionary Church Library
P.O. Box 279
13637 State Street
Grabill, IN 46741

Tib patted Tommy on the head. "Let me down. I gotta go tell Mama that you're gonna get married. It's not a secret from her, is it?"

"Nah. You go tell your mom. And tell her I'm bringing Cammie over to meet her."

～

Ryan's wife, Darcy, was about Cammie's age, pregnant with her second child. After only a few minutes of sitting in Adirondack chairs with a pitcher of lemonade on the low table between them, Cammie felt like she'd known her for years. When Tommy ran off chasing Tib, Cammie leaned toward Darcy. "How often do you travel with Ryan?

Darcy's smile was wistful. "I went with him occasionally before Tib was born, but now this is a once-a-year treat. My dad works here at the track, so we get infield parking privileges." She gestured toward the RV behind them. "This is a rental."

"Is it hard having him gone every weekend?"

"Of course. But I knew what I was getting into when I married that man. I'd rather share him with the race circuit than not have him at all." Darcy rested her forearms on her protruding belly. "Is there any truth to what my little blabbermouth just told me about you and Tommy?"

Cammie shook her head. "Tommy and I are just friends."

"Well, just in case that changes, I'm going to give you my cell number before you go."

With a laugh, Cammie shook her head again.

But before she left, she took the number.

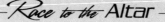

They were walking back across the track when Tommy stopped and took her hands. "Look, we know a lot about each other after all this time, but we haven't spent time together. Maybe we'd find out after one date that we weren't meant to be anything but friends. All I'm asking is for a chance."

"When would we have the second date? A year from now?" *This is so wrong. What am I doing?*

"I get days off, Cam, and I get back home to Charlotte at least once a month. It's not like I'm a homeless drifter. Cammie, I'm not going to grovel. There's something about you that I can't get out of my head, but if you're not the least bit interested, just tell me."

Her eyes burned, but she refused to cry. "I'm. . .committed to Joe."

"Is Joe enough for you?"

A sharp breath jarred her. Thankfully, Tommy didn't wait for a response. She couldn't have given one.

"If you've promised yourself to him, just say the word. The second you're engaged, I'll be out of your life. But you haven't asked me to leave you alone, Cam. There must be a reason for that."

That's what I'm trying to do right now. You're not giving me the chance.

"I have to ask something; you don't have to tell me the answer." His pressure on her hands increased. "Are you better when you're with Joe? Are you guys closer to God because of each other?"

The questions froze her. She hadn't intended to admit that Tommy was getting to her, that his words had found the empty place she tried so hard to ignore. Now he was using the knowledge like a weapon.

"You say all the right things, but you can't follow through. If you had a different job I'd probably be putty in your hands. Maybe I'm selfish; I'm not taking second place to a job." He was staring at her, his eyes saying everything she wanted to hear but couldn't listen to. She blinked, and a tear slid down her right cheek.

Tommy brushed it away with his thumb. "What do you need from me, Cam?"

She took a deep breath and looked into his eyes. "I need you. . .to guard my heart."

Tommy was sitting cross-legged, with his back against the wall, when a tall, familiar form approached. He stood, expecting a blow to the face in seconds. But he only got hit with words.

"What's your game, Garrett?" Joe Jorgensen's eyes were blazing. "Are you after Camela? Maybe I'm just stupid for trusting; it took a couple of buddies to open my eyes. How long have you been sneaking off with her like this?"

Tommy moved only his eyes, from right to left, across the infield. "I didn't exactly drag her into a dark corner."

Joe's jaw muscles bulged. "What are your intentions with her?"

"I intend to pray for her, Joe. I intend to hope that you wake

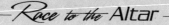
up and realize what you've got in her and treasure her and spoil her and listen to her and give her all the attention she deserves. And if you don't, I intend to step in and do it myself."

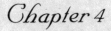

Chapter 4

There was a buzz in the hotel lobby the next morning, a palpable energy. Qualifying for the Carolina Dodge 500 was just hours away. Camela had her own prerace jitters, but they had little to do with tomorrow's race.

Across the table from her, Joe was covering every millimeter of his whole grain English muffin with almond butter, then repeating the procedure with raw honey. He'd brought his own food. Camela hugged her coffee. Her stomach was still on third shift time and nothing at the continental breakfast bar had looked good to her, so she'd wrapped two jelly-filled doughnuts in a napkin. In about two hours they would hit the spot. She had, however, added creamer and sugar to her cup, which defined it as a meal rather than a beverage.

Joe had been strangely quiet all morning, so it surprised her when he said, "You look nice this morning."

"Thanks." Topaz had experimented with corkscrew curls the night before and they were still in, though much looser than he would see them tonight.

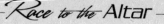

"What're you all dolled up for?" His eyes held a look of harshness.

"This is a preview of things to come."

"So you're still planning on dinner tonight?"

"Why wouldn't I be?"

Joe took a bite of his muffin and chewed slowly, his gaze riveted to her face. "I just thought you might have changed your mind, considering."

"Considering what?"

She didn't get an answer. Camela pushed her coffee cup aside and leaned forward. "What are you talking about?"

"Nothing. We'll talk tonight."

Joe came with her to Bible study. Sitting between him and Topaz was like standing next to a campfire in the middle of winter. Excitement radiated from Topaz as she hung on every word, while every muscle in Joe's body seemed taut. Tommy was still talking about faith, using the story of Ruth to illustrate.

"Read verse 16 with me." Tommy's eyes swept the room, never landing on her, but somehow, in the middle of a group that had grown to over twenty, she felt like they were the only two in the room. "But Ruth replied, 'Don't urge me to leave you or to turn back from you. Where you go I will go, and where you stay I will stay. Your people will be my people and your God my God.'"

Tommy allowed a moment of silence. "Imagine the kind of faith that took. How many of us have what it takes to. . ."

Cammie recited her dinner menu in her head to drown his words.

The jitters stayed with her for the rest of the day. Had an emergency arisen during qualifying laps, she questioned whether she would have had the presence of mind to respond like she should. Thankfully, a minor burn and a steel sliver were the only things that required her attention. Joe invited two of his firefighter buddies to join them for lunch, and Camela had the distinct impression they were there to protect him. His strange attitude muddled her mind even more. Thankfully, no one asked her to voice an intelligent thought during her afternoon med-team meeting.

After the meeting she took a shuttle back to the hotel, and by four o'clock the little galley kitchen of the hotel suite looked like the set for an episode of *Top Chef*. As she cut strawberries and sautéed onions on the two-burner stove, she stared at the clock. Topaz had promised to be there by five and Joe, if he showed up at all, would arrive promptly at six thirty.

As her hands worked, her mind whirled. Had Joe seen her talking to Tommy? He'd never had a problem with it before. Well, maybe a little jealousy would be good. It might be just the thing to push him over the edge. Three hours from now she could be engaged. *Lord, all I want is Your will for my life and Joe's it, isn't he?*

"Of course he is." She said the words aloud to the bowl of spinach she was washing. Joe was an answer to prayer. He was everything she'd ever wanted. Their differences complemented each other perfectly. They were good for each other. They could work through this little glitch.

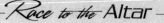

By the time Topaz got back, Camela's jitters had changed to anticipation. Dinner was ready; all she had to do was broil the salmon at the last minute. She'd taken a relaxing bath followed by a sugar scrub and lemon body lotion. Her dress was laid out on the bed, and the diamond earrings were sparkling in her ears.

She stayed in a good mood until Topaz was doing her nails. She'd chickened out of the flames and opted for a vibrant red with tiny diamond glue-ons on each pinky. Topaz was adding a finishing coat. "Joe was sure in a snit today. What's with him?"

"I think he's figured out that Tommy's—"

"A better man than he is?"

Camela jerked her hand away, her mouth and eyes wide open.

"That was a joke! Relax. He's figured out that Tommy worships the ground you walk on. It's about time. So did you have a fight over it?"

A long sigh dragged out of Cammie. "Not yet."

"Eww. So you're getting all prettied up to have a knock-down-drag-out?"

"Maybe."

"Now I know why you want me in the next room." Topaz plugged in two curling irons and pulled an array of hair products out of a leopard-skin bag. "So what are you going to do about Tommy?" Her voice was strangely subdued.

"I told him I won't have a long-distance relationship. And besides, I'm committed to Joe."

Topaz picked up a brush and started running it through Cammie's just-washed hair. "So…then…it wouldn't bother you if I showed some interest in Tommy?"

There was a knock at the door at 6:29. Camela jumped. She'd practiced her defense, but her brain went fuzzy. . . . Joe stood in the hallway, dressed in a black suit, white shirt, and a sapphire blue tie the exact color of his eyes. In his outstretched hand was a bouquet of red sweetheart roses. In the other hand was an envelope.

Camela backed away from the door. She took the roses. "Thank you."

Leaning over the flowers, he kissed her. "New dress?"

She turned around to give him the full affect. With a boldness she didn't quite feel, she asked, "Like what you see?"

"Guess I picked the right color of roses." He handed her the envelope.

Camela set the tissue-wrapped flowers gently on the counter and untucked the flap of the envelope. The front of the card said simply, "I'm sorry." There were two handwritten lines on the inside.

> *I'm sorry for my attitude. I know you wouldn't do anything to change what we have together.*
>
> *Always, Joe*

His arms went around her. "I just overreacted. I shouldn't be surprised that Garrett's got a thing for you."

Camela felt like she'd just stepped off a merry-go-round. She'd been prepared for a fight, not flowers.

He pushed her gently away and held her at arm's length.

"Any guy would be proud to have you. But I've got you." He looked over her. "Something smells delicious."

"I hope you like it." She walked ahead of him to the small table she'd set with her mother's best china and lit the candles. "Sit down, kind sir. I'll only be a moment."

She ladled the chilled asparagus soup into glass bowls and carried them to the table. Joe prayed and then picked up his spoon. Tapping it against the outside of the bowl, he said, "You had all this in your bags?"

"I've been planning this for a while. I thought we needed some time just to focus on each other." She waited for him to reply. When he just continued eating his soup, she said, "Every time we're at Darlington I think of what's changed since we were here last. A year ago you were still in your apartment; now you own a house. I was working in the clinic; now I'm an ER supervisor. What do you think our lives will look like next year at this time?"

Joe looked over her shoulder. "Well, I hope to have my car paid off and have the walls studded in the basement. As far as career, I guess I'm okay with the way things are. How about you?"

I want to have a piece of paper with my new name on it. Camela picked up their still-full water glasses and took them to the sink. "I'd like to travel in the next year. Maybe Cancun, maybe a cruise." *Maybe on a honeymoon.* "Any thoughts about traveling?"

"I wish."

She set the glasses back down on the table with an unintended *clunk*. Joe didn't seem to notice. He was smiling at her. "There is something I'm hoping for this next year," he said.

"Yes?" Her voice came out in a whisper.

"I'm hoping you can get off the night shift."

Camela spread her left hand on the tablecloth, her diamond-studded pinky just touching his hand. "Hmm. You want me around more for any particular reason?"

"Yes." He pushed aside his salad. Reaching across the table, he took her hand in his. "I do."

Her face felt flushed, her pulse rapid. *I do, too! The answer is yes!*

Joe rubbed his thumb on the back of her hand. "The minute you get back on day shift, I'm buying you a full—" He stopped to clear his throat. "A full membership at the health club. We can work out together, maybe even three times a week. You'll have access to the spa for massages and facials and—Camela, are you all right?"

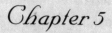

Chapter 5

The clock on the two-burner stove read 7:43 when Joe walked out the door. Cammie plugged the sink, ran hot water, added detergent, and watched the suds peak and climb the stainless steel sides. It reached the top, lapped over the edges into the other sink and onto the counter. Only when a thin warm stream hit her borrowed open-toed shoes did she rouse herself to turn off the water. Mechanically, she reached for a towel and sopped up the excess. Walking to the table, she picked up the two water goblets and brought them to the sink. She stood there, one in each hand, knowing that if she put them in the sink, the water would run over. But she couldn't pull out the drain because she had a glass in each hand.

In the midst of her almost-catatonic state, she was dimly aware of words. They were coming from her radio. Ricky Scaggs singing, "Crying My Heart Out Over You."

Crying. I should be crying. Why am I just standing here? Slowly, she set the glasses down. As she walked toward the radio, she caught her image in the mirror behind the table. The red dress.

Something Topaz had said drifted through the mist in her mind. *"That dress won't be wasted after all."*

Crying in this dress, ruining this makeup, would be a waste. She pushed the POWER button on the radio and walked to the closed bedroom door. Now that the music was off, she heard talking. But it wasn't a movie she was hearing. It was Topaz. Without knocking, she pushed the door open.

Topaz was sitting on the bed, painting her nails. On her knee was her open cell phone. She looked up at Camilla. "Need something?"

"I need to go out."

Topaz waved with her fingertips. "Okay. You guys have fun."

"I'm going out for coffee. And pie. Peach pie. With ice cream. Would you like to go with me?"

"Where's G.I. Joe? What happened? You're acting freaky."

"Dinner is over, and I'm going out for dessert."

Narrowing her eyes, Topaz shook her head. "You don't have a car."

"I'll walk. I need the exercise. In fact, I need a full membership to a health club with a personal trainer and access to massages and facials and waxings and electrolysis and maybe a nose job and..."

Topaz picked up the phone. "I gotta go." She jumped off the bed and grabbed her purse. "You're not going anywhere alone."

⌒

Tommy felt like a spy. Before Topaz had hung up on him, he'd heard Cammie talk about peach pie. That clue and the yellow pages had led him to the third restaurant he'd cased in twenty

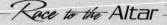

minutes. As he walked in, he saw a flash of red coming out of the ladies' room. He'd recognize that walk anywhere. Sheer layers of red flowed from her waist, and everything about her, from her hair to her fingertips, sparkled. She was more than beautiful.

Quickly, he stepped behind a tall man with a baby in his arms and peered around the man's shoulder. Her eyes stared straight ahead, with a strange, glassy expression. He followed her. The restaurant was dimly lit, and there were ficus trees and Roman statues every few feet to use as cover. A waitress came to their table, and Topaz chatted with her as she filled their cups. Cammie never looked up. Her half-eaten pie sat in front of her.

Lord, if I'm about to make a monumental mistake, please trip me or something. He pulled his cap off and started walking, expecting a shoelace to spring loose at any second. To keep his eyes on Cammie, he sat down next to Topaz.

"Hey, girls. Mmm. . .I love peach pie. I have to have sugar the night before the race. Looks like you do, too." *I have to have sugar? Garrett, that's the worst pickup line ever.* "So what're you two up to?"

A peculiar noise came out of Cammie. Half gasp, half cry of rage. In two seconds, she was gone. He ran after her.

He caught up with her in the parking lot, leaning against a car, clutching her stomach, and sobbing. He put his hands on her shoulders, and she stiffened. "Cam. Talk to me. What's wrong?"

"Everything. My life is wrong." She blew her nose in the cloth napkin still in her hand. "Three years with a guy who can't fit marriage into his schedule for two more years is wrong! Me wanting a guy who wants to spend every minute with me is probably wrong. You and Topaz—" Her head jerked up, and she looked as if she were shocked at what she'd just said. The sobs stopped, and the glassy look returned. "No. Maybe that's one good thing. You'd be really good for her, Tommy. And she doesn't have roots like I do. She could be just like Ruth. Whither thou goest, Topaz will go."

His mouth was open, but he wasn't sure what was supposed to come out. She was talking crazy. "There's no me-and-Topaz anything." A glimmer of understanding cut his confusion. The phone call. "*She* called *me*. She told me about the dinner, and I was saying that I hoped you weren't setting yourself up for disappointment."

"Disappointment?" Her laugh teetered on the edge of hysteria. "Me? Disappointed? Not at all. Joe's not the only one with plans. I have plans. I'm going to travel. I'm going on a long-term mission trip to Mongolia or sign on to a Mercy ship and take care of babies with leprosy or AIDS. Maybe I'll start an orphanage. In fact, I'm going to take all the money I've saved for a wedding, and I'm going to—"

He did the only thing he could think of to stop her. He kissed her.

His lips felt warm and shockingly soft. The kiss lasted only seconds but ended slowly, his lips moving to her cheeks, then her forehead. His hand was on the back of her head and she surrendered to the gentle pressure that pulled her to his chest. She didn't breathe as she felt his lips on her hair, his breath on her cheek.

Listening to his heartbeat, feeling the softness of his jacket beneath her hands, Cammie sighed. It was a breath she'd been holding for years.

She could have stayed right there for hours, but the moment came to an end with the tip-tapping of high-heeled steps that stopped suddenly. "Whoa!"

Topaz. Cammie pulled away reluctantly and walked over to meet her. "I didn't plan this," she whispered.

Topaz grinned. "It's about time!"

"I'm sorry."

"What for? Oh. . .hey, I gave it a serious thought for about five seconds. This boy's custom-made for you, girl." She raised her voice and pointed at Tommy. "You get my roomie home on time. Tomorrow's a big day."

Cammie stuck her elbow in Topaz's ribs. "Tommy has a curfew."

Tommy put his cap on and nodded. "Unfortunately, I do." His hand reached out to Cammie. "Can I talk to you for a sec?"

"Don't pay me no never mind." Topaz waved. "I'll wait in the car."

Cammie touched his sleeve. "I hate those weak women in movies who say one thing with their words and another with their lips."

"I kind of like them myself." His smile was tender. "You're beautiful, you know." He touched the strap at her neck. "You look amazing in red."

"Thank you."

He put his hands on her shoulders again. "I know we could both analyze this to death tonight. But here's the deal. . . . I'm not staking any claims or making any assumptions. So for now, no second-guessing. Let's just let this moment be what it is and get a good night's sleep. Okay?"

Knowing she would think of nothing else for the rest of the night, Cammie nodded. "Okay."

Chapter 6

The ride from the hotel to the track was silent, leaving Tommy, crammed in the backseat of a van between two other guys, alone with his thoughts and his nerves. He'd stuck to his self-imposed race-eve curfew and, true to his word, hadn't allowed himself to replay those last few minutes in the parking lot. He'd been asleep within two minutes of his head hitting the pillow. But today, when he needed to think of nothing but the race, the kiss looped through his brain like a wordless song.

The garage was humming like a beehive, and Tommy welcomed the familiar sounds. Yesterday's laughter and razzing had vanished, and words were few in the choreographed dance to the green flag. The constant white-noise backdrop of air guns whining, punctuated by occasional clanks of tools hitting concrete, the slam of a hood, and the race-day whispers of the crew chief and mechanics would drown the song in his head. For the next six hours, nothing existed beyond these walls. If it didn't say Goodyear or Craftsman, it wouldn't get his attention.

When Skinny stopped with a clipboard in hand, taking food orders, Tommy asked him how long he'd looked for the "long weight." His face turned flag-stripe red. "Somebody told me on the way back to the hotel."

Tommy clapped him on the back. "Hey, it's all part of the rite of passage. Welcome to the gang." He ordered a cheeseburger and soda and handed Skinny a ten. The boy looked surprised, making Tommy wonder if part of the poor kid's hazing was going to include blowing his first paycheck on snacks for the team.

He was leaning against the table, scarfing down the last of his burger, when the crew chief came through, pushing a wheel chair. The boy in it looked to be around ten. His skin was pale, almost translucent; his head was bald. His legs, sticking out of shorts, were too thin. But his smile was enormous. Draped on his lap was a leather NASCAR jacket. At the bottom of his T-shirt it said MAKE-A-WISH FOUNDATION.

Tommy got down on his knees as he was introduced to the boy. "Glad to meet you, Gordon. That's a great name."

"You can call me Gordo."

"I'll do that. So what's the best part about being here so far, Gordo?"

From the pocket of the jacket, he pulled out a laminated picture of himself. "Jeff's gonna tape this to his dashboard. So's I can pretend I'm riding with him."

Tommy nodded and patted the boy's knee. He didn't trust himself to speak. It was the same at every race, with every hurting but smiling kid he met.

Dimples deepened on the pale face. "Who do ya' think's gonna win today?"

"Well, I'm sure hoping it's that red and blue mean machine over there." Tommy pointed across the garage, and the boy nodded enthusiastically. "But you know what I heard the other Gordo say once? He said, 'Whether I win or lose, I'm content with the outcome, knowing I can always trust in God's goodness.'"

"That's cool, I guess. . . ." The wide blue eyes grew serious for a moment and then the grin returned. "But it's okay to hope God wants us to win, isn't it?"

Tommy swallowed hard. "Yeah, Gordo, it's okay to hope."

The first wave of inspectors arrived and checked the fuel cell and carburetor. Half an hour later, Tommy stood and watched as the car was filled with twenty-two gallons of 108-octane fuel, and then he helped push it into the tech line. He held his breath as the inspectors came over and checked the roof flaps with a suction cup and a lift-load gauge. This was the kind of stuff that intrigued him most, and between races, he had his hands into anything that could lower wind resistance and shave a few seconds off their time. The flaps, which prevent the car from flipping over in a high-speed spin, flipped up with less than two pounds of pressure, earning them a thumbs-up. Tommy smiled and breathed. Someday, when he decided to settle down, maybe he'd go to engineering school and study aerodynamics. At the thought of settling down, he asked one of the inspectors a question just to refocus.

Topaz set a paper-wrapped hot dog in front of Cammie. "You

look like a raccoon."

Cammie was sitting at a picnic table, vegetating in the cloudless seventy degrees, grateful for the relative quiet of the raceway grounds an hour before the gates would open. "I didn't do much with makeup this morning."

"Clown makeup couldn't hide those circles. I heard you up at three thirty. Did you sleep at all?"

"Some."

"I'm being amazingly patient here with you in La-La Land. I didn't bug you once last night, but you are working up to talking about this, right? Not spilling your guts builds up deadly toxins."

As she slowly unwrapped the hot dog, Cammie stared at it, unseeing. Taking it in both hands, she raised it several inches, then set it down again. "He kissed me."

"We're talking about Jackman, right?"

"Mm-hum."

"And?"

Cammie closed her eyes. "And it was incredible. I've never, ever been kissed like that."

A long, wistful sigh floated from Topaz's lips. "Don't you ever forget that I was the one who told you to give him a chance."

"I know. But—"

"No 'but'! You're the one who's always telling me that if I turn my life over to God He'll point the way, right?"

Sheepishly, Cammie nodded.

"Well, girl, I think I've got more faith than you do! You waiting for a neon sign or something? What's there to 'but'

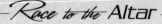

about? I know not a lot of wives go with their men, but you've got that pioneer spirit, girl. And if NASCAR goes through with the permanent med-team idea, they'd hire you in a minute, and you could work every race. It's perfect, Cam. At least until you have kids. From Florida to California, you can see the whole country and still be back home to spend the holidays with your folks."

"But not with my husband. The minute he swallows the last bite of pumpkin pie at Thanksgiving, he'll be in the gym working out like a crazy man to be in shape for Daytona."

"Unlike G.I. Joe?"

Cammie cringed. Topaz smiled triumphantly. "Come on, Cam, you're digging for excuses. No 'buts.'"

Several replies came to Cammie's mind; they all started with "But. . . ." She took two bites of her hot dog. It wasn't sitting right in her stomach. She changed the subject to the other thing that was upsetting her stomach—telling her mother that she'd broken up with Joe. "Can I hitch a ride home with you tomorrow? I'll call my mom and see if she can pick me up at your place."

"Of course. Does Joe know you're not driving back with him?"

"Not yet."

"Do you think he gets that this is finito?"

"Well, after I called him a goal-worshipping cold fish. . ."

A mouthful of Diet Coke slid down Topaz's throat with a loud gulp. "I'm thinking he's probably not going to offer you a ride."

Cammie covered her face with her hand, fingers splayed

across her eyes. "Who was that crazy lady in the red dress last night? I just completely spazzed on him."

"Maybe he needed it."

"All the poor guy is guilty of is not meeting my expectations. Am I nuts to want a guy who wants to be with me more than twice a week?" Cammie's raised her hands, palms up. "I know all his reasons for not getting married until he's financially secure. His parents were horrible with money. There were times when they didn't have food in the house. But I don't want to wait till I'm forty-five to have my first kid! I'm so tired of having to fit into his plan. We have to compare our schedules every month so we can pencil in our weekly date nights. I'm sure he puts 'Tell Camela I love you' in his Blackberry."

"So"—Topaz raised her left eyebrow—"what you're looking for is a guy who's spontaneous, funny, romantic, isn't afraid to embarrass himself in public to show you how he feels. . . ."

With a decidedly unladylike snort, Cammie pulled her phone out of her back pocket, stuck out her tongue, and said, "I'm calling my mommy."

Her mother answered on the first ring. "Hi, baby. Happy Race Day."

"Hi, Mom." She hated the quiver in her voice. "Happy almost-Mother's Day."

"What's wrong, Cam?"

Cammie stood and walked away from the picnic table. "Can you talk? Where's Daddy?"

"He's in the garage."

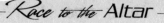

"Okay. I've got kind of a dumb question."

"Ask away."

"If you had it to do all over again, would you still marry Daddy?"

Her mother answered with silence. Cammie listened to the *clank* of dishes on the other end. "Mom?"

"Honey, you can't compare my situation with yours. I was madly, passionately in love with your father, but sometimes life interferes with love. If he hadn't been on the road so much, we would have had a perfect life together. You and Joe won't have obstacles like that."

"But you rode with him for a couple years until I was born, didn't you? Was it still good then?"

Another few seconds of quiet. "It was. For a while. But I needed roots. I just couldn't take living out of a suitcase, sleeping in a different motel every night. I just think God made women to need a nest to feather. . . ."

<hr />

The worship service conducted by Motor Racing Outreach had already started by the time Tommy got there. He stood at the back, scanning the crowd for a familiar blond head. He found her, but there wasn't an empty seat anywhere near her. He had a moment of disappointment that she hadn't saved him a place but let it go as the worship music lifted him. As he sang, he prayed.

Lord God, You've promised to light the path at my feet, nothing more, so I'm not going to stress about the race or about Cammie. I'm just going to leave it all in Your hands. Help me stay focused and honor You today.

The chaplain prayed for protection for the drivers, crews, and fans and gave thanks for the freedom to publicly worship. The time seemed to end too quickly, but Tommy's attention turned just as quickly to not losing track of Cammie. He caught up to her just as she walked out the door and pulled her aside.

With his arm across her shoulders, he bent low. "You look tired but especially beautiful this afternoon. Ready for this?"

She looked up at him with the kind of generic smile reserved for waiters and mailmen. He put his fingertips under her chin. "I don't believe in luck, so how about a kiss for blessing?"

Her eyes widened and she stepped away, out from under his arm. "I can't. I'm sorry. I shouldn't have let you think. . . . I just can't."

She turned and ran.

It was just before 7:00 p.m. and the sun was still low on the horizon, but the raceway lights were already on. The start of the Dodge 500 was just minutes away. Every one of the 65,000 seats was filled.

Tommy took off his hat and put his hand on his chest. The colors were presented and the rumble of voices and stamping of feet hushed. Behind him, the pit was silent, the crew statue still. In this quiet before the storm, all he could hear was the hammering of his pulse.

He bowed his head for the invocation. With the final words, "In the name of Jesus Christ our Lord, amen," the music started and began to swell, raising goose bumps on his arms. Jets screamed overhead and the red, white, and blue unfurled as

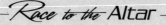

the national anthem reverberated across the stadium.

And then came the words that brought fans to their feet. "Gentlemen. . .start your engines!"

The roar of forty-three cars echoing across the field was sweetly deafening. The vibration made his toes tingle.

The last thing said in their prerace huddle replayed in Tommy's head: *"Don't lose focus."* Nobody knew how much he needed those words. He'd tried to cram Cammie's "I just can't" into a dark crevasse in his brain, along with the jumble of frustration and rejection they'd spawned. Now, when he needed to be clearer than ever, when the safety of his crewmates could be jeopardized by any lack of focus, he knew he wasn't 100 percent. All because of a fickle blond.

The green flag cut the evening air.

On Lap 38, Tommy's radio crackled. "Yellow! Yellow! Yellow!"

In the next pit stall, Lance McCallum's crew shoved their crash cart into place and scrambled like ants on cake crumbs.

There were shouts from every radio. "McCallum hit the wall on Turn 3! Back tire shredded!"

The yellow oval of the pit stall sign swung into the air above them.

"Change four and take a turn out of the left rear."

Tommy tightened his grip on the thirty-five-pound jack and sprang into action with the rest of the crew, perching on the wall like a pack of hungry mountain lions primed to pounce. He checked the jack and then checked it again. Ryan shifted his air wrench from hand to hand; Howie did the same. Beside him, the tire carrier audibly worked on controlling his breathing.

Tommy's feet hit the ground as Jeff slid the Chevy Impala into the stall. He cleared the moving bumper by millimeters, flying into position and jacking 3400 pounds in one dizzying motion. The tire changers dashed out, hitting one lug nut per second. Like the perfectly timed machine they were working on, the crew yanked off the seventy-pound tires and hung new ones while the gas man hoisted his ninety-pound gas cans. Just as Tommy lowered the left side of the car, the track light turned green.

A blur of orange drew his eyes to the right. Smoke pouring from the rear wheel, McCallum's Dodge swerved into pit lane, too fast and out of control. Tires squealed. The back end spun, heading straight for him. Tommy back stepped, felt the wall behind him, lifted the jack. Metal whined against concrete, and sparks shot into the night. . . .

Chapter 7

"W"e've got an arterial bleed! Right femur's smashed!"
Cammie froze. Tommy's foot angled oddly
inward; blood seeped through his pants. His eyes
were wide.

"Maintain pressure, get his vitals, maintain C spine." The
officer took command. "Get his clothes off; let's get an assessment. Dave, get the MAST pants. We'll need the backboard."
The words swirled around her but didn't register.

Suddenly Topaz's fingers bit into her shoulders. "Cam, can
you do this? If you can't, you have to get out of the way. *Now.*"

Like an electric jolt, Topaz's words shot through her. Cammie shook her head. "I'm okay." She pulled on a pair of latex
gloves and within seconds she was positioned at Tommy's left
shoulder.

One of the paramedics kneeled behind Tommy's head and
began inching a cervical collar beneath his neck.

Cammie leaned over so that Tommy could see her without
trying to turn his head. As she did, she pulled her trauma scissors

out of her pocket. "Tommy, do you know who I am?"

His eyes locked on hers. "The girl I love."

Cammie began cutting Tommy's sleeve. "Do you know where you are?"

His face contorted. Beads of perspiration stood on his forehead and upper lip and the color seemed to be draining from his face as she watched. She repeated the question, moving once again so she could look directly into his eyes.

"Darlington." His voice was thin and strained. "Thirty-eighth lap. Tomorrow's Mother's Day."

"Good." He'd heard the questions before. For a fraction of a second her thoughts strayed as she stared at the scar on his forehead, put there years ago by an airborne tire rim. There wasn't much she didn't know about Tommy Garrett. She looked up at the officer. "He's alert and orientated." Her fingers found his radial pulse. She stared at the second hand on her watch as she counted out the beats. *God, save him.* She fastened the blood pressure cuff to his arm. "Any allergies to medications?"

"No."

"Do you know your blood type?"

"O negative."

"Any surgeries other than the appendectomy and LASIK?"

His eyes found hers, surprise mingled with fear and pain. "No."

"Any history of high blood pressure, diabetes, heart disease?" She put the tips of the stethoscope in her ears and pumped the cuff, listening, waiting for the reassuring *blip*. When it finally came, she didn't want to believe it. She pumped the cuff again. There was no question this time. "Pulse ninety-eight.

BP seventy-two over fifty."

Topaz stared at her, Cammie's own fear reflected in her face. Topaz gave a slight nod. "Let's get the MAST pants on."

The Military Anti-Shock Trousers were inflatable pants that extended from the base of the ribcage to the ankle. When inflated, they would pressurize his legs and abdomen, forcing about two units of blood into his upper torso and head. Cammie helped stabilize his upper body while Topaz and the officer slid the pants onto his legs.

Tommy moaned, the sound landing on Cammie like a physical blow. In the distance, she could hear the blades of the CareForce helicopter. "As soon as we get these on, we'll move you to the helicopter."

Cammie touched his face with her gloved hand. His eyes found hers. "No history," he whispered.

Fred Conrad, an ER tech from Darlington's McLeod Medical Center, had secured the cervical collar and was beginning a head-to-toe assessment. As his hands felt along Tommy's left arm, he raised an eyebrow at Cammie. "I take it you know this guy."

As the backboard was set on the ground behind her, Cammie nodded. "We're friends."

Tommy's eyes narrowed and then closed. "For now."

⌒

"Almost there. Two more minutes. Hang on, Tommy."

The move into the ambulance had taken a toll. Tommy's eyes squeezed shut; his hand gripped hers. She had kept up a steady chatter, trying to give him something to focus on. She'd talked him through the move onto the cot, the lift into the squad, and the IV insertion. She took his pulse again. It was weaker than it had been minutes ago. She checked his blood pressure. The reading made her stomach lurch. "Pulse eighty and thready. BP sixty over thirty."

His hand went slack in hers. Cammie pressed her hand against his bare chest and rubbed his breastbone until he opened his eyes. "Stay with me, Tommy."

A weak smile broke through the mask of pain. "Gladly."

Her hold on his hand tightened.

"I. . .need. . ."—his voice faded to a hoarse whisper—"something."

"What do you need?"

"I need"—Cammie leaned forward to hear him—"a date with you."

Part laugh, part cry, the sound that came out of Cammie was accompanied by more tears. "You never give up, do you?" She could tell he was trying to smile again, but couldn't quite force it.

"Never." She leaned even closer to hear him. His breath came in short gasps against her cheek. "Promise. Promise. . .or I won't. . ."

"I promise! I'll go out with you. Just don't you dare let go. Do you hear me?"

A genuine smile spread Tommy's lips. And then he passed out.

Cammie stopped pacing the twelve-by-twelve alcove in the

emergency room waiting area, her gaze riveted to the mute TV mounted to the wall. The race was over and scenes of the accident flashed on the eleven o'clock news. She'd missed the first few words by the time she thought to turn up the volume. "...seriously injured when he was crushed between the wall and Lance McCallum's number 37 Meshcon Dodge. McCallum's car lost control while entering the pit lane with a shredded back tire. Jackman Tommy Garrett was momentarily pinned—" Cammie turned when she heard footsteps behind her. The doctor walked in, wearing blue scrubs, his mask hanging from his neck.

"You're Camela?"

"Yes.

"I'm Dr. Weston. We're sending him up to surgery. Someone will let you know as soon as he's out."

When the doctor left, she called Ryan. She had Tommy's cell and had already talked to Ryan twice. He and the rest of the pit crew would be heading to the hospital as soon as they could get away. Next, she called Tommy's mother.

"Mrs. Garrett? This is Camela Eastman; I'm an EMT and a friend of—"

"Cammie! Is he all right? I've been trying to get a hold of someone who could tell me something."

"He's going to be fine. They're taking him up to surgery—" There was a gasp on the other end. "His right leg is broken, but that appears to be all." There was no need to upset Tommy's mother with all of the details.

"Thank God. They didn't tell much on TV. They showed them putting him on the stretcher. I was so grateful to see you there with him. I tried calling the hospital, but they wouldn't believe I was his mother."

Cammie shook her head, wondering for a moment if the stress had wiped out her memory. She could not remember once, in the three years she'd been to Darlington, ever meeting Tommy's mother.

"You're out of the woods, Thomas."

Tommy opened one eye. He saw a woman with red hair. She had a tiny head and a massive body, and she was dressed all in blue. He closed his eye. "You're out of the woods," she said again. He could see the woods now, like a scene from Narnia, a snow-covered forest. And the woman in blue was standing at the edge of the trees, calling him Thomas. What had he done wrong? Nobody called him Thomas unless he'd done something wrong. He was so very tired. . . .

"Thomas?" This time the blue woman's head and body matched. "Do you want some ice chips?"

No. He wanted sleep. Who was she? The White Witch? It wasn't ice chips in the glass; it was Turkish Delight. He'd sleep her away. . . .

"How's the pain? On a scale of one to ten. . ."

Pain. He gasped. The White Witch pulled a needle out of his hip. "This'll help."

It wasn't just his hip. His whole leg hurt. It felt huge, twice the size of normal, and it throbbed. He needed a rest. . . .

"Tommy? Can you hear me?"

That was not the White Witch. That was an angel. He

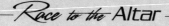

didn't even need to open his eyes to see her blond hair and eyes as blue as the Pepsi Chevy under a Talladega sun. He smiled. "Cammie." He could turn his head now, and his eyes stayed open long enough to appreciate what he saw. "You're going out with me." His eyelids shut against his will. He heard her move, smelled a hint of lemon, and then her lips were brushing his forehead.

"I guess I am."

His eyes shot open. "You are? For real? I was afraid I was dreaming...."

Chapter 8

The hum of the automatic blood pressure cuff was the first sound she heard. The sounds and smells were as familiar to her as home, but the room was dark, with light seeping in around heavy drapes and framing the wide door. It took a moment to remember why she was sleeping in a chair.

She looked up at the clock. 7:14. Sunday morning...the day she was supposed to go home...with Joe.

Her phone vibrated twice, and she flipped it open. A text message from Topaz: *U up? Praying. Yes. I'm praying. Call.*

Cammie dialed. "Hey, it's me."

"What's the latest?"

The sound of Topaz's voice brought unexpected tears. "Demerol's controlling the pain. He's sleeping."

"Good. Have you had time to think through the rest of the day?"

"I'm not going home. That's all I know. I've got the rest of the week off."

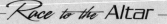

"Let me do legwork and phone calls. Do you need a hotel closer to the hospital?"

"That would be a huge help. I'll have to get a rental car; guess I should make a list."

"Have you talked to Joe yet?"

Cammie rubbed her hand across her face. "No. I don't think he's expecting me to go home with him."

"I saw him looking at you before you got in the ambulance last night. Pitiful. He may be a cold fish, but I think you need to apologize to him."

Cammie bristled. She knew it was true, but since when did this non-Christian friend of hers have all the answers? "I'm not sure if I can right now."

"I know. I'll go get you a room and take your stuff there; I'll come up and see you before I leave."

"You're a godsend."

"Hmm. Nobody's ever called me that. I kinda like it." Topaz was quiet for a moment. "Hey. . .I got a God question for you. Are you up to it?"

"Of course." Cammie stood and walked quietly out of the room. She didn't want to be whispering if Topaz was about to ask a life-changing question.

"Okay. So if I do this thing, if I do the let-go-and-let-God thing, do I gotta change the way I dress?"

"That's your question?" Cammie squinted in the bright light of the hallway and almost missed an aide carrying a food tray. "I'm thinking I have to explain the difference between sanctification and regeneration or predestination versus free will, and all you want to know is if you can keep your leopard pants?"

"Hey. . .it's a big thing. I know God's got me and I'm not gonna get away, but how much do I have to change first?"

"Not a thing. Absolutely nothing. All you have to do is tell Him you love Him and believe Him, and you surrender your will to Him. But then watch out, because *He'll* change *you*."

Five minutes later, Cammie said good-bye with a grin on her face and goose bumps covering her arms. She went into the public bathroom and splashed cold water on her face. As she walked past the nurses' station, her phone vibrated. It was Joe. Her legs turned to rubber, and she stepped toward the wall and leaned against it. "Hello."

"How's Garrett?" His tone was flat.

"He's stable."

"So do you—"

A Code Blue call rang out from the speaker above her.

"You're still at the hospital?" There was a note of disbelief in Joe's voice.

"Yes."

"Are you going home today?"

"No."

She heard him take a deep breath. "Okay. Well. . .'bye."

"Joe, wait. I'm sorry. I was way out of line the other night. But I just. . .you and I. . .all along we've had different goals and—"

"You've always been my goal, Camela. You're the prize. You're what's at the finish line."

Cammie swiped at her wet cheeks. "But I don't want to be anyone's prize. I don't want to be scheduled into 'on' days, and I don't want to be waiting on a pedestal at the finish line. I want to run the race, too, right next to. . ."—she couldn't say the word *you*—"somebody."

"So is Garrett your somebody?" He didn't wait for an answer. "I bought a house for you, Camela. Are you going to give that up for a guy who lives in a hotel?"

With a deep, steadying breath, Cammie did her best to release the anger he'd triggered. He hadn't taken her along to look at the house he'd bought, hadn't included her in the remodeling plans. She had no doubt that he loved her, but like the chrome light fixture he'd just hung in his dining room, she was an accessory to be installed when it was her time on his to-do list. "No, Joe. There's no somebody."

⚊⚊

Cammie stood by the window at the end of the hall, the phone still warm in her hand, staring out at the hospital grounds and beyond. The dogwoods seemed lit from within, glowing pink and red in the morning light. A pair of reddish-brown wrens chased each other in the leaves of a palmetto.

Topaz had just given her heart to Jesus Christ; Cammie should be bombarding the heavenlies with praise instead of wallowing in her own self-pity. And she needed to shelve her personal issues to be there for Tommy. She had just voiced the thought in her head when Joe called again. This time, her knees didn't weaken; her muscles tightened like steel. Whatever he had to add, she didn't want to hear it. But she answered it anyway.

"Listen, Camela. We've been rubbing each other the wrong way for a long time. I guess opposites attract, but that doesn't necessarily mean they should stay together. I'm never going to like surprises, and you're never going to like tofu."

She could tell he was smiling, and for some reason it made her want to cry. "You deserve a woman who loves lists and calendars and can grow sprouts and make homemade yogurt."

Joe laughed. "And you deserve a guy who can write songs for you."

"Joe. . .I need you to know that I'm not leaving you for Tommy. I'm here as a friend, but we're going our separate ways."

"Well, I guess God alone knows the future. Be happy, okay?"

There was no stopping the tears. "You, too."

She went back to the bathroom and let herself cry, then dried her face and prayed her way down the hall. She walked into the darkened room, closing the door partway behind her. A song played in her head. *"For you are good, for you are good, Lord, you are good to me. . . ."* She walked around to Tommy's left side and rested her hand on his arm. He didn't move. *Father, thank You. For so much. For Joe's understanding and the time we shared, for drawing Topaz to You, for saving Tommy. Please bring him through this recovery without a problem, and show me. . .* She stopped in midsentence, not sure where she'd intended to go with it, why she'd stuck herself in the middle of a prayer about Tommy's recovery.

Show me. . .show us. . .Your will, Lord. "Amen."

"Amen."

Cammie jumped. Tommy's right hand moved slowly until it came to rest over hers. He gave her a weak smile. "Hey, beautiful."

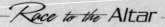

"Hey, yourself. I think you just had the longest NASCAR nap on record." She turned on the dim light over the bed. "Are you in a lot of pain?"

"On a scale of one to ten, I'm only about a fourteen."

Cammie picked up the call button. "I'll get you something."

"Not yet. I don't want any more drugs until you tell me what happened. It's all a blur. Where did we place?"

Skirting around the part about his blood pressure dropping to forty over twenty, she told him most of the details. He seemed more interested in the fact that they'd ended in second place than anything else.

Tommy squeezed her hand. "Well, I'm here; I'm breathing. God is good." He fell back to sleep, and Cammie pushed the call button.

When he woke again, he reached out for her. "Talk to me," he whispered.

Cammie pulled her chair closer and took his hand. "What do you want to talk about?"

"Anything. I just like to hear your voice, even if I'm in and out. Tell me everything I don't already know about you."

"Okay. Wait. . .have I ever met your mother?"

"No."

"When I called her she acted like she knew me."

"It might be the life-sized poster of you hanging on my bedroom ceiling."

"*What*?"

"I'm kidding." He winked at her. "I sent her the picture I

took with my phone the other day. And I have mentioned you once or twice." He smiled and closed his eyes.

"You can be such a brat." She pushed the hair off his forehead. "Ryan's called three times. He and Darcy are coming later with some of your clothes and stuff. I think the whole team is coming by again. You're loved."

For the next half hour, Cammie rambled about anything that came to mind. . .the beagle puppy she got when she was eight, losing her first tooth while riding on a Ferris wheel, doing surgery on her dolls and stitching them back up with red yarn. She told him about her first job, her first date, and her first kiss. She listed her pet peeves.

"I hate bathroom stalls without purse hooks and waitresses who call me 'Hon.' I don't believe in wasting calories on cheap chocolate. If your finger doesn't melt a hole in it in ten seconds it's not worth bothering with. I like pineapple and Canadian bacon on pizza and nachos instead of popcorn at the movies. Ooh, movies. . .old ones, especially with Jimmy Stewart. My all-time favorite is *Mr. Smith Goes to Washington*. I love docudrama. After I saw *Doctors Without Borders*, I signed up for a two-month mission trip to Nigeria. I want to go back there. . . ."

She talked until she was sure he was sound asleep. An hour later he woke again.

"Your mother called." She smoothed the sheet. "She'll be here in twenty minutes."

"You'll like her." He pressed his lips together twice. "Cotton mouth." Cammie filled his water glass and helped him sip from the straw. He smiled weakly. "Thanks. She'll like you, too." His

eyes swept the room. "It's Sunday, huh? Feels like I've missed days. When are you heading home?"

She stared into brown eyes that were hard to turn away from. In spite of the pale, haggard look, there was something about Tommy Garrett's face that felt like home. Even now, in the midst of his pain, she had the feeling he was studying her, reading between the words, once again seeing her soul. "I'm not."

"Not?"

"I'm not going home. Not until you do."

Chapter 9

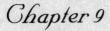

Cammie paused in the middle of the hall. Did she really hear guitar music? She stopped in the doorway of Room 342. From where she stood, it looked like the IV tube was hooked directly to the neck of the guitar. She stifled a laugh.

Tommy's hair, normally tamed under a red cap, reminded her of the Raggedy Andy dolls made by the hospital auxiliary back home. The one-size-fits-all gown had slid off his right shoulder. Muscles rippled to the strumming of the strings. His usually soft brown eyes held an intensity that made her breath catch.

"I never thought I'd see. . ." Tommy picked up a pencil and wrote something in a notebook.

Cammie knocked on the doorframe.

He jumped, smiled, and closed the notebook. "You scared me."

"After what you've put me through, you deserve to be scared."

"Come here." He reached out to her, and she gave him her hand. He pulled her to him and kissed her.

She didn't fight it. She knew there were reasons why she

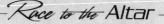

should resist, but not a one was coming to mind. It was a short, sweet kiss, and she was disappointed when it ended. Tommy patted the bed, and she walked around and sat on his left side, facing him. "What did the doctor say?"

"The good news is I'll be able to walk just fine."

"And the bad news?"

"There's a chance I'll have some permanent nerve damage." Tommy looked past her. "He figures I'll have full use of my leg, but it's doubtful that I'll ever regain the strength and flexibility I had before the accident." He looked back at her, his eyes clouding. "Looks like my jackman days are over."

Cammie's heart did a strange flip. Was this the way God was going to answer her prayers? The thought brought instant guilt. She put her hand over his and tried to show only the half of her mixed feelings that genuinely grieved for the loss of his dream. "I'm so sorry."

Tommy's hand turned over and held hers. "I'm having a hard time remembering that God is in control. I was struggling with being out just for the season; this is tough to swallow."

"Would you stay on full time as a mechanic?"

"I don't know. It sure would lose some of the thrill if I wasn't on the crew."

Again, Cammie felt the stir of hope and tried to squelch it. "What are your chances of working at the Hendrick Complex?"

"I'm sure they'd have a place for me in Charlotte. And. . .I'm praying about going back to school."

Cammie smiled. She could see herself baking a peach pie while he studied. "You'd be the best engineer NASCAR's ever known."

His lips pursed, and he kissed the air in her direction. "It's not the timing I had planned, but there will be perks to being grounded." He winked at her. "Hey, will you do me a favor?"

"Anything. . .almost."

"Will you do some shopping for me?"

"Sure. What do you need?"

"Toothpaste."

"They don't have toothpaste here?"

"I want some that doesn't taste like a hospital."

"O. . .kay. . ."

"Oh yeah, and something red."

She tilted her head to one side and decided not to take the bait. It turned into a staredown that lasted almost a minute until Tommy blinked and laughed. "You look amazing in red." He pressed a roll of bills into her hand. "You need a change of scenery and a little fun; go buy yourself something nice and come back and show me."

Her trip to Magnolia Mall had started with a resolve to only look at tops but ended with a black pencil skirt in a smaller size than she usually wore and a sleeveless lipstick-red silk blouse with rouching on the sides that was shockingly slimming. Out of her own money she splurged on strappy black sandals and a choker with a carved pewter slide.

It felt odd walking into a hospital in heels, but she couldn't help the spring in her step. The knowing smiles and quickly hushed voices as she walked past the nurses' station were embarrassing, though she'd assumed all along that she and Tommy

were a major topic of conversation.

Barb and Shauntelle, two of the nurses she'd spent some time talking to, were standing outside Tommy's room as she approached. They smiled at her, Cheshire Cat smiles, then waved into the room and left.

At the doorway, Cammie stopped. The lights were dimmed; the drapes closed, the TV tuned to a music channel. She took two hesitant steps. Battery-operated candlesticks lined the perimeter of the room at two-foot intervals. White icicle lights looped between the curtain rod, TV, and bulletin board. She was walking into a setup.

A hot/cold surge of nervous anticipation coursed through her. She took a tight breath and walked in.

Tommy was sitting up in bed. His feet were bare, and he wore a pair of black shorts over his cast. Above the shorts was a long-sleeved light blue dress shirt, the cuffs folded back, and a dark blue tie. His guitar sat next to him on the bed. He stretched out his right hand to her. "My lady in red. You look incredible."

He was smiling his approval, but with a seriousness in his eyes that scared her. She set her purse on the floor and handed him the toothpaste she'd bought. "You didn't really need this, did you?"

"No. I just needed you distracted." His eyes ran from her hair to her shoes. "And now *I* am."

The thought occurred to her that she'd probably never distracted Joe from anything. She looked around the room. "The entire shift was in on this, weren't they?"

"Delivery!" A teenager walked in, holding a pizza box.

Tommy paid him, then set the guitar on the floor, freeing a space on the bed.

Cammie kicked off her shoes and sat beside him. "Is this legal?"

"Just think of it as a very wide couch." He reached across her to the bedside table where a single red rose lay beside a gold box of Godiva chocolates and a DVD case labeled MR. SMITH GOES TO WASHINGTON. She looked down at the pizza box at the end of the bed and knew beyond a doubt that there was pineapple on the pizza. As he put the rose in her hand she suddenly felt like crying.

"This is, by far, the most amazing date I've ever had."

"It better be." He ran the backs of his fingers along her face. "Talking you into it almost killed me."

When the movie ended, Cammie realized her thoughts had been far from Jimmy Stewart. She was too preoccupied planning a future with Tommy Garrett. Sitting just like this, side-by-side, for the next eighty years would be nothing short of perfect. In the two hours and four minutes the movie took, she had planned a Valentine's Day wedding, followed by a Florida honeymoon that would include the Daytona 500. She had envisioned serving side-by-side on month-long mission trips to Mexico and Jamaica. Whatever job Tommy ended up with, she hoped it would have that kind of flexibility. She had named their three children and decided on colors for their first apartment.

When Tommy shut off the TV, she shifted back to the

present. As he pulled his arm away from her shoulders, the absence of his body heat chilled her. He lifted his guitar, and Cammie moved to give him room. He played several chords. "This is for you."

> *"I never thought I'd see the day*
> *Your Pepsi blues would look my way.*
> *Too short and ugly to compete*
> *With muscled dudes over six feet,*
> *I never thought this funny face*
> *Would get you to go on a date.*
> *But when my hopes began to lag,*
> *I saw you waving a green flag.*
>
> *"If I knew how, I would get tall for you.*
> *If I could walk, you know I'd call for you.*
> *By now you know how I can fall for you*
> *Because I'm so over the wall for you."*

Cammie sniffed and made a melodramatic show of pretending to mop up tears. "You wrote that for li'l ol' me?" She sniffed twice more. "That was so touching. I'm honored. Thank you." She kissed his cheek and laughed. "You definitely need to record it."

Tommy shook his head. "Famous country singers have to travel a lot, you know. It messes with relationships."

"I've heard that." She put her hand on his cheek. "You know. . .this is a very handsome funny face."

"That was a compliment?"

"Definitely." For a moment she simply looked at him, thinking she would never get tired of that face. "Thank you for an amazing night."

"Does that mean you'd chance another date with me?"

"I guess I'd consider it if you asked."

He set the guitar down and reached out for her hands. "Camela Eastman, will you go out with me—I mean stay in with me—tomorrow night?"

She nodded. "I'll even arrange the details. As I recall, you like peach pie, too."

"I do." He ran his thumbs across the backs of her hands. "Can we pray before you leave?"

"Of course."

Tommy bowed his head. "Almighty God, we come together to praise You. You are awesome and mighty, and Your ways are perfect. Thank You for giving us this time together. Father, we commit every moment of our future to You."

Unable even to echo his "Amen," Cammie simply nodded. Nothing he had done in this entire fairytale night had touched her quite like this.

Chapter 10

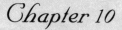

Tommy sat in the wheelchair staring at the window. He'd stayed up late working on a song and hadn't slept well after that. His leg had been hot and throbbing in spots all night and now felt cold and heavy, but he wasn't about to complain. After eight days in this room, he was finally going home. His mother would be here with her van in less than an hour. Cammie would arrive to say good-bye in a matter of minutes. He wasn't ready for that.

They'd be less than three hours apart, and she'd promised to make the trip from Raleigh to Charlotte as often as she could, but he'd grown accustomed to having her by his side every day. She'd cried last night when she said good night. The pain of watching her walk out of his room had prompted the lyrics he'd worked on until 3:00 a.m. He fingered the paper in his hand; it was getting damp from constant folding and unfolding. Lacing his fingers together, he commanded his hands to be still. He didn't want to look like a nervous wreck when Cammie walked in.

Five minutes later, she was silhouetted in the doorway,

wearing white shorts and a red sleeveless blouse. Her hair was still wet; there was something strangely intimate about seeing her in the morning with shower-damp hair. It deepened the sadness her tears had started; he was missing her already.

She walked toward him, one hand behind her, and bent to kiss him. He put his hand on the back of her head to hold her there. As he inhaled the fresh citrusy scent of the lemon body cream she loved, he made a mental note to buy her a case of it. When she tried to pull away, he protested. "Not yet," he whispered against her lips. She smiled then, making it impossible to continue kissing her.

"I have a souvenir for you." From behind her back, she brought a brown teddy bear, about five inches high, dressed in a red and black NASCAR jacket and a red bandana. In its hand was a flag that said DARLINGTON—TOO TOUGH TO TAME. She set it on his cast. "This is your stand-in Lady in Red from the Lady in Black."

"Thank you." Touching the bear, he struggled to rein in his emotions. He couldn't remember the last time he'd cried. Probably Dale Earnhardt's funeral. But the humor that usually got him through difficult situations seemed inaccessible at the moment. "I'd much rather have the original, but she'll be good company until I have the real thing." He pointed to his guitar on the bed. "I wrote something for you."

"Again? I'm going to have my own album pretty soon. And then you'll get famous and be on the road all the time and that really—"

He said the last three words with her. "Messes with relationships."

He took the guitar and motioned toward the recliner. When she sat down, he positioned the wheelchair facing her. "Even when I become a world-renowned country singer, this song will always be for your ears only."

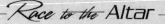

Fingers of anticipation tingled upward from the small of her back. Cammie stared at Tommy's untamed hair as he bent over his guitar. From the moment she'd walked in the room, she'd sensed something restless in him. Even two hours before a race he didn't look this nervous. His hands were shaking; his face looked almost as pale as it had in the ambulance. Instinctively she knew this was more than just a song.

He played several chords and then looked up at her. Those chocolate eyes, reading her in a way that still unnerved her.

At that moment, his cell phone rang. Tommy shook his head. "My mother." He pulled his phone from his pocket and answered it. With his first few surprised words, Cammie knew it wasn't his mother.

"Wow. Thank you. Honestly, I've never considered it. I'm honored."

Cammie watched him. His eyes had a dreamy, faraway look. As a smile spread across his face, she tried to guess the other end of the conversation. A knot of dread was forming in her stomach.

"Of course. I'll call you when I get settled at home. Thanks, Jeff. God bless."

Cammie could see him almost literally come back to the present as he closed the phone. "That was Jeff?"

He nodded. "There's going to be an opening next season for a hauler driver."

Surely that wouldn't be something Tommy would be interested in. She wanted to believe that, but the look on his face told her otherwise. "That was nice of him to think of you." She'd hoped to sound neutral, exposing none of her shattered emotions, but it came out sounding stilted, almost patronizing. As if she'd said it was nice the other little boys still wanted to play with him.

"Yeah, it was." He looked down at his watch and then smiled like a man with a secret. "Now where was I?"

He began to play, the soft notes flowing over Cammie like spring rain, slow and gentle.

But she couldn't feel them. She *wouldn't* feel them.

How could he go on as if nothing had changed? Beyond the shadow of a doubt, she knew where this was leading. As close as they'd become in the past week, as much as they'd shared, he had yet to put it into words. He had yet to say "I love you." That's what the song was about, she was sure of it. But how could he? Those eyes that seemed able to read her every mood. . .couldn't they see what his words on the phone had done to her?

"I've always been the type
To pride myself
On taking life as it comes.
No five-year plan,
No long-range goals.
I'm an easygoing man.

"Always thought I'd handle
Most anything
The good Lord sent my way.
But then He sent you,
Spun my world around,
And nothing's made sense since."

Her fingers dug into the vinyl upholstery. If he told her he loved her, he'd expect an answer. She couldn't say she *didn't* love him.

"All I know
Is I can't let go.
I'm an easygoing man,
But going my own way
And living without you
Is more than I could stand."

As the song went on, Cammie kept her eyes on the guitar, and not his face. Finally, he set the guitar down and took her hands. Silence echoed in the room until she drew the courage to look into his eyes.

"I love you, Cammie." He ran his fingertip along her face. "Will you marry me?"

She couldn't breathe. She had only enough air in her lungs to push out two words. "I. . .can't."

~

She shouldn't be driving. Even after half an hour of sobbing as she stuffed her suitcase and packed her things into the rental car, even after a cup of vending machine coffee and twenty minutes of praying out loud in the car, tears were still coming so heavy she couldn't blink fast enough to clear her vision.

She'd done the right thing. She'd answered with her head, not her unstable emotions. Her mother's words echoed in her head: *"Sometimes life interferes with love."* Wouldn't Tommy driving a car hauler across the country for nine months out of the year come under the "life interfering" category? It wasn't a chance she was willing to take. Maybe Topaz was right, maybe it would be perfect "at least until you have kids." And it was true that Tommy wouldn't be on the road forever. But a lot could go wrong before he was ready to give it up. She wasn't going to let her kids go through what she'd grown up with. She wasn't going to end up like her mother.

Maybe, if all he'd said was "I love you," she would have stayed, would have tried to explain her fears to him yet again. But. . .her thoughts were spinning. . . . Had Tommy Garrett really proposed?

Lord, what's this all about? What was I supposed to say? If he'd asked me before the phone call I would have said yes. I do love him. I do want to spend the rest of my life with him. We'd be good together. . .not just for each other. . . . I could see us leading Bible studies in our home together, doing mission trips together. It's the together *part I need, Lord. I can't do a long-distance marriage, and I don't even know if I'd be allowed to ride with him. . . .*

She needed to talk to someone. With no idea who to call—her mother, Topaz, one of her friends from church, or maybe Darcy—she fished her phone out of her purse. As she did, it

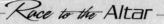

rang. She glanced at the display. It was Tommy. Suddenly light-headed, she said a weak "Hello."

"Cammie? This is Shauntelle. It looks like they're going to take Tommy back to surgery, honey. Sounds like he has a blood clot in his leg. They're doing an ultrasound right now. But he's gonna be jus' fine; don't you worry."

Breathe. Steady. Think straight. "I'll be there in twenty minutes." She put her blinker on, though she couldn't even see the next exit.

He's going to be fine. They caught it in time. Are you sure? He could lose his leg. Or worse. . .it could travel to his heart or lungs or. . . Stop it! I deal with emergencies every day. I know the procedures. He's going to be just fine. But the repair to his femoral artery is still. . . But he's young, he heals fast. . . .

For the next ten minutes she argued in her head like a woman with multiple personalities. When she reached the surgical floor nurses' station, she couldn't even remember where she'd parked her car.

Shauntelle's wide hips cleared the corner of the counter and plump brown arms enveloped her. "His mama's in the waiting area. I'm thinking she's needin' a hug, too. I'm prayin', and I'll let you know first thing we hear something, okay?"

"What happened?"

"That stubborn man of yours just happened to mention on his way out the door that half his leg had felt hot for a couple days, but today it was cold. If he'd told us sooner. . ."

Cammie walked numbly into the waiting area and put her arms around Julie Garrett. As the minute hand on the wall clock jerked in slow motion, the two women prayed, talked, and drew support from each other in the silences. Cammie had just handed Julie a cup of coffee when she spotted the basket of Christian books she'd looked through many times in the past week. She'd read the historical romance about the young bride on the Oregon Trail. She picked it up and reread the girl's prayer on the last page. Her final words were, "Sometimes love isn't enough. . .unless it's Yours."

Tears stung her already-burning eyes. She set the book down and picked up another one. *Sacred Marriage* by Gary Thomas. The subtitle leaped off the cover: *What if God Designed Marriage to Make Us Holy More Than to Make Us Happy?*

As the words slammed her spirit like a sledgehammer, Shauntelle appeared in front of her. "He's in recovery. He's fine. The doctor will be out in a minute."

Tommy's mother stood up. "Thank God."

"Can I see him?" Cammie's fist pressed against her lips.

"We don't. . ." Shauntelle stopped and smiled. "Guess being a nurse ought to have its privileges. Come with me."

Cammie followed her to the recovery room, where she reached across the metal railing and took his hand. Tommy opened his eyes and closed them again, but a smile crinkled his pale face. "You're back."

"I'm back. For good." She kissed him on the lips; his feeble attempt at a response was endearing. "If you haven't given up on me, my answer is yes."

"Give up? Never." His eyes closed again.

"I love you. And I'm sorry I made this all about me and my fears. It's about so much more. . .about how God will use our marriage for His glory. My mother's right that sometimes life interferes with love, but God intervenes in life! I don't know how He'll work out the details, but even if you're only home two days a week or if I'm sitting next to you in a semi, with God's help we can make—" His deep, even breathing stopped her. She smiled. She'd have years to explain herself.

⬿

The White Witch was back again. Tommy opened one eye and saw her hooking up an IV bag. She was talking to someone far away. . . . Who? Where was he and how long had he been gone? The faraway voice was familiar. Cammie. . . The White Witch was talking to Cammie. . .about roses and stephanotis and babies' breath. He closed his eyes. Just a short rest. . .

He woke again. Where was he? Cammie was there. . .telling the White Witch about red velvet dresses with sweetheart necklines. Bridesmaid's dresses! Cammie was getting married! How long had he been unconscious? Days? Weeks, maybe? Something must have gone terribly wrong. She'd said she couldn't marry him.

The last thing he remembered was Cammie running away, crying. She'd said she couldn't marry him; she'd said "I can't." It had taken him a few minutes to figure out why she'd turned him down, and then his mother was there and his leg was throbbing and his head felt funny and the next thing he knew they were taking him back to surgery. He never got the chance to tell her he wasn't going to take the hauler job. He never got the chance to tell her that he'd meant what he said in the song—that living without her was more than he could stand. He'd missed his chance, and now. . .how much time had passed? Cammie was marrying Joe after all.

But why was she here? To break it to him in person when he woke from his coma? If he could raise his hand, he'd clamp it over her mouth and stop the chatter. How could she be so heartless? He licked his lips and forced his eyes open. Strange. . . she was wearing the same red blouse she'd worn when she said "I can't." He tried to talk, but nothing came out. He swallowed and tried again. "You're. . .getting married?"

She bent over him, her smile wide, her cheeks flushed. The scent of lemon made him ache with wanting to hold her. Before he knew what was happening, her lips were on his. He turned his face to the side. This wasn't right. . .unless. . . "Wait. . . What. . . ? Who. . .are you marrying?"

Cammie's laugh was like sunshine, making his senses suddenly sharp. He looked past her; he was still in the recovery room. Her breath was warm on his cheek; her lips brushed his ear. "I'm marrying you, funny face."

BECKY MELBY and her husband Bill live in Wisconsin. They have four married sons and six grandchildren. Working part-time at her husband's chiropractic office, playing with grandkids, motorcycle rides with Bill, reading and writing delicious Christian romances, and all things chocolate fill her time. She and Bill also host a small group Bible study. Her desire for her writing is to glorify God through His gift of words.

CATHY WIENKE is also a Wisconsin resident. She and her husband Brian have two sons and a daughter, two grandchildren, and a spoiled Maltepoo named Pooh Bear. Brian and Cathy are fulfilling their dream of building a log cabin in northern Wisconsin. With their family they enjoy ATVing, NASCAR races, Packer games, and trips to Disney. Cathy serves in an outreach ministry at a teen girls' prison. She loves reading good Christian fiction and devotes time to painting room murals.

Becky and Cathy have been friends for over thirty years. They have coauthored three Heartsong novels, which appeared in a 3-in-1 collection, *Wisconsin Blessings*, in February of 2006. For more information, go to www.melby-wienke.com.

Winner Takes All

by Gail Sattler

Dedication

Dedicated to my brother Richard,
NASCAR junkie and willing research guinea pig.
Thank you!

Chapter 1

T hank you—and good luck at the Richard Petty Experience. I hope you do well." Lynda Blakeson tucked the receipt into the bag, smiled, and handed it to the customer. In typical fashion, the father had the NASCAR hat out of the bag and on his son's head before they left the store.

At least this one actually put the bag into the garbage can and didn't drop it on the ground.

With no other customers currently in the store, Lynda returned to her stock lists. Now was the time for the stock to be purchased, sorted, inventoried, and priced. The next big race wasn't for a month yet, but when that date rolled around, she would barely have time to breathe. During the week of the race, Talladega would be home to over 170,000 tourists needing food, camping supplies, gas, and countless souvenirs, and Lynda wanted to provide for a good percentage of those needs.

Laughter and voices echoed from the office in the back, where her boss and storeowner, Kathleen, was listening to a sales pitch from a vendor.

The laughter trailed off when Kathleen's cell phone rang. In the silence, Kathleen's gasp echoed in the empty store.

Lynda froze. She didn't want to listen, but with the door open, she could hear Kathleen clearly.

"How bad?" Kathleen asked, her voice choked and filled with emotion. "Will Jolene. . . ?" She went silent.

The salesman left the room and joined Lynda in the store.

He smiled awkwardly. "I think Kathleen needs some privacy."

Lynda felt shaky. "Jolene is Kathleen's daughter."

The salesman glanced around nervously. "This might be a good time to check my voice mail. I'll step outside. Excuse me."

Lynda waited for him to leave, intending to take advantage of his absence to pray for Kathleen's daughter before any customers came in.

As she composed herself, she looked outside through the glass door.

The salesman was tall—six foot one in his shoes, according to the security markings on the doorframe. In addition to being lean and trim, he was a very handsome man. In contrast to his steel blue eyes, his hair was so dark it was almost black. Cut short and gelled into a current style, it suited his prominent nose and strong facial features. The dark frames of his glasses matched the color of his hair and complimented his dark grey suit. The total package proved quite easy on the eyes.

He pushed a few buttons on his cell phone, snapped it closed, and then stepped forward to the lamp standard in front of the building. He removed his glasses and leaned against the pole. He closed his eyes then lowered his head, resting his forehead in his hand.

He sighed and became still.

It looked like he was praying.

All Lynda could do was stare.

Kathleen burst from her office into the store. "Jolene's been in a bad car accident. Although, according to her husband, who is with her at the hospital, her injuries aren't life threatening, it could be months before she's able to walk again. Little Brittany is still in school, and she doesn't know yet. I have to go."

Lynda felt sick. "Don't worry about the store. I can look after things here."

Kathleen took two steps and stopped. "I believe you can. In fact, I'm going to stay in Birmingham for as long as they need me. I'll leave you in charge of the store." Kathleen's voice quieted. "My daughter will need my help. I've been thinking of going into semiretirement anyway, which means giving you more duties and responsibilities as I take more time off. Let's consider this as a trial for you. God bless you, and I'll call you in a few days."

Before Lynda could respond, Kathleen stepped outside and ran to her car.

The door had barely closed when it opened again, and the salesman walked in.

Lynda ran her fingers through her hair. "It's not life threatening, but it is bad. Kathleen's going to Birmingham to help."

The salesman stared out the door, in the direction Kathleen had left. "This might sound callous, but should I be speaking to you about the sales meeting? As tragic as this is, we all still have to earn a living."

Lynda gulped. "I guess so."

He extended one hand. "My name is Rob Williams. And you are?"

Lynda's hand trembled as she returned his handshake. "Lynda Blakeson."

"I'm pleased to meet you, Lynda." He reached into the inside pocket of his suit jacket and pulled out a DVD case. "I'm promoting a new NASCAR computer game, approved and licensed and ready to mass market. My laptop and the sample game are in Kathleen's office. May I show it to you?"

Everything was moving so fast, but Rob was right—the world couldn't stop. Kathleen had asked her to run the business, and that was exactly what Lynda was going to do.

"Sure," she said. "I just have to keep an eye on the store because now I'm the only one here."

"Then I'll give you the quick version. My marketing plan is to set up a demonstration table to personally show NASCAR fans the game and let them try it out before they buy, which is the best selling tool."

Lynda watched the demo, but her mind was shooting in a million directions.

She would have to reschedule the staff, work the extra hours herself, plus buy and stock new merchandise—or choose not to order it, starting with this new game.

Their current items were meeting the needs of the transient customer base. Tourist trends were predictable, and the profits were steady and consistent.

But was she merely supposed to keep with the status quo?

Lynda dreamed of owning her own business, but Talladega wasn't exactly a booming metropolis outside the two times a year when the racing fans arrived.

This changed everything. With Kathleen wanting to ease out of the store, Lynda wanted to ease in, which meant possibly buying a share of the ownership when Kathleen returned. Lynda felt confident she would have first consideration to buy it outright when Kathleen wanted to sell.

What happened in Kathleen's absence would prove that Lynda could—or couldn't—succeed.

Lynda didn't want to be like the fearful servant in the New Testament who, when entrusted with his talent, was afraid to take a risk to increase his master's investment and buried what he had been given. When his master returned and saw no profit, what little the servant had was taken away.

Was this God's nudge—a prompting for Lynda to take the risk and show what she was made of?

She stared at Rob.

Was carrying his product a risk she was supposed to take? She didn't know him, nor did Kathleen. He'd sought them out, for reasons she didn't know.

Yet she'd watched Rob pray for a stranger, unashamed, and not concerned that his private moment with God might not have been so private.

That alone made her want to trust him. His game seemed interesting enough. In fact, if she hadn't been working, since it was a NASCAR racing game, she would have played it through.

Since she liked it, her gut feeling was that other NASCAR fans would, too.

She gulped. Seeing that he wasn't ashamed to pray in public

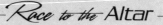

gave her more courage to speak her mind. "I need to pray about this. Not just about carrying your game, but about managing the store while Kathleen's gone."

His eyebrows rose, and he broke out into a wide smile. "I think that's a great idea. Would you like me to pray with you? After all, there's a lot at stake in this for me, too."

He smiled, and Lynda had to remember to breathe.

Working in the fringes of a male-dominated industry she saw a lot of handsome men, but with or without his glasses, Rob easily qualified as the most handsome man she'd ever seen.

In addition to his masculine appeal, wearing the glasses made him look scholarly. Brains, plus brawn. The perfect male.

It terrified her, but perhaps this was another test.

Lynda didn't like tests, but tests were part of life and often what made a person grow the most toward his or her potential. The NASCAR races she depended upon for her living were a test for the drivers, sometimes a test of life itself, for the sake of catching their dreams.

She'd already passed her first test, one that started over a year ago.

This was her next test, this one for her dream.

It was time to move forward and not bury her talent in the sand.

"Yes, I'd like to share in a time of prayer with you, but I'll need to wait until the store closes, which isn't until eleven o'clock."

Rob's smile didn't drop. "That's okay. I have nowhere else to go. I can wait."

Chapter 2

The moment Lynda turned her back, Rob broke out in a sweat.

The closer he'd come to her, the closer he'd come to panic.

He didn't know if this was his best dream come true or his worst nightmare taunting him.

All his life, even before he'd fully understood what it meant, everyone had called him a nerd. As a child, when he'd been trapped in the house by illness, God had provided his family with a computer, and sometimes it was the only thing that kept him sane. The only thing he loved more than his computer was NASCAR.

His childhood dream had been to be a NASCAR driver. As an adult, he'd tried, but no matter how well he'd done in the dirt track, because of his medical history, he'd been unable to get sponsorship. Now, the only thing he drove was his Toyota. He poured all his energy into his computer and made his living as a programmer.

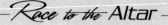

But when he wasn't sitting at his desk working on his boss's latest project or at church worshipping the God who saved his life, Rob had become the best NASCAR driver he could be— on his computer. At first, he would play any racing game he could find, but he'd been driven to create his own game, to his own specifications, by his personal love of NASCAR.

When his computer game was the best it could be, he'd jumped through all the hoops to get it approved by NASCAR, including all the licensing and legalities. Now was the time to move forward—into marketing. He'd accumulated all his vacation time, banked overtime, and received an additional leave of absence from his job, with his boss's blessings, to see what he could do with his dream.

He'd been pretty sure of himself, until he saw Lynda Blakeson.

He didn't know if this was a sign, or if God was playing a joke on him.

Either way, he was here. He had to see it through, even if it meant his complete and utter humiliation.

The object of his dreams—or nightmares—broke into his thoughts, which was just as well. "Would you like some coffee? We've always got a pot brewing."

"I think I would. Thanks." He tried to smile graciously, but he didn't need coffee. His heart was already in overdrive.

"I don't mind if you want to use Kathleen's office if you have work to do."

"It's okay, I'm all caught up with everything, but there's always e-mail to check."

She smiled, sending his stomach into a knot. "Just like voice mail. Whatever would we do without them? Let me show you where the coffee is."

He followed, like a puppy, desperate to be with her, whether she acknowledged him or not. She showed him the coffee station and poured a cup for herself; then she watched him as he made one for himself.

Instead of retreating to the back office, he remained at the coffee machine. Like someone who stayed at the scene of a train wreck, he couldn't stop looking at something he didn't want to see, but he couldn't drag himself away.

"It's not busy," she said as she wiped up a spill left by the last customer. "Why don't you bring your laptop to the front counter? Then I can have a better look at your game now and not make you wait. Your time is valuable, and I'm sure you have better things to do."

Actually, he didn't, and it wouldn't have mattered what other valuable things he had to do. He was a moth drawn to a flame. He was going to get burned. He just knew it. But still, he kept getting closer and closer. . . .

Rob shook his head to clear his thoughts. "Uh. . . sure. . . I'll be right back."

He kept telling himself it was better sooner than later, but yet, he didn't want the fantasy to end.

As his laptop booted up, a customer came into the store. Rob watched Lynda, mesmerized the entire time as she helped the woman find just the right size filter for her kerosene lantern. He was still wondering what had brought him here, to her.

"I'm back. I'm ready."

Rob didn't know if he was ready. "You'll probably want to

choose your car and select your driver, then make a slower practice run around the track before you start racing."

She flipped through the selection screens quickly as she designed her car and picked a number, telling him that she'd played similar games before.

"Do you have female drivers?" she asked as she flipped past a few choices.

His stomach tightened. "Yes. One."

He could tell when she clicked on the only female driver he'd created.

She froze solid. Her face turned to stone.

Her eyes narrowed, and her mouth stiffened.

"Who are you? Is this someone's idea of a sick joke?"

Rob pulled at his collar to loosen it, even though his tie wasn't real, it was a clip-on. "Believe me, I'm probably as shocked about this as you are."

"I doubt that. Who put you up to this? Who did this?"

"No one. I did. Every component of this game is programmed and designed by me exclusively."

She closed the laptop so sharply he cringed.

"Get out."

He grabbed his laptop and tucked it under his arm before she did something violent with it. "Please, I'm asking you to trust me. There's a reason this happened, and believe it or not, it really has nothing to do with you. At least it wasn't supposed to. When I met you today, it was like my life flashed before my eyes."

She crossed her arms across her chest tightly as though she were hugging herself, but Rob couldn't blame her. If the situation had been reversed, he didn't know how he would have reacted.

"There is an explanation," he muttered.

"I can hardly wait to hear it."

Rob's gut clenched. This wasn't something he wanted to share, especially with a stranger.

If only he'd picked another store as a first attempt at marketing his game, but he'd had a good and valid reason for choosing this store that had nothing to do with the staff. Or at least it hadn't—until he walked in the door.

He kept his laptop cradled safely under his arm. "The woman in my game was supposed to be my idea of the perfect woman. Or rather, she was supposed to be the antithesis of the world's most awful woman." He ran his fingers through his hair as he searched for words to explain better. "It was kind of a joke, but not the funny kind. I certainly never expected to find that the perfect woman was real." He lowered his voice. "I especially didn't expect to actually meet her. But here you are."

Lynda's teeth clenched so hard he wondered if she was going to need a trip to the dentist.

Rob gave her a weak smile. "You're not married, are you?"

Her eyes narrowed even more. "I still want to know who put you up to this."

Being cautious, he set the laptop on the edge of the counter, where she couldn't reach it easily. "No one." Unless it was divine intervention. Rob didn't know. All he knew was that his brain seemed to be in another dimension. "I deleted all the pictures I had of her except a few that had other people in them. Let me

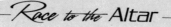

show you. And please forgive me for getting personal, but this is the truth."

He pulled up a photo of his best friend's wedding. He'd been the best man, so the photo was of Jason with his new wife and himself with Brenda.

He zoomed in on Brenda. "We were engaged when this picture was taken. She did some things that hit me like a sucker punch to the gut, and I finally saw her for the person she really was. Maybe it was childish of me, but my best retaliation was to make my female star driver everything she wasn't."

He pulled up the digital image of the perfect woman he'd created and positioned it alongside the picture of Brenda for comparison.

His ears burned, so he knew he was blushing, but he couldn't stop as he turned the laptop for Lynda to see the pictures. He didn't need to look at her as she studied the image. He'd designed her every feature from the passion of his heart. But he looked at her anyway. He couldn't *not* look.

"Here is the enemy—and the perfect woman, who is everything she's not."

He studied Lynda's face as Lynda studied Brenda's.

Brenda's blond hair and light blue eyes were the direct opposite of Lynda's black hair and dark brown eyes. Lynda was structured and physically fit, maybe a little chunky, like she was comfortable with herself and didn't care—compared to Brenda who was always on some kind of diet, even though Rob figured she was always about five pounds underweight.

Brenda's face was delicate, almost fragile, her features perfect, her chin small, and her nose cute and dainty. Her hair was always professionally artistically cut to frame her face, and he couldn't remember ever seeing her without makeup.

In direct contrast, Lynda's nose and other features were prominent, not that she was ugly—far from it. She was pretty, too, but in a distinct and almost tomboyish way. She had high cheekbones and a heart-shaped face, with a little bump on her nose, something he'd always thought showed personality and strength, which was why he'd made his perfect woman that way. Her hair was long and wavy, cascading casually over her shoulders the way it wanted to, naturally, without guidance from a curling iron.

He knew Lynda wasn't wearing any makeup because he could see a small scar above her left eyebrow—something his perfect woman didn't have.

Yet.

He could always add it in the next version. After all, a perfect woman should be heroic in some way. Maybe she would have suffered a race car accident, or saved a little old lady from a mugger.

"This is me," Lynda muttered. "It almost feels like I'm looking in a mirror, except I'm digital."

He'd created that digital Lynda. Just like something out of a fantasy movie where the computer nerd designed a perfect woman through some science only available in the movie industry. In Rob's case, though, the perfect woman of his dreams was no hologram. She was real—and very much alive.

"Click the prompt over there and drive the car. See how it feels." He told his heart to slow down and forced himself to breathe. "It will really feel like you're behind the wheel. You can

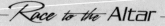

have your choice of the keypad or a controller. I have a steering wheel for the PC in my car, if you want. I just have to go get it."

To Rob's profound relief, she plugged in the controller he offered and took her car for a test lap around the cyber track.

"This is good," she said as she rounded the last curve. She then clicked it into "real race" mode and took it for a few laps around the track with the computer-generated drivers.

"You can make your choice between a number of raceways. I've got this level set on the Talladega Superspeedway, since that's where we are. I've also got choices of Daytona International, Chicagoland, Indianapolis Motor Speedway, Bristol Motor Speedway, and Homestead–Miami."

"I like it, but if I carry your game in the store and let you do your demonstrations, you've got to take me out of it."

"I can't. Thousands of copies of this have already been burned."

She dragged one hand down her face. "I'm sorry, I'm finding this really strange. I think the worst part is when you called this character perfect. It's me, but I'm far from perfect."

She may not be perfect, but the way she denied her attributes rather than being flattered told him a lot about her already.

When he'd designed his perfect woman, it wasn't because he was a randy, postpubescent teenager. He'd done what he'd done for a valid reason. Brenda had hurt him, deceived him, and played him for a fool. It had been his way of dealing with the heartache. Keeping his mind busy while Brenda's complete opposite, at least physically, helped him heal.

He'd constructed this perfect woman from the leadings of

his heart. Now that she was here, for real, he wanted to learn what she was like and see exactly how opposite to Brenda she really was.

And working with her in the store for the next month and a half would provide that opportunity.

Chapter 3

Lynda watched Rob set up his display area while she remained behind the counter.

It had been a restless night. It felt like only a few hours since she'd last seen him. And now he was back.

She didn't know what to think. Of course she admired what he was doing. He had used the talent God had given him, not burying it in the sand, and made something good. She wished him every success, especially since his success would also add to her success in increasing her Master's talents and earning her a reward.

Except that she still hadn't quite come to terms with being a personality in his game.

It might have been flattering if he hadn't called the character that bore her face *perfect*.

She wasn't perfect. She was far from it. Yet, she was not quite as imperfect as she'd been not all that long ago.

She was still coming to terms with her new appearance— and now she couldn't have found a more shocking reminder of what she'd become. Her face had become manifested in a stranger's fantasy.

In her younger days, everyone always told her that appearances weren't important, yet her life proved that wasn't true. Now that she looked different, people treated her differently, and many times, it hurt.

Rob approached her and slid a key across the counter. "I've locked the computer to the display so it will be secure, but here's a key in case you've got to move it when I'm not here. Could you ask whoever opens the store to turn it on and set it to the demo mode? When people play the actual game they're more likely to buy a copy, but I'm still planning on being here whenever possible to help walk customers through the initial steps."

"How often do you expect to be here?"

"I wish I could be here the whole time the store is open, but I do need to sleep. Hopefully I can be here every day from noon until you close at 11:00 p.m. until this season's race is over and all the racing fans have gone home."

Lynda's stomach clenched. "People don't really start coming in droves until about two weeks before the actual race. Many come when the pretrials start, but most come just a few days before the real race. Right now, the only people who are here are those who want to take advantage of the preseason displays and activities."

"That's okay. I only have a finite amount of time, and I have to make the best of it. After the race is over, I'll have to leave the game and any marketing with all the vendors who chose to sell it and go back to my day job, no matter what happens. I want to make the best use of my time until then."

She tilted her head, crossed her arms, and studied him. "Just where is your day job? There are not a lot of businesses in Talladega that could utilize a full-time programmer."

"Birmingham. I lease one of those newer loft apartments downtown. It's great. I walk to work in about five minutes. Longer if I get sidetracked at Starbucks." He checked his watch. "It took me fifty minutes to drive here, without stopping for coffee. I'm thinking it will take me probably just over an hour in rush hour when it's time for me to come in the morning. I'm not used to that kind of commute. I shudder to think of how much money I'm going to spend on gas."

His eyes lost focus for a few seconds, then widened, and he looked out the window, staring off into nothing.

She didn't know him very well, but she had a feeling that he'd just had some kind of idea, and she had a hunch she wasn't going to like it.

"When I did my demographics of the area to choose which store would best meet my needs, I chose this one because it was closest to the campground, which is my first target market."

Lynda blinked. "Target market?"

"Families camp more than singles, and families with boys buy most computer games. People who travel in motor homes often have a computer or laptop with them to keep the kids occupied while the parents are driving. I've done my research. After a week of racing activities, it would be an added bonus to have the kids doing their own racing on the way home, on the computer."

"That's why you picked this store? It's the closest one to the biggest campground?"

"Pretty much. Being close to the campground gives me an

idea. I could save nearly two hours a day in travel time if I got a campsite." He pulled a PDA out of his pocket and called up the calculator feature. "Two hours a day, seven days a week, four point three weeks in a month—that's over sixty hours, which is over five whole days lost by driving back and forth." He knit his brows. "I don't like to waste that kind of time."

"You're going to live in a tent for a month?"

"No. I have a friend who owns one of those little round silver trailers. I could probably borrow it for a month—or rent a motor home, just to drive it here and park it. The campground has hookups and electricity. I've already checked."

"Right. Your target market needs electricity for their computers."

"You got it. Do you live close to here?"

"I don't think anyplace in Talladega is far from anywhere else. But yes. I live down the block. I walk to work in three minutes because the nearest Starbucks is out of town. But sometimes I stop and talk to my neighbors."

"It looks like a nice community."

"Yes. I like small town living."

"I've never lived in a small town. When I was a kid we lived in a very busy neighborhood, near the big hospital. Always lots of noise and lots of traffic."

She couldn't imagine it. Naturally the area surrounding the track was very busy when a race was on, mostly from the partying in the campgrounds. The noise from the track when the cars were racing was sometimes deafening. But that was temporary and worth it for the thrill of the races.

Lynda turned toward his display, which looked like the

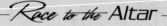

driver's seat of a car and included an accelerator pedal on the floor. He'd painted it in bright racing-car colors, his choices red and yellow, using the number 27. "That's pretty nice. Got any special reason for the number?"

"That's my age. How old are you?"

"Excuse me?"

"I was just curious about how old you are."

"Old enough to not want to tell you."

He grinned. "Fair enough. But I figure that you look about twenty-five. Am I close?"

Lynda gritted her teeth. If he was digging for information about his fantasy woman, he could guess all he wanted. "You're close, but you'll never know."

From the quirk of one eyebrow, she could tell she'd said the wrong thing. She'd unwittingly made it a challenge. She didn't want to do anything to encourage him to do anything other than sell his game and make money for Kathleen's store.

"Okay, you win. I'm twenty-six."

"Perfect," he said, barely loud enough for her to hear.

"Listen, if you're comparing the real me to your fantasy me, you can forget it. I'm not a curiosity item."

"That's not what I meant. I meant that twenty-six is a good age for a female driver. So I did well."

She decided to let it go.

"Now that you're all set up, what are you going to do? It's still not the busy season, although more and more people are coming for the Richard Petty Experience."

"I know. My first plan is to capitalize on those people."

"Have you ever done the Richard Petty Experience?"

"No. I did better than that. I did some competing in dirt track a few years ago, but I had to quit."

"That's too bad. But it's tough to get into even the Busch League."

"Yeah. Too expensive for my budget," he grumbled, but didn't elaborate.

It made her wonder if he'd done well, but not well enough to get sponsorship. If so, it would have been a shame, but racing was a dangerous sport and not for everyone. If computer racing met his needs, and he could also earn some money from it, then God truly had blessed him.

"I'm all ready for the crowds," he said as he rubbed his hands together, "even though I know the busy season won't start for a while yet. But now that I have a place all set up, it's time for me to start my online marketing campaign. I also need to send out my newsletter."

Lynda took that as her cue to return to checking her camping stock. Today was Friday, so the weekend campers would start arriving soon, which was the bulk of her business in the nonracing seasons when the children were in school.

It felt strangely comforting to have Rob in the store all afternoon. Except for racing season, one person worked alone. The only times there were two working in the store was when Kathleen, as the owner, worked in her office or during the shift change.

On schedule, Mary arrived at five. Lynda introduced her to Rob and explained what Rob was doing. Just as he'd been to her, he was gracious and cheerful and told Mary he was looking forward to spending time in the store with her.

However, when Lynda picked up her purse to leave, Rob approached her.

"I was wondering if I could take you somewhere for supper? It would be easier to talk when there aren't any customers interrupting. Do you have plans?"

There hadn't been many customers that day. However, the arrival of the weekend campers would soon change that.

"No, I don't have any plans, although we don't have to go out. We have some delicious sandwich wraps in stock. We could sit in the office and go over what you need."

"I was actually hoping you could show me around town." He checked his watch. "The sun won't set for a couple of hours, so we've got plenty of time."

She cleared her throat. "If you want to see Talladega, I can show you the whole thing before sunset if we go now. If you don't mind eating while you're driving."

He nodded. "That sounds good. I know you walked here, so I'll drive."

Chapter 4

O ver there, to your right, is the historic Ritz Theater. It's an Art Deco theater from the 1930s. They restored it just over ten years ago."

Rob knew he had a stupid grin on his face the whole time Lynda showed him the town. He couldn't wipe it off.

Talladega in the off-season was nothing like his home city of Birmingham. Talladega was small. His demographic study was fairly current and said the city's resident population was under 20,000. The existing businesses and recreational facilities matched the population. Not much, but adequate. And quiet.

He suspected that his desire to live here temporarily was more of a need to get out of his rut and away from his routine than to truly market his game. If he had to be honest with himself, it was still too early to start serious marketing. When he took the leave of absence from his job, he'd intended only to start feeling out the area, but when he saw the proximity to the campground, his mind was made up, and he had no more need to search.

That meant he had a couple of weeks of downtime before he needed to get serious. Yes, he'd be at the store marketing his game, but for the next two or three weeks, mostly he was on vacation.

"I'd like to go to the Davey Allison Memorial Walk of Fame on Sunday. Would you like to join me?"

"I go to church on Sundays."

"I do, too. I meant afterward. If you don't have other plans. I've got a few loose ends I'll have to tie up on the weekend since I'm going to be disappearing until mid-October. If not on Sunday, then how about another day? Taking the walk would be a great initiation into my temporary move to Talladega."

"I guess."

He'd hoped for more enthusiasm than that, but for now, it was good enough.

"I'd also like to go to the Motor Sports Hall of Fame one day. It's been years since I've been there."

She nodded and turned to look out the window. "Me, too."

He drove past a Piggly Wiggly. "That reminds me, I'm going to have to do a little grocery shopping every couple of days. My friend's trailer has a fridge and freezer, but they're not very big. Do you know the Pig's hours?"

"No. Sorry."

"What else is in Talladega that you think I'd be interested in?"

"There are hiking trails, if you're into that sort of thing."

"Actually, I am. I do a lot of walking. It's good exercise and doesn't cost a lot."

"That's true."

They drove for a while longer, but it wasn't long before they were almost back where they started.

"There's my church, down there."

Since there were no cars behind them, Rob slowed as they passed it. "It's small, but bigger than I thought it would be. My church at home has about five hundred people every service and lots of weekday activities."

"We have a social committee, too."

He waited for her to say exactly what it did, but she didn't.

"Are you always this talkative, or is it me?"

She glanced at him, then turned again and looked out the window as she spoke. "I'm sorry, but I'm finding this all a bit strange. I can't figure out what it is you're trying to accomplish."

"I just want to get to know you a little. It's not every day a man meets a woman he draws without having met her first."

"But it's only because of what I look like that you want to get to know me. What if I had red hair and green eyes? Or if I were only five feet tall? It would have been different."

He paused for a minute. "No, given the circumstances, I would still have wanted to get to know you and how your store operates. You know your client trends and the trends of this area better than I do. The better my game does, the better for both of us."

Finally she looked at him. "That makes sense, I guess."

"I can understand that you're feeling awkward. So let's just pretend that you're not in my game and take it from there. Okay?"

Rob also had to admit to himself that he was starting to feel lonely, especially in the evenings. He'd been going out with Brenda for a couple of years, and they'd been engaged for four

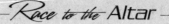

months of that time. At first he'd kept himself busy, but now that he'd finished all the programming and testing for his game, his evenings had been rather empty. Living at the campground would totally cut him off from everyone he knew, so it would be even worse.

More than most people, he knew what it was like to live life alone.

As a child he hadn't been able go outside to play with the neighborhood children very often, and he certainly couldn't get involved in sports. He'd spent most of his time alone in his room. Besides his computer, his primary contact with people was his mother sitting on the edge of the bed, reading to him, or the doctors and nurses in the hospital. His mother had homeschooled him until he was in his teens, because she'd been too worried about him to send him to public school. His primary social interaction had been at church, but because of his limitations, he was mostly a "Sunday-only" friend to the busy teen crowd. Knowing his limitations and the risks, he'd been grateful for the few friends he had.

It wasn't until he'd healed from the last surgery and had been given a clean bill of health at age seventeen that he could finally have a normal life. He'd done all he could to never live that lonely existence ever again.

When he and Brenda were a couple, they naturally spent a lot of time together. Their breakup was sudden and unexpected. He'd never felt so alone, because unlike when he was a child, he couldn't go running to his mother, and life and careers were pulling him and his guy friends in different directions.

Being alone and lonely was what motivated him to complete

his game. Now here he was.

He looked at Lynda. Not that he was looking for a marriage partner in a woman who was a virtual stranger to him, but he was looking for a friend away from home.

"Okay," Lynda said, turning her face to look out the window again. "I'll do my best to ignore the fact that the woman in your game is a dead ringer for me. Still, I want to clear the air right now. I'm not going to dinner with you. I want to do everything I can to help you, because if your game does well, my store will profit, too. But business and pleasure don't mix."

Rob blinked. He'd taken clients, both male and female, out for meals, and he'd never gotten a reaction like this. He didn't think he'd done anything wrong or offensive by asking, but obviously he had.

"I'm sorry if you took that the wrong way. I thought we should get to know each other a little, so you could trust me, since I'm going to be spending so much time in your store, a lot of it unattended."

Her eyes widened; she gulped and then ran her fingers through her hair. "No, I'm the one who should apologize. Even if we didn't have business interests together, I should be welcoming you into our community since you're going to be living here for longer than the average camper."

Rob turned briefly to see her face. She really did look distressed, which made Rob wonder if she'd recently been burned by love, too. Only he'd managed to work it out of his system by making an anti-Brenda. It just happened that his anti-Brenda was Lynda.

"It's okay," he said. "As it says in Galatians, 'Carry each other's

burdens, and in this way you will fulfill the law of Christ.'"

She smiled weakly at him. "Of course. Getting on the right track, the campground is only a few minutes from the store. When do you think you'll make the move?"

"Probably on Sunday night. There's a guy at church who's just moved back into town after being away for a missionary project. He'd probably love to stay at my place while he looks for something of his own."

"That sounds like a great idea. He can look after your plants and any pets, if you have any."

"I don't have any plants, but I do have a pet—a chinchilla. I thought I would just bring her with me. I'm not sure if I trust her with a stranger."

"You'd trust your home with a stranger, but not your rodent?"

Rob felt himself bristle. "Chinchillas may be rodents in the strict sense of the word, but she's a great pet. She's quiet, soft, easy to care for, and never gets fleas." And she made enough noise so he never felt totally alone.

"Have you ever been camping before? A trailer can get very hot inside during the daytime when it's all closed up and you're at the store. It isn't the place to leave an animal unattended."

"I never thought of that." He didn't really want to leave his pet at home, but he didn't want to spend two hours a day driving, either.

Lynda sighed. "If you're really going to camp for the time you're marketing your game, I suppose you can leave your animal at my house. It has a cage, doesn't it? I don't know anything about pets except dogs and cats."

"Yes, she has a cage. I can pick her up when the store closes, so you don't have to listen to her at night."

"Night?"

"Chinchillas are nocturnal. That's why she's a great pet for me. She's just waking up when I get home from work. She's at her best in the early evenings."

"Okay. . ." Lynda's voice trailed off. "I think this concludes our driving tour of Talladega. Unless you want to go out of town so I can show you the entrances to our hiking spots."

"No, I'm good. I should probably head home right now and make sure I really can borrow Matt's trailer and start making other arrangements. If you'll just give me directions to your house, I'll take you home."

Chapter 5

W ell, rodent, what would you like for supper today? Carrots are the Tuesday special. Enjoy."

Lynda watched Chiquita Chinchilla, otherwise known as Chikki, munch happily away at the carrot slice she'd offered.

Lynda had never had a pet before, but Rob's little rodent was a good choice for a busy person.

Yet, as busy as he was, Rob never appeared rushed. He never seemed stressed, not even when his boss called him this morning on his cell phone about some kind of emergency at his real job. Rob had tried to explain what to do in some kind of high-tech lingo, but his boss couldn't fix the problem. Rob had simply apologized to her, even though it wasn't necessary, put his game on demo mode, and left. Quietly and without protest, even though he didn't like the long, boring drive.

Yesterday, she'd seen him in action when a cranky customer couldn't steer the car properly on his game. Rob explained it quite well, then finally set it into slow motion until the man could do it, and then he put it back into real time. His patience was a sight to see. The man hadn't bought the game, nor had he thanked Rob for his time. After the man left, Rob had simply laughed and said it was the man's loss.

She'd never met anyone like him.

She wondered how he was doing, fixing his boss's problem. He'd expected to be back at suppertime, but he still hadn't returned by the time she'd closed the store at eleven o'clock.

Lynda continued to watch Chikki, who was indeed nocturnal. The world was settling down for the night, but Chikki was raring to go.

Even though there was bound to be overnight scampering, Lynda hoped Rob had the sense to stay in Birmingham for the night instead of driving the highway at midnight.

She'd just started scraping another carrot for Chikki when a car pulled into her driveway.

She opened the door just as Rob raised his fist to knock.

She raised her arms to shelter her head. "What are you doing here? I expected you to go home."

He froze, then quickly thrust his hand behind his back. "I didn't want to intrude on Steve. It's his place until I get back. Besides, I had to come and get Chikki."

Lynda straightened and stepped back so Rob could enter. "I wouldn't have minded. Today I picked her up while I was waiting for you. She's the softest little thing. And you're right, she is cuddly, although she was a bit nervous with me at first."

Rob smiled and followed her inside, heading straight for Chikki's cage. He picked her up, carrot and all, and petted her while she nibbled away. "That's probably because you were

nervous. Thanks for looking after her. I'll leave you alone. Sorry I'm so late. Glen messed it up even worse when he was trying to fix it. He thought he was doing me a favor by trying. I told him I locked him out of the database so next time he'll have to call me first."

"Are you allowed to do that to your boss? I would think. . ." Lynda's voice trailed off as she watched the last of the carrot disappear. "I just thought of something. You've probably been working the whole time you were gone. Did you have supper?"

He shook his head. "No time. But I didn't expect to take so long, either."

She suspected that he had been in a rush to pick up his little pet so it wouldn't be a nuisance. He probably hadn't taken the time even to get something at a drive-thru on the way to her home.

"Almost everything is closed by now. Instead of cooking, I have some leftovers in the fridge, if you're interested."

"No, I can't, I—" The grumbling of Rob's stomach cut off his words. His cheeks darkened. "Maybe I can. I am kinda hungry. Thanks."

Leaving him with his pet, Lynda hurried into the kitchen, cut him a large slice of lasagna, put it in the microwave, then returned to the living room.

"It will be ready to eat in two minutes. Would you like milk or juice with that?"

"Whatever is easiest, or you have the most of. I appreciate this."

"It's not a problem. I don't want you to go hungry."

She watched as he put Chikki back into her cage and

snapped the door closed.

"You were probably up at sunrise, weren't you?"

"Yes. I'm used to quiet in the mornings. The rustling from the other campers wakes me up, especially when the young kids start running around outside."

"Then this has been a long day for you. It's nearly midnight."

"Yes, I can hear that little excuse for a bed calling me. I don't think I'll have any trouble sleeping tonight. I might even sleep in. At least for a little while."

"Then I should give you a key to my house. The person who usually opens the store called in sick, so without Kathleen, that means I have to open at seven. You'll need to get in to drop Chikki off."

"Good idea. As long as you don't mind."

"Not at all. There's the beep; your supper is ready. The kitchen is this way. As you can tell, Chikki had some supper while you were gone."

He grinned. "So she's no longer 'your rodent.' She now has a name?"

Lynda felt herself blush. "Don't push your luck. She's still a rodent."

"There's still progress. At least she's a 'she' instead of an 'it.' You like her. You're weakening. I can tell."

Lynda snorted, then turned to lead him down the short hallway into the kitchen.

When she took the plate out of the microwave and turned around, Rob wasn't behind her.

She retraced her steps and found him standing in the

hallway, examining her photos hanging on the wall.

"Nice. Must be your family. They all look like you. Whose wedding?"

"My brother's."

"I can sure see the family resemblance. I hope you don't mind, but can I ask you something?" He paused, looking at all the pictures, studying everyone in them...especially the picture of herself. Taken two years ago... It was her brother's horrible wedding pictures that made her finally see herself as the world saw her and do something about it.

Lynda cringed. Waiting for the inevitable questions.

"You must be the photographer, I don't see you in any of these photos. But this must be your sister. She looks a lot like you. Really a lot. You could almost be twins. Are all of your family members believers?"

Lynda sagged with relief. "Yes. We all still go to the same church, too. You'll probably see everyone next Sunday."

He smiled. "That would be nice. I want to meet people while I'm staying here. I can't spend all my time working." He turned to face her. "I know you said you didn't want to get personal and mix business with pleasure, but does that extend to the rest of your family? Can you introduce me to your sister?"

Lynda could barely speak. "What?" she finally managed to sputter.

His expression became serious. "I can respect your reasons for not wanting to go out with me. But I have to admit, now that I'm unattached again, I am looking for someone. This time, I'm going to be smarter about it. I want to know that her faith is solid before things get too far. Which means before the first date. And if it works out, an hour isn't too far to drive. It wouldn't be like a long-distance relationship or anything. If nothing happens, then I'll simply have made a new friend for the short time I'm here."

"But. . ." Lynda looked at the picture. He really had no idea. But then, they'd only just met less than a week ago, and he hadn't met any of her friends or relatives yet, only the people she worked with, who weren't going to say anything about her past life. "Don't you care that the woman in this picture is so"— she gulped and forced herself to say the word—"fat?"

"A little, I guess. But the most important things about a person are what's inside, and that starts with a good relationship with God and being at peace with yourself. Of course, it's a health risk to be so overweight, which is bad, but I'm not the picture of perfect health, either."

She looked straight into his eyes. Aside from being a little pale, he looked fine. Very fine, actually.

"Are you not feeling well? Do you want to lie down?"

"It's okay. I was pretty sick as a child, but it was all corrected. I'm fine now. I just sometimes get tired faster than everyone else. You haven't answered my question."

Lynda looked at the picture, but her eyes didn't focus. "I don't have a sister," she mumbled.

"Then who. . . ?" His mouth dropped open as he stared at the picture, then back to her, a reaction she'd seen often from people who hadn't seen her for a long time. Once they figured out who she was, the shock was hard to hide.

"There's nothing wrong that would make you lose so much, is there? Just tell me to mind my own business if it's something

you don't want me to know."

"I appreciate your concern, but it was nothing like that. I just finally made up my mind to do something about it." It hadn't been easy, and at times she still struggled with discipline. "According to the charts, I still have another ten pounds to lose, but I can't seem to get the last of it off."

"Not that it's up to me, but I think you look good as you are. Great, in fact."

She was sure that was only because of his computer-generated image. She knew where she was supposed to be, but she couldn't do it. She was close, yet so far.

"Thanks. Now let's get into the kitchen before I have to put that piece of lasagna back in the microwave again."

His stomach grumbled one more time before he made it all the way into the kitchen. Still, even though she knew how hungry he was, he paused to pray before he began to eat.

"Mmm. This is great. Thanks. I needed this. I want to return the favor."

"It's just leftovers. All I want is for you to do well selling your game. So that means I want to keep you healthy and strong, which means fed."

He nodded. "It's easy now, but when the crowds start coming, for that one big week, I want to be at the store from opening at seven through closing at eleven until the day of the NEXTEL Cup race, when I'll have a booth. I had better start taking my vitamins now."

"Or eat your spinach."

"I hate spinach. But Chikki loves it. And speaking of Chikki, I think it's time for me to take her back to the trailer. Thanks for dinner, and I'll see you tomorrow."

As she watched him go, she had the feeling that with her admission, she'd suddenly fallen from the pedestal he'd put her on.

It was just as well. She didn't want him to feel anything for her except a shared desire to succeed on their combined business venture.

She watched the taillights of his car disappear down the street.

It didn't matter if he still would have asked her out when she was big. The only reason he was interested in her now, as she was, was because of his fantasy woman.

And it was a fantasy for her to think otherwise.

Chapter 6

R ob stood, stretched, and sat down again, grateful for the lull. It was still a month before the big crowds were due, but being Saturday and with the weekend campers, it had been a busy day in the store.

All afternoon the flow of people had been constant. He'd managed to sell nearly a dozen games since he'd arrived at lunchtime. Even though the profits weren't enough to make a day's salary, he was still happy. He was there for promotion, not discount volume.

He looked up at Lynda, who was straightening a pile of T-shirts that had been left in disarray by a pair of overzealous shoppers.

When she saw him watching her, she smiled. "It looks like you've been doing well today," she said as she patted the refolded pile.

"Yes. I also just got a notification that someone else joined my racing club."

"Racing club?"

"I started an online club, exclusive to my game. Gamers can race each other instead of the computer-generated drivers. Anyone, anywhere on the globe, has the potential to become a NASCAR driver, racing real people, not just a computer program. In a cyber sense, of course."

"That sounds like a good idea."

"I hope so. I have a note about the Web site packed with every game."

Already his club was starting to take off. He finally had more members he didn't know joining because of the game rather than people joining just because they were his friends. Word was starting to spread, and that was what he'd been praying for.

Another thing he'd been praying for in the past week was an opening with Lynda.

She'd drawn a dotted line in the sand between them that he wasn't allowed to cross. He didn't know why, and until he figured it out, he wouldn't dare pass into territory in which he wasn't welcome.

Yet he was welcome in her home, as long as he was with Chikki.

For a person who said she didn't like rodents, Lynda was developing a fast fondness for his chinchilla.

His pet was making more progress that he was. He needed to find a way to change that, but he didn't know how. So far, all he had was when they were together in the store, when it wasn't busy.

"Am I still invited to your church tomorrow?"

"Of course. It's not large, but I'm sure you'll meet some very interesting people."

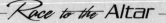

Meaning, he thought, *other women.* But he didn't want to meet other women. He wanted to spend his time with Lynda.

"We didn't last week, but now that I'm here, would you like to do the Davey Allison Memorial Walk of Fame with me?"

"I can't. I promised I'd take my first-grade Sunday school class out for a picnic lunch and then keep them busy for the afternoon. Unless. . ." Her voice trailed off.

He waited, giving her time to think.

Her eyes lit up. "Unless you want to help. We can take them to the Walk of Fame and go around the park. That would be such fun!"

"Uh, I guess there is no Chuck E. Cheese's in Talladega, is there?"

Her eyes narrowed. "If you don't want to go, just say so."

His mind went blank. He didn't interact with children. He didn't know anything about them. He hadn't interacted with children even when he was a child.

"I'm not sure what to do with the kids."

"Just make sure no one gets lost or separated from the group. Besides, I'm sure you'll win their hearts quickly, and they won't want to get too far from you."

He wasn't sure what she meant, but he was beginning to think that this would be his only chance to see her on Sunday.

He tried to imagine what it would be like. He couldn't picture her in church, behaving like a schoolmarm in front of a bunch of hyperactive kids. Instead, the image that burned in his mind was of Lynda dressed in NASCAR driver duds, her helmet cradled under one arm, while the kids followed her in a line, like the Pied Piper of racing.

Rob shook his head, and the image cleared. He wasn't a geeky teen boy living with the perfect computer-generated woman he'd created, like in a B-grade movie. Lynda was a very real person—a good, moral, upright Christian woman. She was probably an excellent Sunday school teacher, and the children in Talladega were no different from the children in Birmingham.

"Sure. It sounds like it could be fun. I guess."

He was going to spend the afternoon with her, away from the store.

It didn't matter that they wouldn't be alone.

After all, they were just children.

How hard could it be?

Chapter 7

Lynda grimaced along with Rob as she pressed the towel containing the bag of ice to his head.

"Does that hurt?"

He gritted his teeth, then smiled weakly. "I refuse to answer on the grounds of incrimination."

In other words, yes.

"I don't know what to say. If it wasn't for you, Kyle would have been seriously hurt."

"What was he thinking when he climbed on the memorial wall? Didn't it occur to him that he might fall off?"

"He's just a kid. I'm sure you did things like that when you were little."

"Never."

Lynda flinched at his sudden, and very definite, denial.

She could imagine what he was like as a child. He was probably very studious and no doubt spent a lot of time at his computer. She remembered him saying that he'd been pretty sick as a child, but when he was feeling well and out with the

other boys, she would think that he'd been just as wild and ram-
bunctious as the rest of them. He was tall, fit, and had amazing
stamina. She had no doubt that he'd done his share of climbing
and showing off, just like the other boys, especially when there
were little girls around.

Unless he was very conscientious about damaging his glasses.
She didn't know how well he could see without them. Today his
glasses had been knocked off as he dove to catch Kyle when he
saw the little boy starting to fall.

Before she could respond, Kyle's mother hurried back into
the room with another package of septic wipes.

Rob cringed. "No. Please. It's okay. It's clean. It just has to
heal."

Lynda sympathized with him. She was sure that they'd wiped
all the dirt off the abrasions on his arm, but when it started to
heal, it was going to hurt every time he moved. But at least his
elbow wasn't broken. It was a good thing he'd been wearing jeans.
If Rob had hit the ground with bare legs, his leg would have been
as badly scraped as his arm from the skid on the cement.

Evie's voice trembled when she spoke. "I'm so glad you're staying for dinner. I just wish there was a better way to thank you."

He smiled at Evie. "Don't worry about it. I'm just glad Kyle
wasn't hurt."

Lynda smiled at his graciousness, then looked up at Evie.
"Is there anything I can do to help?"

"Everything is just simmering. It's probably best if you just
hold that ice in place until the swelling goes down."

She was pretty sure that Rob could have held the towel all
by himself, but she wanted to hold it.

Evie stood in front of Rob, looking like she was unsure of his affirmation that the abrasions on his arm were clean enough. Finally, when it was clear that Rob wasn't going to take the box of wipes from her hands, she set it on the coffee table. "I don't believe we've met before. Are you from around here?"

"No. I'm from Birmingham."

Evie smiled. "It's so nice to see Lynda finally dating and now bringing you to church. Doesn't she look great?"

Lynda cringed. "But we're—"

Rob raised one hand, covering Lynda's hand with which she held the towel, halting her words. He smiled up at Evie. "Yeah, she does."

The timer on the oven dinged. "I have to check things. I'll call you when it's time to eat." She hustled off before Lynda could correct Evie's assumption.

"How could you let her think we were dating? I told you that business and pleasure don't mix."

Rob shrugged his shoulders. "It seemed important to her. Did you see the look in her eyes? She's just happy for you. We both know we're not really dating, and why, so there isn't a problem."

Lynda sighed. She'd seen similar sentiments to Evie's before. When Lynda had lost enough weight that she no longer had to shop for clothes in the larger-sizes stores, many of the ladies from church had suddenly turned into matchmakers.

They didn't understand that she hadn't changed anything except her outside appearance. When men who she'd once been interested in started calling, Lynda was no longer interested in them. They'd not been interested in her until she wore a smaller size. Their sudden attention told her everything she needed to know. That wasn't what she wanted in a relationship.

But how to find someone who could love her for what she was inside, she didn't know. When single women outnumbered the single men in her church, she was always left as the last choice. Now that men were actually calling—after ignoring her for so long—she couldn't trust their motives.

The difference with Rob was that she knew his motives. His reason for being interested in her was definitely unique.

When she was with him, she felt comfortable. Perhaps it was because he'd been honest with her from the first time they'd met. His motives were simple, even understandable and honest. Besides, the fact that he was leaving after the NEXTEL Cup race gave her a safety net.

It had been so long since she'd been on a real date, perhaps it wouldn't be such a bad idea. At least knowing when he was leaving, she knew what to expect.

She removed the ice from the lump on his temple. "I think this worked. It's gone down a lot." She stepped back. "Maybe you're right. It might keep things less complicated if we just let everyone think we're dating. We could even go out a few times. I'm sure you don't want to explore Talladega alone. Although, if you're planning on spending every evening at the store until it closes, that doesn't really allow much time for sightseeing."

He stilled as her words sank in. "That would be fun. I'd really like that. I don't have to be at the store every single hour of every day. At least not until the final week. It's not like I'm confined to a desk all day like I would be back at my day job. I can put it on demo mode, and we could go out and do something any time

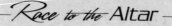

you haven't scheduled yourself to work. Even mornings. Just tell me when and we can—"

Kyle appeared at Rob's feet, a shy smile on his face. "Daddy's home, and Mommy says supper is ready."

Rob smiled at the small boy. "Thank you, Kyle. Want to show me where to go?"

Kyle broke out into full smile. "In the kitchen," he said and ran ahead, leaving them to follow.

Lynda walked into the kitchen, feeling lighter than she had for a long, long time.

Brad, Evie's husband, shook Rob's hand the moment he entered the room. "Thanks for catching Kyle. I don't know what gets into that kid sometimes. Sorry you got banged up."

"Just a few bruises, nothing serious," Rob replied.

Brad turned toward Lynda. "I hear Tyler's going to be doing a pit tour this time."

"Yes. He told me."

Rob turned to her, as well. "Who is Tyler?"

"Do you remember those wedding pictures you were looking at? Tyler was the best man at Andrew's wedding. He worked really hard, and he made it into a pit crew last year. He's been traveling, and he hasn't been home since February. But he e-mails me every once in a while to let me know what's happening on the race circuit and what he's doing with himself."

Rob's face tightened, and his eyes became unfocused for a second; then he quickly returned to his usual relaxed self. The change happened so quickly she just might have imagined it, except she knew she hadn't.

"I guess you're really looking forward to seeing him."

"Yes. I am." Tyler was the only one of her brother's friends who had never said a single mean word to her—to her face or behind her back. He'd also been very supportive during the times she'd struggled with her diet and exercise plan. Since he stuck to his own strict physical regimen, he'd nominated himself to be her personal trainer, whether she wanted one or not. She credited much of her success to Tyler's help, even though she hadn't always appreciated it at the time.

Brad turned back to Rob. "How's your game selling?"

Rob's brows knotted. "My game? I'm sorry, but I don't remember meeting you before. Have we met?"

Brad grinned. "This is a small town. Word travels fast. Do you have a copy with you? If you do, I'd like to try it after we're finished eating. Maybe I'll even buy one."

Evie elbowed her husband in the ribs. "Don't you think you're a little too old for computer games?"

Rob pressed one palm over his heart. "This isn't just a game. It's racing. NASCAR for everyone. Besides, a man is never too old for computer games. At least not good ones. And besides, who's to say he's not buying it for Kyle?"

Brad winked at Evie. "See?"

Rob paused. "I don't know if we should desert everyone to go play games, though."

Lynda patted him on the arm. "Go ahead. I don't mind. I'm sure Evie doesn't, either."

When everyone was finished eating, Rob and Brad disappeared into the room with the computer while Lynda helped Evie clean up the kitchen.

"I didn't know he was the one who's set up in your store,"

Evie said as she filled the sink with soapy water. "He's not what I expected."

"Expected?"

"Don't let Brad know I said this, but he's so handsome! When you finally scored, you scored big-time."

Lynda gritted her teeth. This was exactly what she'd lived with all her life, but from the opposite side. It didn't matter that he was handsome or not. What mattered was that he was smart. Funny. Kind. A man of God. Loyal. Hardworking. Dedicated. He had a soft spot for defenseless animals and little boys who fell off places they shouldn't have been. The list went on. And she didn't even know him that well.

Maybe, just maybe, she should get to know him—before he left and she'd never see him again.

Then she would know what kind of man to look for, when she got the confidence to start looking. Eventually it would happen. She didn't want to be single forever.

She turned to Evie. "Brad is handsome, too."

Evie grinned as she scrubbed at the roaster. "Yes, but he likes to think he's the most handsome man in my world. I may be married, but I'm not blind. Good luck to you."

"Yes, but—"

"Evie!" Brad burst into the room. "You should see this. Lynda is in Rob's game!"

Evie turned to her, an obvious question in her face. Lynda knew the story, but she couldn't give the reason because it was personal and not her story to tell. "It just kind of happened."

"I have to see this," Evie said, and she was out of the room in seconds flat.

Lynda spent the rest of the time sitting on the couch, watching Kyle and Rob construct buildings out of plastic bricks while Brad and Evie raced in the den.

Rob raised his arms over his head and stretched when Kyle ran to his bedroom to retrieve the base section for their ever-expanding structure.

"He sure is a cute kid. Busy, but cute."

"Yes, he is."

Rob listened to the clattering that echoed down the hall as Kyle searched for his missing piece. "So, how do you feel about kids?" he asked.

"I like kids. That should be obvious. I teach Sunday school."

"I mean, about having kids. Of your own. After you're married, of course."

"I guess I'd want kids. I haven't really thought about it much. You?"

"Yeah. Even after considering the risk, I do."

"Risk?"

He sighed heavily. "The risk of a heart defect."

She stared at him. "I don't understand."

He looked up at her. "I've got a congenital heart defect. Although it's not genetic. It was caused by some medications my mother took when she was pregnant. I had a miserable childhood and then some major surgery that finally corrected it when I was seventeen, followed by regular testing. The last set of tests said that, if I'm careful, I'll probably have an average life span. So, knowing that, would you marry me?"

Lynda nearly forgot to breathe.

"I hardly know you." She'd been to church with him exactly

once, and he'd never met her friends, except now with Evie and her family.

He smiled at her, and her breathing really did stop. "I know. But if you did. Would you consider someone who wasn't the picture of perfect health? I know you can't speak for every woman on the planet, but do you think that would make a difference?"

Her heart pounded at the realization that she'd misunderstood. It was a hypothetical question.

She also told herself not to be disappointed.

"I don't think it would. I wouldn't refuse to marry someone just because they drove a car in heavy traffic, which would increase the likelihood of a car accident."

Since she knew that he'd been very hurt from the breakup of his engagement, she wondered if his health were an issue. However, Kyle's return prevented her from asking. Besides, if he wanted her to know the details, he would tell her. If not, it wasn't her place to ask.

Not long after Kyle's return, Brad and Evie also joined them, rather sheepishly.

Brad handed Rob the money for the game, grinning through the entire transaction. "That game is great! If I had a bigger monitor, it would feel like I was in a real car."

Rob nodded. "I designed it specifically to have realistic vehicle dynamics. I calculated tire grip in different conditions, and the wear before a pit stop and tire changes are needed. Suspension, handling, tire pressure, wedge, gearing, anti-sway bar. Everything. There are racing tips from some of the greats—Greg Biffle, Dave Blaney, Kurt and Kyle Busch, and my personal favorite, Dale Earnhardt Jr, to name a few."

Brad's grin widened. "I just joined your club, too. I think it's great that you have Lynda in there. Would it be hard to make a driver that looked like me? Or is that too much to ask?"

Rob thought for a few seconds. "It's possible, I suppose. Not on the game itself, because the content is now under NAS-CAR's control and regulations. But I could for the club. I'm just not sure how long it would take. It's a lot of programming."

"Let me know how much it would cost. I'm interested."

"Cost? But—"

Brad held up one palm toward Rob to cut off his words. "I didn't mean for you to do it for free. Your time is valuable. I was thinking about the reaction I'd get from the guys at work. It would be worth it for me."

"Okay. I'll let you know."

Lynda stood. "I think it's time we got going. I have to open the store in the morning, and I have to check what stock was sold over the weekend before I do that. It's going to be an early morning."

Rob also stood. "It was great meeting you both. Thanks for supper. And I'll be in touch."

Chapter 8

"Hi, Rob," a husky feminine voice drawled behind him. His fingers froze on the keyboard. All the formulas in his mind crashed.

Rob spun around.

He blinked to clear his vision, but nothing changed. The object of his nightmares really was there.

He forced his vocal chords to function. "What are you doing here?"

She smiled. The same smile that once set his heart into overdrive now turned it into a cold, hard rock in the center of his chest.

"I came to see how you're doing with your game." Her voice lowered to an even more husky pitch. "And to tell you how much I've missed you."

"You shouldn't have come."

"I had to. We need to talk."

"I figure all the talking that needed to be done has been done. Now if you'll excuse me, I'm quite busy. Good-bye, Brenda."

He called up his file, knowing his concentration was blown, but he could at least read what he had done to keep himself busy until she left.

Rob gritted his teeth, sensing her still standing behind him. Of course, nothing could be so easy. He wanted to know how she found out where he was, but he hadn't made it a secret. His friends all knew where he was, and he'd even given Steve the phone number at the store, just in case he forgot to charge his cell phone and something needed his attention at his apartment.

"I guess you're still angry with me, and I can't blame you. I came here to tell you in person that I'm sorry, and I'm asking if you'll forgive me."

"We've been over this already. Nothing has changed."

Her voice dropped to barely above a whisper. " 'Be kind and compassionate to one another, forgiving each other, just as in Christ God forgave you.' That's Ephesians 4: 32."

Slowly, he turned the chair around again to face her.

"You pick one verse to memorize. I can just see you picking that one. I've got news for you, Brenda. I've prayed and prayed about this and about us. I have forgiven you, which is what God wants me to do. But He doesn't command me to trust you and set myself up to get kicked again. God wants us to be compassionate. He doesn't want us to be stupid."

"I know. But what I did was wrong."

"Yes, it was."

Her eyes became glassy, and silent tears started to flow. "I made a mistake. A big mistake. I'm sorry."

"No, Brenda, you made more than a mistake. You made a choice to do what you did. I thought about it and prayed about

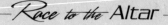

it, and it's over. I think you should go home." He checked his watch. "Shouldn't you be at work? Or did you lie to them, too, and phone in sick?"

She stiffened. "I asked for the day off to take care of an urgent personal matter. I thought we could talk."

"There's nothing to talk about. I'm sorry, but I don't love you anymore."

Brenda gasped, pressed her hands over her mouth, made a choking sound, and ran out the door.

Rob stared after her, not really seeing anything.

Plain tears, he could handle, but not this.

He felt dead inside. Numb.

He'd known that, one day, he would have to talk to her again, but he hadn't anticipated her begging or an apology. He certainly hadn't expected her to seek him out or to go so far out of her comfort zone.

"Rob?" another female voice sounded behind him.

He turned around, slowly this time.

Lynda stood before him, her eyes big and wide. Sympathy surrounded her like a halo.

She was the best thing he'd ever seen.

"That was her, wasn't it?"

"Yeah," he muttered, hating that his voice came out like he was strangling.

Without a word spoken, she reached down, clasped his bigger hand with her smaller one, and pulled gently, coaxing him to stand. "Let's go into Kathleen's office, where it's private."

Like a lamb being led to the slaughter, he followed.

Once inside, she didn't speak. Gently, she closed the door

behind them, pulled him closer, and then wrapped her arms around him, just tight enough to feel snuggled, emphasized by her tiny hands pressed into his back.

He leaned into her, nestled his cheek into the hair at her temple, slipped his arms around her, and held her in the same way.

She didn't say a word. Which was good, because he didn't feel like talking.

Her touch told him she cared enough about his struggles without needing to talk about them to death. Her warm touch told him without words that he wasn't alone, which was what he needed.

He hadn't talked to anyone about Brenda, about how she'd turned his life upside down and stomped his soul flat. He'd kept it all locked inside, where such things belonged.

The only time he'd said anything to anyone was when he tried to explain as briefly as he could to Lynda why he had her image in his computer. He hadn't said much, but even that little bit had lifted a weight off his shoulders.

She gave him a little squeeze and sighed. With the sound and the gesture, a sense of relaxation seeped into him, right where he needed it.

He hadn't planned on something like this happening, but he was glad it had.

He needed this, and he needed Lynda.

Was meeting her divine intervention? He'd asked himself that before, and he still didn't know.

For the first time, he needed to talk about what happened.

But not now. There was no one tending the store. A thief could have backed a truck in and taken everything, for all the

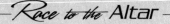
time they'd been behind the closed door.

Slowly he backed up. His heart pounded as he reached up and slowly touched Lynda's cheek with the tips of his fingers. "I'm good. Thanks. Now let's get back to work."

Chapter 9

Every time she had a chance, Lynda sneaked a peek at Rob.

She'd seen Brenda's picture the first day they'd met, but seeing her in person was like a kick in the solar plexus.

Brenda was gorgeous. Thin. Classy.

And Lynda was. . .just Lynda.

She didn't want to feel jealous, but she did.

Brenda had also left sobbing her eyes out.

It had been hours, but it still felt like only minutes.

She'd never witnessed a lovers' spat before, and she never wanted to again. She'd felt like she was intruding, but she couldn't escape—she had a store to run, and Lynda couldn't abandon it.

Lynda reached up to straighten the rack of Richard Petty sunglasses when the bell tinkled, signifying someone else had entered the store.

The expensive sunglasses in her fingers nearly hit the floor.

Brenda was back.

Poised. Regal. Her step was so dainty she almost floated.

Lynda wanted to call out to Rob that Brenda was back, but she couldn't because there were customers in the store, three of them surrounding him while he ran through the demo of his game.

Without announcing herself, Brenda stepped behind Rob, blending in with the mother, father, and son who were watching Rob's cars roar down the oval track.

Fortunately, he didn't notice she was there.

Lynda watched. . .because she couldn't *not* watch.

She'd heard his spiel so many times she had it memorized.

He'd displayed the warm-up track, the choices of "real" raceways, the cars, and next was the choice of drivers.

Lynda watched Brenda's face. She seemed genuinely happy for Rob, a completely different person than the first time she'd walked in.

Rob smiled as he handed the father a case, obviously having made a sale, then explained about his online game. At that point, Brenda must have heard enough, because she walked away from Rob and over to the sales counter.

To her.

Lynda tried to relax and smile politely. "Can I help you with something?"

Brenda smiled graciously. "I need something to drink. Do you have. . . ?" Brenda's voice trailed off. Her eyes widened, then narrowed into slits. "He's put you in that game! You're the woman driver. It was supposed to be me, but it's you! How. . . ?" Brenda's face tightened, she turned and stomped toward Rob at the same time as the happy family approached the counter with their new purchase.

Lynda focused her attention and her manners on her customers, but it wasn't easy. Brenda didn't shout, but the harshness in her voice was unmistakable, as was the accusation in her pointing finger.

Lynda hurried with the transaction, hating to rush anyone out of the store, but she didn't want the family to think Brenda was an unhappy customer—nor did she want to explain the situation.

Just as the door closed behind them, Brenda spun around and headed toward the exit, except this time instead of crying, she was the epitome of rage.

The second Brenda left, Lynda turned toward Rob. He remained seated at his console, staring at the door through which Brenda had just passed, like he'd been blindsided by a truck.

"I'm so sorry," he muttered as he stood and walked to the counter. "I would never have thought she'd be back."

"She said it was supposed to be her in your game."

"I never promised her that. Even if I did, when we split up, that would have erased any obligation." He shook his head. "I can't believe it. She accused me of cheating on her, and that's why I've got your picture in the game instead of hers."

"That's ridiculous. We hadn't met at that time. Besides, I thought you finished the game after you split up. Even if it really was me, I mean the real me, you could have chosen whomever you wanted your drivers to look like."

"I know." He sighed. "I think she's trying to minimize what she did. You see, we didn't split up because I was cheating on her. One of the reasons we split up was because she was cheating on me."

"One? You mean there were more reasons than one?"

"Another reason was because she only went to church because I did, not because of any faith of her own. She believed in God as the Creator of the universe, but nothing more—it wasn't personal. And then, to make it worse, she lied about it. I still can't believe she would lie about her relationship with God. I mean, it's God! You do not lie to God. Then she said it wasn't important; it wasn't like God was going to send a bolt of lightning and strike her down."

"She said that?"

"Yes. She tried to gloss over it and kept telling me how much she loved me, and like a fool, I believed what I wanted to believe. The end came when my best friend saw her with her other boyfriend, and a few days later, I did, too. She wants me to forgive her and take her back, but anything I felt for her before is gone. I trusted her. First she lied to me, and then she cheated on me. I can't believe I was so gullible." He made a weak laugh. "I also can't believe I'm telling you this. Especially here. In the middle of the store."

Lynda stared into his eyes. The pain she saw was real and fresh, and her heart broke for him. It was such a weak word, but above all, Rob was a *nice* man. He was easy to trust, because trusting came easy to him, which was probably why he was so hurt.

She wanted to cry for him, but he didn't need that—he needed her support. She didn't want to hate Brenda, but it was hard. Tonight she would remember to pray for her, as in praying for your enemies.

"I think that trust and fidelity are the backbone of a marriage, too. The man I marry will have to share my level of faith, as well."

His eyes softened. "You know, it's not quite an hour's drive between your place and my place. That's not really so far."

Lynda gulped. She wanted to believe that was a hint, but the thought of Rob actually being interested in her as a potential wife frightened her more than the thought of being alone. "I'm not sure I'm ready for that kind of thing yet."

"That's okay. I thought I was, but today, I'm not so sure anymore, either."

Lynda leaned toward him, resting her elbows on the counter between them. "I have an idea. I know what will make us both feel better. Tyler's in town to do pit tours, and they start today. He got me a special pass. Do you want to come with me?"

She'd always been good in a crowd, when no one was in a position to get individual attention. There was safety in numbers, and the pits were always well populated before the start of the races.

"Say the word, and I'm there."

"Good. Mary's coming in about an hour, and when she gets here, we're gone."

Chapter 10

Rob looked up at Tyler as he shook his hand. At six feet tall, he usually looked down on everyone else, but Tyler was at least two inches taller than he was.

He was also built like a professional wrestler, which made sense, because Tyler was the fuel guy.

Rob couldn't picture himself picking up an eighty-pound tank and running it across the pit to have the car fueled and back on the track in the required 12.5 seconds.

He stood back while Tyler showed everything to Lynda, who was hanging on his every word.

Rob didn't want to feel jealous, but he did.

"We're allowed to have seven over the wall," Tyler said, pointing to the two-foot wall separating the pit from the storage area. "The only time we come over the wall is when the car arrives."

Lynda's eyebrows quirked, and she stared at the wall. "Really? But it seems like such a beehive of activity when the car comes in."

Tyler grinned, resting his hands on his hips. "It is. We have more guys who stay behind the wall. One of them holds out the sign on a long stick that shows our driver where to stop. They're going very fast out there, and they can't slow down any more than they have to, because every hundredth of a second counts."

She nodded. "That makes sense."

"Then there's another guy who stays behind the wall and gives the driver a drink with a stick, and another one who cleans the grill with a stick."

"They must have very strong arms to do that."

"Yes. You'd be surprised how hard it is until you try it. Then there's the pit crew chief who gives us all direction by radio, so he doesn't have to go over the wall, either. The crew that does go over the wall totals seven guys. A jackman, two tire guys, two helpers, the fuel guy." He patted his own chest. "That's me. The seventh is a catcher, who holds a can to catch any spills, which is required by the rules. One of us pulls off the windshield cover. Then, in hopefully less than 12.5 seconds, we're done and the car is back on the track, and we're back on the other side of the wall. And watching it all is a NASCAR official, who comes over the wall to make sure no one cheats."

"Wow," Lynda said, gauging the distance a man had to master with the stick over the wall and not whack anyone or anything.

Rob stepped forward. "Are there ever any women in the pit crews?"

Tyler nodded. "Some, but not many. It's very physically demanding, and we all have to be expert mechanics. Sometimes you have to do more than the basics, in not a lot of time. Now

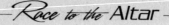

let me show you what's on the other side of the wall."

Tyler gave them both a very interesting explanation of the tools and equipment stored, ready for use within a second's notice.

When Tyler was showing Lynda a very expensive-looking tire-pressure gauge, two other pit crew members, dressed in full NASCAR duds, joined them.

"Hey, wanna introduce me?" one of them asked, stepping between Tyler and Lynda.

Tyler shoved the new guy out of the way and slipped one arm around Lynda's shoulders. "This hot babe is Lynda, the sister of a very good friend of mine, if you catch my drift, boys. Fortunately for you, she's still single and looking for Mister Right. Which you may or may not be. I'm taking applications, and anyone who dates her has to pass my inspection."

The three of them jostled around with playful pushing and shoving, but deep down, Rob didn't think Tyler was kidding.

Rob wondered if he would pass muster. He kept himself in decent physical condition because he had to, but it was nothing truly strenuous or muscle building. He did just enough to keep himself toned. He lived by his brain, not by his physical strength.

He thought he saw Lynda cringe as she stepped back. "Sorry, guys, but I'm with someone."

All three men turned and glared at Rob.

He smiled and waved. "Sorry, guys. She's mine." At least, in his dreams, she was. "Come on, sweetheart. It's time for supper. Let's go." He stepped forward and slipped his arm around Lynda's waist.

Tyler's mouth dropped open. Rob didn't know if that was a good or bad reaction. "How about that?" Tyler mumbled as Rob led Lynda to the parking lot.

Rob didn't take his arm away until they arrived back at his car. He quickly disengaged the lock, and they both slipped inside.

"Where do you want to go?"

"It doesn't matter. Wherever you want."

He grasped the steering wheel, but didn't turn the engine on. "Is something wrong?"

She shook her head. "No. Not really. It's just that when men do stuff like that, I can't help but wonder what they're thinking. Things like that never used to happen to me. I'm still the same person. Life is so unfair."

He reached to her and brushed her cheek with his fingers. "It sometimes seems that way, but God has a reason for everything He allows to happen."

She looked at him with sad, big, wide, gorgeous eyes, and he lost it.

"And I'm sure there's a reason for this," he said, his voice low and husky. "I just haven't figured it out yet."

He cupped her cheeks with his palms, leaned forward, and kissed her.

When she made a little whimper, he lost it even worse.

His heart pounded, and his brain sizzled.

He tilted his head, and kissed her again, this time more slowly and with more of his heart involved.

He was falling in love with the woman of his dreams.

When he broke away, he didn't want to stop looking at her,

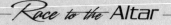

but he had to in order to drive.

"Where do you want to go?" he asked, when he figured his voice would finally work.

"Uh. . .anywhere you want."

He wanted to ask her what was cozy and romantic in Talladega, but he didn't want to let her know what he was thinking, nor did he want to do anything to jeopardize what had just happened.

"I have an idea," he said. "Let's go to your place to pick up Chikki, and I have the perfect place in mind. It's cozy, friendly, very casual, and the food is great."

She smiled. "That sounds good. Where?"

"My trailer. For a barbecue."

He didn't let her obvious shock that he was cooking dampen his enthusiasm. He was a decent cook, and this was the time to prove it.

In record time, he had a couple of pieces of chicken on the grill.

"The potato salad is bought, but I cut the carrots all by myself."

"I'm impressed. Except I think they're more for Chikki than for us."

"I'll never tell."

When the chicken was cooked to perfection, they paused to pray for their meal, and began to eat.

"This is really good. Thank you."

He wanted to tell her that he would make her a really good husband one day, but he kept his sentiments to himself. "You're welcome" was all he said.

After supper they walked around the campground. He wanted to hold her hand, except she insisted on taking Chikki, who happily nestled into Lynda's arms while they walked slowly around the campground.

"I can't believe that it's only a few weeks until the big race. But already the campground is starting to fill up. Pretty soon every place a camper or tent can go will be filled."

"That's why I'm here. To sell my game to the crowds. I've booked a booth for the day of the big race. Would you like to work it with me? It will be fun."

It would also his last day in Talladega before he had to go back to work in Birmingham, and he didn't want to be separated from Lynda on his last day there.

"I've never done a booth, but I'm always willing to try something new. But before then, just wait until you see what it's like in the store. Next weekend, the big rush begins."

"That's the moment I've been working up to. I can hardly wait."

Chapter 11

W hat are you doing?"

For once, Rob didn't answer. His face was locked in concentration as he steered his car on the screen.

Today he looked even better than he normally did. He was dressed in NASCAR racing gear, his colors red and yellow, with the number 27 emblazoned on his jacket.

"Wow. How fast are you going? Everything is just whizzing by."

Again, he didn't answer.

The checkered flag waved in front of him, and his car slowed. "I did it!" He waited for the points to tally. "This is the qualifier. I'm in."

"I didn't realize you were racing for real. Sorry. Is this a game race or a club race?"

"Club. What about you? You joined, and there happens to be a driver who looks just like you. You should do the qualifier, too. I can look after the store while you do that."

"Okay." She shouldn't have agreed so easily, but she truly enjoyed Rob's game. Besides, since she was one of the characters, she had to race.

The time went by quickly, and even though she didn't place first, she did qualify.

As the day went by, Lynda could see that the calendar had indeed marched on. The store was very busy, even busier than the previous season, which meant that many had come just to get Rob's game. The best part was that while they were there, they purchased their supplies, too.

Rob checked the time. "I promised my boss I'd do something for him. Would you mind giving a pitch for me if anyone comes in?"

"Sure. I think I have most of your pitch memorized by now, anyway."

He grinned, nodded, then pulled up a program and started working on some kind of code. Lynda left him alone, and everything was going well until Brenda walked in.

"I'd like to buy one of those T-shirts and a hat in the same color. And the sunglasses."

Lynda wondered if Brenda was really interested in the NASCAR products or if she was trying to gain Rob's attention.

Lynda was about to ring up Brenda's purchases, when Brenda raised a hand.

"Wait. I need to try it on."

"Try it on? It's a T-shirt. Just hold it up."

Brenda grabbed the T-shirt and pranced to Rob's display. "What do you think?" she asked as she held it up to her chest, making sure she pressed it down in all the right places.

"Nice," Rob muttered, without looking up from his computer.

"What about the color?"

"It's fine," he said as he typed.

She slipped the sunglasses on and puckered her lips. "Do these suit me? Or should I buy the other ones?"

"Buy whichever ones have better UV protection."

She waited for him to say more, but he didn't. She made a *humph* sound and returned to the checkout counter. "That's everything for me."

Lynda thought she heard Rob mutter, "I certainly hope so," but she wasn't absolutely positive.

Seeing Brenda again brought all her fears and insecurities to the surface once more. If she had to compete, Lynda was sure to come out the loser.

"Good riddance," Rob muttered as the door closed behind Brenda. He shut down his program and got up to make a fresh pot of coffee for a couple of guys who walked in while Lynda helped a family select some camping supplies. A few more people hovered in different places, waiting for help.

Two more men came in, but this time, Lynda recognized them as having purchased Rob's game earlier that day.

They sauntered to the T-shirt rack, and one of them began reading labels.

Lynda smothered a grin. It was good to see someone read the washing instructions before they made a purchase. Proper care would lengthen the life and clarity of the decal, which was the point of the shirts, especially considering the price.

"Good day, gentlemen. Can I help you with something?"

"Yeah. My girlfriend says not to buy anything that you have

to dry clean. I don't know how to tell if. . . Hey! You're the woman in that new game." He elbowed his friend in the ribs. "Look at her! She's real!"

He turned back to her. "Are you in the club?"

"Yes, of course."

He elbowed his friend again. "She's in the club."

"I'm not deaf," his friend grumbled. "I heard her."

The first man read her name tag. "She's the manager here," he said, as if she wasn't standing right there. "A real person."

The young man glanced at Rob, who was busy with another demo. He almost elbowed his friend again, but this time, his friend moved. "Wouldn't it be something if I could be in there, as one of the drivers, with my own face in the game? And if I could show Brittany? She'd think I was so hot."

He turned to Lynda. "If he made you in the game, do you think he could make me?"

Lynda thought of Rob's promise to Brad. "Maybe, but you'd have to ask him, not me."

They were gone in a split second, hovering over Rob until he was finished with his demonstration. They bombarded him with questions, then left happy, telling Lynda the answer.

Lynda didn't have a chance to speak to Rob again until she locked the doors at 11:00 p.m. By then, the two young men had started an online chat group and announced that they were personally going to be driving in the game. Rob now had three more requests from people who also wanted to be characters.

The same as every other night, Rob gave her a ride back to her house to collect Chikki.

"Are you going to put those two in the game? How many

have you got now?"

"At last count, seven."

"I hope they don't expect you to be done tomorrow."

"They don't. Everyone knows they have to wait their turn, and the lineup is getting longer."

"Have you thought of putting your own face in there? It's your game, after all."

"Naw. My ego doesn't need it. Besides, my name is on the copyright in nice big letters. But since you're the person whose real face is in the actual program, not just in the club, I need to ask if you can be more involved in the racing. You're good for publicity. The best selling tool I have is word of mouth from satisfied customers. I've already asked Brad to race often. But face it, the guys aren't as interested in seeing him as they are in seeing you. There was some chatter on the loop about you, too. They all want to see how you drive."

"Me? I like the racing, but I don't want people to watch me."

"Sorry, but I didn't plan this. Now that more racing fever is starting, it's impossible to stop. It's also good for sales. Please?"

She looked up into his eyes. He really didn't know what he was asking.

All her life, she'd been ignored, even deliberately cast aside. Suddenly, because of the way she now looked, the opposite was happening.

It frightened her, because she didn't know what to do.

She thought of how the NASCAR drivers handled their notoriety. Some, of course, handled it better than others.

She closed her eyes, able to picture her favorite drivers over the years and how they'd faced the crowds, in wins and in losses.

She thought of her favorite driver, Kyle Busch, and how he'd once changed teams.

She clearly remembered in the spring of 2006, Jimmie Johnson took his first Talladega win in the Aaron's 499. She'd got the day off work and been there, in person. It had been a great race and a great day. Jimmie had learned and moved forward from all his mistakes. He hadn't let his past hold him back, and he won the NEXTEL cup. He'd been jubilant, and the crowd was jubilant with him.

Lynda wanted to be jubilant, too. She'd worked hard to overcome what had held her down all her life. Just like Kyle Busch, she'd also changed teams. She could now be a winner. She had a goal, and that was to help Rob sell his game, earning a commission on every sale—which would prove she had what it took to manage and then ultimately buy the store when the time was right.

"Okay, I'll do it. Would you like to stay for a cup of tea? This might be your last chance to relax."

"I would love to, but I really should get home and get working on those faces. From here, time is going to be tight. I'll see you tomorrow, same time, same place."

Chapter 12

R ob fumed inwardly as once again, Brenda sauntered
out of the store.

She'd made an appearance at least three times a
day since she first arrived in Talladega.

He wanted to tell her to leave and not come back, but every
time she came in, she also stopped to buy something. Brenda
now owned more sunglasses than she'd wear in a lifetime, and
every color NASCAR hat made. She'd even bought an emergency road-kit, complete with a self-charging flashlight and a
set of tools that she didn't know how to use—or name.

She was a nuisance, but she was a paying nuisance.

He couldn't turn away business for Lynda when every sale
was important. Therefore, he gritted his teeth and said nothing,
even though it hurt.

He hadn't wanted this to happen. Since Lynda wasn't opening
up emotionally to him, he'd wanted to show her how successful he
could be with his business savvy and his showmanship. Instead,
she'd been dragged into the middle of his personal problems.

He wanted to make it right and take her with him on a real relationship. But time was running out.

The race was on. Not a race on cultured pavement, but a race to show her that he could be the man to bring her to the finish line of life, and love, before the checkered flag brought everything to a stop.

He motioned to Lynda to join him in Kathleen's office for a few minutes to gulp down a quick lunch. The store had been so busy that they'd kept working. Both their stomachs were grumbling, and it was time to take a short break.

Rob grabbed a couple of sandwich wraps while Lynda got their coffee. They hurried into office, but kept the door open in case they had to cut their break short.

"I hope Mary's going to be okay out there alone."

"We won't be long," he said between bites. "By the way, I hear the club is divided fifty-fifty about us."

"Oh?"

He grinned. "Everyone agrees that the two of us are the best drivers and that one of us is going to win the trophy, but it's divided right down the middle about who is going to win—you or me."

"That's easy. Me." Lynda flicked her hair over her shoulder and turned the television in the corner on to the Craftsman Truck series, in progress. "I remember the first time I saw a NASTRUCK race. I was just a kid, and I was afraid to go in a pickup truck for years."

Rob smiled. "Yeah. Those are pretty powerful machines. When I was in my teens, my dad got a Chevy truck, so I used to dream about being Mike Bliss."

"I remember some of his early races. I think. . . Oh, no. She's back."

Rob didn't have to ask who Lynda was referring to.

This time, Brenda was at the small display of pet products, examining a dog leash in blazing NASCAR colors with NASCAR logos running the entire length.

She didn't even have a dog. She said she was allergic to them.

"That does it," he snapped.

He strode out of the office and stepped between Brenda and the display rack just as she was starting to reach for a Flying Wheel rope toy.

"I've had enough. Seeing you a hundred times a day isn't going to change my mind. What do you think you're going to accomplish?"

Her voice came out sounding choked. "I'm trying to show you that I'm sorry and that I can be a nice person."

"By maxing out your credit card on stuff you don't need? Give me a break. You're also not being very nice to Lynda. You owe her an apology for being so rude."

A tear rolled down Brenda's cheek. "You'd make me apologize? Don't you love me at all? Just a little bit?"

He thought about all their time together. He thought he'd loved her, but most of their relationship had been a lie, at least on her side. She didn't share his love for God. She didn't like the computer. He doubted that she even liked his friends. Now she thought she was too good to apologize to Lynda.

He'd had enough. "I'm sorry, Brenda, but it's over. You have to accept that and move on, as I have."

She glanced toward Lynda. "Because of her?"

"You know that it was over before I met Lynda. It was over when I found you with Josh. I felt like you ripped my heart out. I can't go back. I'll never be able to trust you. I don't know what you want in a relationship, but if you could sneak around on the man you were supposed to be marrying, I don't think you know, either. Good-bye, Brenda. I'll probably see you around town. Good luck, and I hope you find what you're seeking."

Again, Brenda glanced toward Lynda. "Can we be friends, then? Maybe you'll think of me and invite me to your wedding."

He froze at the word. He hadn't thought specifically about a wedding, but now that it had been said, that was exactly what he wanted.

He turned around, wondering if proposing to Lynda in Kathleen's office might give them something to look back at and laugh about in their retirement years, but Lynda wasn't in the office. Her half-eaten sandwich was in the middle of the desk, and she was back in the store, trying to help a dozen customers find what they needed quickly and get back on the grounds of the superspeedway.

But that was okay.

Tomorrow, after the big NEXTEL Cup race, the club's trophy race was scheduled. They would be sitting side-by-side, Lynda on her PC and him with his laptop, racing for the championship.

He didn't know which one of them would win, but even if he didn't get the trophy, if she told him that she loved him, then they would both finish as winners.

Chapter 13

The roar of the cars made Lynda's ears ring, even at a distance.

Rob stiffened at the sound of the crowd, which was shouting at something that was happening on the track. "Is every race like this? Believe it or not, I've never been on the grounds during a race."

Lynda smiled. She was glad they were seated safely in their booth, unaffected by the crowds, except for proximity. "Talladega Superspeedway seats 170,000 people. Every seat is full."

At the same time, they looked at the small closed-circuit TV in their booth, so they wouldn't miss the race.

"I see lots of empty seats when the camera pans the crowd."

"The race is three hours long. During the whole race, people walk around, buy souvenirs, visit with friends, check out the grounds, and eat. It isn't until the last few laps when everyone is in their seats at the same time. It's a sight to see. What's really something is when the winner takes the checkered flag. The roar of the crowd is louder than the cars."

"I'll bet."

They stopped talking while some people stopped to browse through their booth. Rob's game was selling well, and Lynda brought some NASCAR-licensed souvenirs, which were also being eagerly snapped up by racing fans.

"You should have seen the campground this morning. Every possible space that could have something on it is taken. And the food! It's like a never-ending banquet. Strangers are feeding me. There's everything. Cajun. Hot dogs and corn. Ribs. Pork chops. And pulled pork!" He grinned and rubbed his stomach. "Soft pretzels. Everything you could think of. Lots of beer, too, but I passed on that. People barbecuing in the back of their pickup trucks. And get this. I couldn't count all the people out there with good old-fashioned charcoal instead of propane. I've never seen anything like it."

"Fun, isn't it?"

"Yeah. The energy in the air is like lightning. Everyone seems connected."

While Rob watched the crowd, Lynda watched Rob.

This was it. The end of their project. They'd succeeded.

Tomorrow, it was time for him to go home.

It was over.

She didn't know when it happened, but she'd fallen in love with him. The hard part was that for the first time in her life, she thought she'd felt some warmth back, instead of pity, or worse, disdain.

She couldn't help but love him.

Every day she dreamed of the day he'd kissed her and dreamed that it would happen again.

But it hadn't. He'd done nothing romantic since then, but that was her own doing. She'd wanted to keep their relationship professional because it was safe that way

Except that today was the day of the NEXTEL Cup race and their last day together.

She didn't want to be professional anymore.

Yet she didn't know what to do.

"Look!" Rob said, motioning with his head in the direction of the booth next to them. "Is that Sterling Marlin?"

"Maybe. I saw him race a few years back. He's spectacular. Did you know he started out working in the pit crew for his dad, Coo Coo?" She wished she could have shared some of her past experiences from other races, but the crowd of people didn't give them much opportunity to talk.

The only time they didn't have a crowd of people at the booth was, as she'd said, during the last few laps of the race and then during the winner's burnout and drive through Victory Lane.

People were soon back on the grounds and at the booths and displays, and the crowd didn't settle down until well into the night.

As they packed up the booth, even though she was tired, she could barely contain her excitement.

"I can't believe how much we sold," she said as she folded the remaining T-shirts and stuffed them into a box. "I don't have to count or tally to know that sales are way above last year. Kathleen is already making arrangements for me to buy into the store. I couldn't have done this without you. I don't know what to say."

She crunched up some newspaper to protect the mugs she'd

had on display. Through the crinkling, she thought she heard Rob mumbling.

She nearly dropped the mug. She thought he'd said, "You might want to say 'I love you.'"

"What was that?" she asked.

His ears turned red, and he cleared his throat. "Nothing worth repeating. Need some help?"

She noticed he'd already finished packing up, but all he had was his laptop and accessories and a few games.

"I'm pretty much done. Almost everything we brought sold. We can carry this all out in one trip."

"Good thing, in this crowd."

They made their way off the grounds slowly, then to her house.

But tonight, instead of going to sleep, it was time for another race—the final season race for the club.

Because the real NEXTEL Cup race had run, they'd decided to do a scaled-down version of the five hundred miles.

They'd set her computer up on the kitchen table so Rob could be beside her with his laptop.

"You ready?" he asked, while he tested his steering wheel.

She looked through her cyber windshield on her monitor to oversee the hood of her car, brightly painted in blue and white, a big red 5 on the hood, as well as the name and logo of her sponsor, which happened to be Kathleen's store.

Rob had even bought her a matching helmet, which he made her wear to get her more in the mood.

She turned to look at him, wearing his red and yellow helmet. Of course, he also had a NASCAR jacket and matching pants in his colors, because he'd had the outfit specially made as part of his marketing plan.

"Yes, I'm ready. You?"

"Raring to go."

They signaled the other racers that they were ready, waited for the sequence of lights, and they were off.

Lynda drove for all she was worth, but as they got to the end, she fell behind. At the final lap, she climbed back into second, but she couldn't overtake Rob, and he got the checkered flag.

He hooted with joy, did a cyber burnout like a real NAS-CAR driver, and then took his car for a spin down Victory Lane.

There was no champagne, but Lynda brought a couple of bottles of carbonated lemon-lime soda out of the fridge, shook one, opened it, then handed it to him. He laughed, choking while he tried to drink the bubbles so it wouldn't spill all over her kitchen floor.

They returned to their computers while the other club members e-mailed Rob a picture of a trophy, and then they e-mailed Lynda a picture of a second place ribbon.

Lynda hit PRINT, but when she turned to Rob to hand him the picture, he was holding out something toward her.

"This isn't happening the way I thought it would. I really thought you were going to win, and I was going to give this to you as a victory prize." He reached for her left hand and stroked one of her fingers.

Her ring finger.

"You didn't win the race, but you still won my heart. You

started off as a fantasy, but I got to know you as a real person and fell in love with you. I got you this as a symbol both of how we met and how much I love you."

He gave her a gold ring with five stones, which was the number of her car. Two stones were blue, so they were likely sapphires. The white stones were opals. In the center was a large, beautiful diamond.

She gulped, and her heart pounded. A diamond. She'd only known diamonds as the center stone in a ring to mean one thing.

"What is this?" she stammered.

"I was hoping it could be an engagement ring. Will you marry me, Lynda? Please say you love me."

"I. . ." She was almost afraid to believe it, but she'd fallen in love with him so fast. God had truly blessed them both, because Rob loved her, too. "I love you. Yes, I'll marry you."

He kissed her so fast she nearly dropped the ring, but she held onto it like a lifeline until he released her.

"I don't want a long engagement. How would you like to elope? We can have our honeymoon at the next NASCAR race, which might be Martinsville, but I'm not sure." He paused. "If Glen will give me more time off work."

He stopped to think.

Lynda reached for his hand. "Even though Kathleen's daughter is doing much better, I can't leave the store until Kathleen is back. Maybe we should just wait. Just not for long."

Rob gently grasped her hands and massaged her wrists with his thumbs. "Or we could get married right here, at the Talladega Superspeedway. The race is over, so that means we

could get married on speedway property. We can decide on a honeymoon later."

Lynda nibbled on her lower lip. "I have a feeling that as soon as I tell her, she'll race right back."

Rob grinned. "Then we can race to the speedway and get married."

Lynda gave his hands a gentle squeeze. "Gentlemen, start your engines."

Grabill Missionary Church Library
P.O. Box 279
13637 State Street
Grabill, IN 46741

GAIL SATTLER

Gail has written many award-winning novels and novellas for both Barbour Publishing/Heartsong Presents and Steeple Hill/Love Inspired. Gail loves to read books with a happy ending, and that's why she writes them that way. When she's not writing, Gail keeps busy in her church, where she plays bass guitar (loud) for her worship team. Outside of church, she plays in a local Jazz band, and that's loud, too. Gail lives on the west coast, where you don't have to shovel rain, with her husband, three sons, two dogs, two toads, and a lazy lizard named Draco, who is quite cuddly for a reptile. Visit Gail's Web site at www.gailsattler.com.

A Letter to Our Readers

Dear Readers:

In order that we might better contribute to your reading enjoyment, we would appreciate your taking a few minutes to respond to the following questions. When completed, please return to the following: Fiction Editor, Barbour Publishing, Inc., P.O. Box 719, Uhrichsville, OH 44683.

1. Did you enjoy reading *Race to the Altar*?
   ❑ Very much—I would like to see more books like this.
   ❑ Moderately—I would have enjoyed it more if _____
   _____

   _____

2. What influenced your decision to purchase this book?
   (Check those that apply.)
   ❑ Cover   ❑ Back cover copy   ❑ Title   ❑ Price
   ❑ Friends   ❑ Publicity   ❑ Other

3. Which story was your favorite?
   ❑ *Clear! Clear! Dear!*   ❑ *Over the Wall*
   ❑ *The Remaking of Moe McKenna* ❑ *Winner Takes All*

4. Please check your age range:
   ❑ Under 18   ❑ 18–24   ❑ 25–34
   ❑ 35–45   ❑ 46–55   ❑ Over 55

5. How many hours per week do you read? _____

Name _____

Occupation _____

Address _____

City_____ State_____ Zip_____

E-mail_____

If you enjoyed

then read

Sugar and Grits

Southern Hospitality
Enriches Four Mississippi Romances

Mississippi Mud by DiAnn Mills
Not on the Menu by Martha Rogers
Gone Fishing by Janice Thompson
Falling for You by Kathleen Y'Barbo

Available wherever books are sold.
Or order from:
Barbour Publishing, Inc.
P.O. Box 721
Uhrichsville, Ohio 44683
www.barbourbooks.com

You may order by mail for $6.97 and add $3.00 to your order for shipping.
Prices subject to change without notice.
If outside the U.S. please call 740-922-7280 for shipping charges.

If you enjoyed

Race to the *Altar*

then read

CAROLINA CARPENTER *Brides*

*Four Couples Find Tools for Building Romance
in a Home Improvement Store*

How to Refurbish an Old Romance by Janet Benrey
Once upon a Shopping Cart by Ron Benrey
Can You Help Me? by Lena Nelson Dooley
Caught Red-Handed by Yvonne Lehman

Available wherever books are sold.
Or order from:
Barbour Publishing, Inc.
P.O. Box 721
Uhrichsville, Ohio 44683
www.barbourbooks.com

You may order by mail for $6.97 and add $3.00 to your order for shipping.
Prices subject to change without notice.
If outside the U.S. please call 740-922-7280 for shipping charges.

HEARTSONG
PRESENTS

If you love Christian romance...

$10.⁹⁹

You'll love Heartsong Presents' inspiring and faith-filled romances by today's very best Christian authors. . .Wanda E. Brunstetter, Mary Connealy, Susan Page Davis, Cathy Marie Hake, and Joyce Livingston, to mention a few!

When you join Heartsong Presents, you'll enjoy four brand-new, mass market, 176-page books—two contemporary and two historical—that will build you up in your faith when you discover God's role in every relationship you read about!

Mass Market, 176 Pages

Imagine. . .four new romances every four weeks—with men and women like you who long to meet the one God has chosen as the love of their lives—all for the low price of $10.99 postpaid.

To join, simply visit www.heartsongpresents.com or complete the coupon below and mail it to the address provided.

✂-------------------------------

YES! Sign me up for Hearts♥ng!

NEW MEMBERSHIPS WILL BE SHIPPED IMMEDIATELY!
Send no money now. We'll bill you only $10.99 postpaid with your first shipment of four books. Or for faster action, call 1-740-922-7280.

NAME _____

ADDRESS_____

CITY_____ STATE _____ ZIP _____

**MAIL TO: HEARTSONG PRESENTS, P.O. Box 721, Uhrichsville, Ohio 44683
or sign up at WWW.HEARTSONGPRESENTS.COM**